METEOR

Lizzie's War: Book 2

Kevin O'Regan

Core Books

Published by Core Books

Paperback edition ISBN: 978-1-7392206-3-1
A CIP catalogue for this book is held by the British Library.

CONTENTS

PROLOGUE

Like the maggot in the apple, the worm in the bud, betrayal destroys us more surely than the knife that spills blood. Insidious, unobserved, it eats away at the core, the heart, until the rot is at last revealed. It is not just betrayal of country, of friends, but of ourselves and what we could have been. Corruption like cancer grows, destroying feeling, integrity, life. But which is worse, to betray one's country or one's family? It is the conflict between rival loyalties that undoes us.

"If this were played upon a stage now, I could condemn it as an improbable fiction."

Fabian in Twelfth Night by W Shakespeare

Thursday 4Th March 1943 02.00

CHAPTER 1

Silently, slowly, a dark pole broke the surface of the sea. It was a calm night, a light south-westerly wind hardly troubling the water, small waves washing softly on the sand as the tide began to retreat. Hazy cloud high in the heavens hid the stars and the moon, now waned to the slenderest of crescents, gave almost no light.

Any observer would have seen nothing in the darkness, no movement to alert the suspicious mind. Some ten minutes passed and then the faintest sound of disturbed water reached the shore, hardly audible above the hiss of the creeping and receding waves on the beach. No ear received it. Slowly, around the pole, a dark form rose above the water, higher and higher until a much larger, long shape parted the surface.

Inside the vessel, the Kapitan lifted his left arm smartly, the four gold stripes around the cuff causing him to smile in satisfaction, and consulted his watch. "Exactly as the plan. It is 0200 hours and we are right under the British noses."

The Oberleutnant by his side smiled. "All is ready Herr Kapitan."

The Kapitan nodded and the Oberleutnant strode away from the bridge to the despatch section beneath the conning tower. Two men in dark outdoor coats stood in silence whilst other crewmen lifted a kayak up the tower, passing it to colleagues above. Others followed, clambering up the metal ladder with two boxes of equipment and two full kitbags.

1

The Oberleutnant held out his hand and the taller man shook it. "Viel Glück Hans or should I say Harry?" He presented his hand to the shorter man. "Good Luck, Bob, as they say in English. Now you are both English." He smiled. "It is a high tide, a spring tide as they call it. You won't have far to walk up the beach." Then he clicked his heels smartly together and raised his right arm in the Nazi salute. "Heil Hitler."

Both men responded in kind and climbed slowly up the ladder, Hans first. They stood side by side in the conning tower, eyes adjusting to the darkness.

Bob shivered. "Thank God it's calm. Me, I'd get seasick on a kid's boating pond."

A crewman showed them down steps onto the deck and they walked a short way until they were abreast of the kayak which was now in the water alongside the hull. It looked tiny, puny against the leviathan of steel. They were helped down a ladder to the canoe which was being held steady by two more crewmen. Hans with his lean, fit frame was able to board the kayak in one agile movement. Bob, wheezing and swearing under his breath, nearly tipped the small craft over before finally settling into it, exhaling with relief.

"In two days, we'll be back. Same place, same time," he called softly.

Both men put paddles against the side of the submarine and gently pushed themselves away. The tiny craft swayed a little but Hans, who was closer to the bow, began to paddle and the momentum stabilised the craft. Bob fell in with his stroke and they headed towards the shore. It took only some ten minutes before the kayak scraped on the sand of the beach. Hans stood confidently and swiftly stepped out, using his paddle to maintain his balance. The kayak bobbed up at the bow and, grabbing the rope that was tied there, he pulled it another yard or two up the beach.

"Thank you my man. Very kind." With a similar precariousness to his boarding of the vessel, Bob also alighted and both men looked back out to sea. The hull of the submarine had already sunk beneath the surface leaving only the conning tower just about visible. Bob took a large torch from his coat pocket and flashed it twice across the water. Moments later, the submarine had been swallowed by the dark sea, leaving only a strange flatness on the surface.

"This is it then Hans. We're on our own now."

There was only the faintest trace of a German accent in the reply Hans made. "Yes Bob. As you say we're on our own now. Let's get the boat under cover up the beach."

Bob grabbed the bow rope. "Right you grab it as well – I'm not doing it on me own. We can drag it."

"We should lift it…leave less of a trace."

Bob looked one way along the beach and then the other. There was not a light to be seen, no sign of any human habitation nor activity, just the concrete blocks strewn along the upper beach against tank invasion. "I don't think we need to worry about that out here. I reckon we could have come in a landing craft and no one would be any the wiser."

"The English can't be that useless can they? They must have lookouts."

"Believe me Mate they are that useless. How else could I have blown up that factory a couple of months ago?"

"We will not risk it so let's be quick."

Hans took hold of the rope and the two men trudged up the sand hauling the kayak. The weight of the equipment boxes and kitbags caused the rear of the boat to gouge a track in the soft sand and their boots made big impressions, pushing a little pile of sand backwards with each step.

Towards the top of the beach, the sand was more stony and the going easier but by the time they reached the grass line, Hans was breathing heavily and Bob blowing like a steam train. He looked both ways, trying to make out anything that might provide a hiding place for the boat.

"Blimey. There's not much here is there?"

"That's why it's a good place for a landing. There must be something, a fisherman's hut perhaps."

"We'd be better off leaving it here. Put it in a hut and the fisherman might wonder where it came from."

"Good point Bob. Let's just turn it upside down and leave it in the long grass. If someone sees it, they'll assume it belongs to a local."

"Right. Let's do it. Then it's a long walk I'm afraid."

Hans took a torch from his coat pocket and carefully panned it across the ground in front of them. They dragged the kayak into the longest patch of grass they could see and turned it over so that water would not fill it. It's grey hull lay like a sleeping seal.

"That'll be fine. Ok map." Bob fumbled in one of his pockets and pulling out a map, unfolded it. Hans held the torch beam close to it. "Right, we've landed here, just north of Gibraltar Point...hopefully. It's hard to tell in this light. Mind you it's hard to tell anyway on account of it being so bloody flat round here. We must be south of Skegness though, otherwise we'd be walking straight into an army camp. They took over Butlins, see, but that's to the north side of Sgeggy."

"So we need to find this road into Skegness. There is a lane here look; we just have to cross the scrubland to get there." Hans took a small compass from his pocket. "We head across this way."

"Yep. We certainly don't want to be south of Gibraltar Point as that would lead us straight into RAF Wainfleet. Mind you, they'll be looking for incoming aircraft." Bob surveyed the dark, empty landscape. "I bloody hope they've dropped us in the right place."

"There is a channel of water here, look. If we can find that, we know where we are."

"I wouldn't count on it chum - there's bits of water all over this place and they change daily as the sand shifts."

"Ok but we must go and try," said Hans.

"Agreed. We need to find a suitable vehicle in Skegness, something like a tradesman's van that won't attract attention so early in the day." Bob's tone was casual.

Each man slung a kit bag over a shoulder and lifted a case of equipment.

Robbie McBane flipped over onto his back and breathed out. His sleep had been fitful and now it seemed he was not going to slip back into that blissful state. He had resisted looking at the clock though its insistent tick, audible through the towel he had dumped on top of it, made him sit up. Flicking on a small torch, he looked at the time. Just three o'clock. He could do with another three hours before getting up but his mind was full of the strange conversation he had had with his RAF Police boss.

Flight Lieutenant Belding had been very cagey. "You need to get yourself to RAF Northolt by eleven hundred hours. You'll be picked up in an aircraft and taken to RAF Cranwell. You'll be there for a couple of nights at least. Your job is to check on security arrangements and see that no harm comes to your fellow passengers."

"So what's so special about RAF Cranwell? Why can't I just drive there?"

"It's quite a trek up to Lincolnshire you know. The other people going will be flying and you need to be with them. If there's something special at Cranwell, I'm sure you'll be told."

Robbie was silent for a moment, trying to decide whether he should ask for someone else to be sent. It sounded all very tame and a bit of a non-mission. Belding could read his thoughts.

"I've chosen you Robbie because I was asked to put my best man on this mission. You did a superb job at RAF Silverstone last month. This is a vote of confidence."

Robbie was of course flattered but could not help speculating about the mission. He had now been in the RAF Police Special Investigation Branch for two years, having come south from Glasgow after his fiancé had been killed in a German bombing raid. He respected Belding and knew that he would have given him a fuller briefing had he been at liberty to do so.

He did doze off a couple of times but, when awake, time seemed to crawl by. He was relieved when the alarm clock rang at six. He was up quickly, washed and shaved and eating his porridge by six forty hours. He listened to the news on his wireless set at seven o' clock as he sipped a large mug of tea. Interesting how in RAF service, one automatically used the twenty-four hour clock to define time rather than the usual twelve hours as on the BBC.

He had packed his overnight bag the previous evening. All he needed to do was put in his wash bag and the picture. He lifted the photograph tenderly from his bedside cabinet. Catriona, the young woman he had been due to marry before her life had been cut short by a German bomb in Glasgow almost two years to the day. He always took her photograph with him, having made what he thought was a binding decision never to consider another partner. He slipped the photograph in its frame between some clothes in his bag.

Last month, that resolve to cherish Catriona's memory for the rest of his life had been shaken when he encountered a young woman who was every bit as lovely and as lively as Catriona had been. He was not ready yet to relinquish the grief of losing Catriona, felt it would be a betrayal of his love for her. But, at the same time, this new young woman had slipped past his defences into his heart. She was not ready for a relationship either she had said, so there was no danger, but he hoped he would meet her again, that, one day, he could find happiness with another. He looked in the mirror; would his red hair deter her or perhaps the suggestion of sadness he could not remove from his eyes?

So much tragedy in this war, so many people grieving just because a madman like Hitler wanted power.

Belding had authorised a lift for Robbie to Northolt from his accommodation at Burnham Beeches. At zero eight-thirty hours sharp, the car pulled up outside his block and a young airman stepped out smartly. Robbie was at the window and, lifting his bag, walked down the stairs. He opted to sit in the front, not feeling as a sergeant that he was of sufficiently high rank to lord it in the rear. The airman was quiet, respectful, speaking only when addressed by Robbie. There was little conversation, therefore, as they drove the fifteen miles to the airfield.

They arrived a few minutes before nine hundred hours and the guard at the gate directed them towards a building which housed the Officers Mess. Robbie thanked the driver and told him not to wait. He was greeted by a corporal who took him to a small meeting room with a highly polished wooden table surrounded by padded chairs. The smell of furniture polish was strong.

"You've got a bit of a wait, Sir. I think your transport's not due until about eleven hundred hours."

"I'druther be early than late, Corporal."

"Yes sir. Air Chief Marshal Sir George Stanley is taking the same aircraft as you. He should arrive here in a while. Would you like some coffee?"

"That would be most welcome, thank you." He sat down and resigned himself to a couple of hours of boredom.

CHAPTER 2

Lizzie looked at the young woman sitting at the end of the row of chairs behind her in the briefing hut. She returned the look, smiled weakly and turned away. The tight bun of hair at the back of her head suggested someone efficient, precise.

"Looks like there's nothing for us to do." Lizzie laughed briefly. The sudden quiet of the briefing room at White Waltham was a little unnerving after the usual banter of the daily chit distribution session and Lizzie wondered why she had not been tasked with anything. "I'm Lizzie Barnes. I don't think we've met – we've certainly not flown together before."

The other woman turned back. "Alice Frobisher. No we've not met. I'm a navigator."

"That explains it. I don't usually get a navigator…have to try to work out where I'm going myself."

"That must be hard."

"It certainly is. The week before last, I flew a Wellington up to Silverstone – it's a new training base. Just skirt round London and follow the A5 said Trueman."

"You found a body didn't you? I heard about it."

"Yep and I was stuck up there for the best part of a week. Still, I helped find the killer. I went to the funeral of the dead girl on Monday. Trueman let me take an aircraft to fly up there. I was glad I went…pay my respects. So sad…just nineteen. Her parents had already lost their son in France…you know in the retreat… Dunkirk"

"Must be terrible for them. So much sadness in this war."

Lizzie looked carefully at Alice. An unspoken sorrow seemed to haunt her eyes and told a different story to the well-groomed and implacable exterior presented. She said nothing for a minute or so, looking out at the airfield of White Waltham. Already, the first plane was taxiing out to the runway – one of her lucky fellow Air Transport Auxiliary pilots starting his or her mission for the day. One never knew what one would get – that was part of the attraction. One day it was delivering a new aircraft from the factory to the base from which it would operate, the next it was flying an important person somewhere. That's why Lizzie loved it: the variety, the anticipation each morning.

"I wonder where Trueman has got to?" Commander Trueman, who was the senior officer at White Waltham airfield in charge of No 1 Ferry Pool, had disappeared into his office several minutes before, telling the two young women to wait. "D'you get to fly much...I mean if they don't assign a navigator..."

"Yes I do. Most days. It's just there's not many of us so we're in demand." Alice smiled, a flash of warmth breaking the austerity of her sharp features. Sharp but fine, delicate, beautiful.

Just then Trueman's office door swung open and the man himself stood in the doorway. "Lizzie, Alice...in here please."

The two women followed him into the office and Lizzie shut the door behind her. A man, probably in his late thirties Lizzie guessed, was sitting on a chair beside Trueman's desk, his legs stretched out before him and an amused smile playing on his lips. Supercilious was the word that came to Lizzie's mind. His dark hair was neatly groomed and his face, handsome certainly, betrayed a good bone structure. Trueman signalled them to sit. The office was not large so they were all quite close to the desk at which Trueman now sat.

"Let me introduce you to Mr Grainger who is from the Ministry. This is Second Officer Barnes and Navigator Frobisher. We have an important mission for you both. You are to fly to Brockworth airfield in Gloucestershire to pick up an Arthur Healey who is an engineer with the Gloster Aircraft Company."

Trueman rose and leaning forward, handed Lizzie a chit and Alice a sheet of paper.

Lizzie glanced at the chit. "Is the Gloster shorthand? I thought it was the Gloucestershire Aircraft Company."

"It was, " Trueman smiled, "but some of our allies had difficulty with the pronunciation – Gloo- ces-ter-shire, the final syllable rhyming with fire – so it was simplified."

"The Americans I bet."

"It's not my place to say." He smiled. "When you pick up the said Healey, you will fly him to Northolt and pick up two more passengers. You'll then fly them all to RAF Cranwell in Lincolnshire. You will need to stay there tonight and probably Friday night, tomorrow in other words, as well. You will then fly your passengers back to the same airfields, that is the two passengers to Northolt and Mr Healey back to Brockworth. Then you can return here. Accommodation will be provided as usual at the base. I've assigned you an Anson Mk 1 for the trip."

"May we know what Mr Healey's role is and the reason for his visit?" Alice spoke with quiet assurance.

"I'll let Mr Grainger answer that."

Grainger drew his legs in and sat a little more upright. His voice was a drawl as if it were an effort to speak to them. "No is the short answer. You both signed the Official Secrets Act when you joined the ATA. That's right isn't it?" He looked at Trueman who nodded his head. "That signature means you can never disclose anything that you see, hear or do if it is deemed secret."

"I think we are aware of that Mr Grainger. We frequently do things that are important to national security."

Grainger's eyes narrowed. Clearly not a man who liked to be challenged. "This task is top secret. You must not allow yourselves to reveal anything about it. Is that clear?"

Alice looked a little frightened by his tone but Lizzie was not going to be intimidated. "So what is the mission?"

"You'll be told what you need to know as and when. Just follow your instructions. I will be accompanying you."

Lizzie looked at Trueman. "Are we to leave right away?"

"As soon as you're sorted and ready."

Lizzie stood up. "Give us twenty minutes to check the aircraft over and we'll see you outside Mr Grainger." She left the office with Alice behind her. "He's a bundle of fun isn't he?"

There was a flash of amusement in Alice's eyes. Not quite so reserved as she appeared then.

"This'll do nicely. The Prince of Wales – very patriotic. A pub is better than a boarding house – fewer questions asked. It's close enough but not so close as to arouse suspicion." Bob killed the engine of the van. "Now remember, we're from Skegness to do a roofing job in the area – just keep it vague – and we just want a room for the night."

"I've got it. I'm not an idiot."

"No, but we've got to get our story right. And your name is Harry ok?"

Hans, now Harry, swore softly and yanked the door handle. The two men tumbled out of the van, slamming the doors behind them. Bob hitched up his trousers and led the way into the pub, glancing at his watch. Just after nine. They had parked up a mile or so away in the entrance to a field and waited until the day had woken. Birds chattered in the crisp morning air and Bob inhaled deeply.

"It's good to be home you know…not that I lived around here. A Londoner me."

Hans tried the door but it was locked. He knocked on it impatiently. He was tired and they faced an uncomfortable wait in the van until the evening. To keep their story authentic, they had decided they would check in to some digs and then go off in the van to make it look as though they were working.

At last the door was tugged open and a burly man was standing in front of them. "Yes? What is it?"

"We are wondering if you would have a room for tonight. My partner and I are doing a job here today and tomorrow so…"

The landlord looked Hans up and down and then turned his scrutiny on Bob. "Where're you from?"

"Only Skegness," Bob chipped in. "It's just with the petrol rationing, we have to avoid doing too much driving about. You know how it is."

The landlord appeared to soften. "Don't I just. Come in."

Hans had to duck to enter. They were led into a saloon bar. A faint smell of frying wafted through from an open door into the back. The landlord's bald head, almost spherical, gleamed in the light from a sconce.

"Just the one night is it?" Hans nodded. "And do you want two single rooms or a double – twin beds o'course."

Hans opened his mouth to speak but Bob jumped in. "The twin'll do fine."

"Righto. I just need some names."

"I'm Bob Edwards and my mate here is Harry Smith. Is that breakfast I can smell?"

"It is yes. Do you want some?"

"Yes please. That's making me hungry that is. Work can wait for a bit, eh Harry?"

When the landlord had ambled through the door beside the bar presumably into the kitchen, Hans pulled Bob's arm. "Why a twin room? Why not single rooms?"

"In one room, there's no risk of someone playing one of us off against the other."

"What do you mean, play one of us off…?"

"Look just trust me. I come from this country and I've done this kind of job before. We've got to keep everything realistic. Two roofers would not fork out for single rooms – least not round here they wouldn't, tight bunch of…"

Ten minutes later, they were sitting at a table with a hot cooked breakfast in front of them and steaming mugs of tea. Bob's eyes lit up when he saw the food and he wasted no time shovelling it into his mouth. Hans ate with more care, cutting the sausage into precise chunks and the scrambled egg substitute into neat segments.

The landlord came through to collect their plates. Bob looked up, smiled and rubbed his paunch. "Lovely that. Don't usually get such a good brekky in...at home. By the way, are we ok for some dinner tonight...about six?"

"Of course. Not sure what's on the menu but I'll let the Missus know you'll be in to eat."

"Lovely. Well we better get on our way. Roof won't fix itself! Ta ta, see you later."

They returned to the van and Bob started the engine. "Stroke o' luck this." He took a large breath and belched loudly. "Pardon me. I mean finding a roofer's van with ladders on top and not locked. Means we can stay inside the back, no one can see us. Perfect."

"We need to keep it out of sight as much as possible. Let's check things out at the base, work out where we get in, where we film from and everything."

"Yeah, a bit later, okay? You need to relax Hans – sorry I should call you Harry from now on. Don't want to let anything slip."

Bob drove out of the village and eventually turned onto the road that would lead them to the base. Hans spotted a track leading off into woodland and Bob reversed, the van swerving drunkenly as he did so.

"For God's sake take your time. You'll have us in the ditch."

"Not me pal. I've driven getaway vehicles backwards, forwards, any which way and never had a crash. You're in the hands of an expert." Bob grinned at Hans.

They found a small clearing off the track and Bob pulled into it. Having stretched their legs for a while, the two men sat, one either side in the back of the van. After leaving the beach, they had walked into the outskirts of Skegness from their landing point and snooped around looking for a suitable vehicle. Of course there were cars around but they were all locked and in drives or outside houses whose occupants may have been disturbed by the sound of an engine starting in the early hours. They had found the van in a side street. Bob pulled open the driver's door and pushed the starter button. The engine had fired into life and Hans had clambered into the passenger seat as Bob let in the clutch.

They were soon cruising along the main road to Boston, running parallel to the shore. Hans had been nervous because the van had "Allen Roofing" emblazoned on each side. It was too conspicuous. "What if they report it missing and the Police search for it?" Bob seemed unconcerned. "Don't worry. We'll talk our way out of it…or I will anyway."

Now, fed, watered and relaxed, Bob slumped down, leaning his head on his kit bag. He was soon asleep, his wheezing becoming snores which prevented sleep for Hans. "Bloody fool, " he muttered to himself, "why did I get him? He's a liability."

CHAPTER 3

"Let's get this aircraft sorted." Lizzie looked at Alice. "Have you got the co-ordinates on the paper he handed you?"

"Yes...all in order. Should be no problem. The cloud cover is quite low so you may need to fly above it. Probably no visual clues, otherwise we could have found the A40 and followed that for much of the way."

"I spend my life following roads. It'll be great to have someone giving me flight directions for a change. How long have you been with ATA?"

"I joined last year. I'd already had some training in navigation."

"Rather you than me. Not sure my Maths is up to it."

"That's what most people say but it's not that difficult. Just have to be methodical."

"Yes but that's not easy when things get hairy. There must have been some moments when your pilot went astray and you didn't know where you were."

Alice smiled. "I watch the compass carefully and the air speed indicator. I know the direction and strength of the wind so I keep track of where we are. If you're going astray I'll tell you."

Lizzie looked at Alice. She was smiling and her manner was pleasant; Lizzie felt she would be rock-solid in a crisis. She had a quiet, calm assurance which gave confidence. The two women had been donning flying gear and parachutes in the kit room as they talked. They left the room and found Trueman waiting outside.

"Ladies, just a word of warning. Be careful around Grainger. He has powerful contacts in the MoD. We can't afford for him to go back telling tales about us. You'll be picking up a very important officer at Northolt as well. Remember that the intercom allows you to talk to each other but there is a button which allows you to address the passengers via a speaker in the cabin. For God's sake make sure it's off unless you do need to say something to them. We have had one or two very unfortunate situations in the past where the passengers have heard some remarks between the aircrew that were better not heard."

"So no discussing Mr Grainger's choice of socks." Lizzie smirked.

"Quite, Lizzie. I'm sure I can trust you though that devilish look in your eye causes me some concern."

"I'll keep an eye on her, Sir." Lizzie was pleased that Alice was showing some spirit. She felt sure she would thaw further as they spent more time together.

"Yes...I know...that's why I chose you."

"So you don't really trust me?"

"I'd trust you with my life in an aircraft, Lizzie, but your tongue is a bit of a liability."

"I merely maintain my right to be respected for what I do."

"And so you should but...be careful on this trip. It's top secret." Trueman turned to Alice. "You know of course that they have camouflaged Northolt by painting houses and gardens on the hangar roofs. It's in the middle of housing estates anyway so it can be tricky to find."

"Thanks for the tip, Sir. I'll try to make sure Lizzie doesn't land on a busy road."

"Yes, she did make an attempt to do so last month."

"That was just a scare tactic."

"Well it certainly succeeded. I'm told the poor young man who was in the forward gunner position has not been the same since!"

Lizzie laughed and watched Trueman walk back to his office. "I'm glad he's got a sense of humour."

Lizzie and Alice strolled out to the apron where the Anson

was waiting, its nose stuck in the air, the frame visible through the large passenger windows. They had only just climbed aboard when Trueman emerged from the building with Grainger who was carrying a suitcase. Trueman watched him heft his suitcase into the hold and take his seat in the passenger section; he shook his hand.

"Have a good trip. You'll be alighting at Northolt on the return I assume?"

"Yes. Thank you Commander Trueman. I hope your confidence in the pilot and navigator is well founded."

Lizzie looked at Alice who grimaced. Trueman closed the door and Lizzie started the two engines. They coughed and spluttered into life. As they warmed, she and Alice carried out the pre-flight checks. With their radio mouthpieces on, the two women quietly confirmed each procedure until Lizzie asked if Alice was ready. She assented and Lizzie radioed the tower.

"White Waltham tower, this is Anson Kilo 8717 requesting permission for take-off."

"Kilo 8717 you are cleared for take-off. Have a good trip."

Lizzie flicked the intercom switch on the panel in front of her. "Mr Grainger, this is Second Officer Barnes, your pilot. We have been cleared for take-off. Please make sure your seat belt is on. There is a parachute under your seat though we hope you won't need that. We have a lot of cloud cover but the South Westerly wind is not strong. It should be a comfortable flight." She flicked the intercom switch off and looked at her watch. "Nine twenty hours," she said to Alice. "Do we have an ETA?"

"Flight time is thirty minutes so nine fifty hours give or take a few minutes."

"Let's hope they have the coffee brewed." Lizzie pulled back the throttles and taxied to the end of the runway. She turned the plane to face the long line of concrete and then pulled the throttles back full. The engines roared and the Anson shook as it rolled forward, gathering speed and bumping over the runway. The tail lifted and, moments later, the aircraft left the runway.

"Now comes the exhausting part...for you." Lizzie grinned at Alice. "The wheels have to be lifted by hand pump. So when you're ready..."

"One hundred and forty pumps I believe. It's about time they motorised it." Alice began to pump, counting aloud. Slowly the wheels retracted and the sound of the wind over them lessened until they were fully home. "Your heading needs to be 280 degrees which should allow for the wind drifting us slightly northwards."

"Roger that." Lizzie made a slight adjustment to starboard and brought the aircraft onto the desired heading. The ceiling of cloud was already approaching, the first wisps of grey mist fleeing over the wings like ghosts. Soon they were lost in it. "This is the bit I don't like. I'm always fearful that we'll find another aircraft in the cloud. Flying blind does not make for a comfortable trip."

"We'll soon be above it and then we can enjoy blue skies and sunshine while everyone down below is feeling depressed."

And sure enough, after several minutes, the Anson rose above the low cloud and the sun graced them with its light. The cloud below now looked white and fluffy, a complete blanket covering the land. Above them, wisps of cirrus spread like feathers over the dome of blue, softening the light. It was beautiful and Lizzie breathed deeply, the old excitement that flying always gave her infusing her body.

"Beautiful isn't it?"

"I never tire of it. It's as if we have escaped into another world, a world of light, leaving darkness behind us."

"It's just a shame that we have to come down."

The two young women laughed and settled back, the drone of the engines filling their ears.

Sergeant Albert Swallow could see the end of the envelope projecting from his pigeon hole as he approached the rack.

Interesting. It must be his little sister – she was the only one who wrote to him. In fact she was the only person he had in the World. He took the letter from the rack and looked at the hand writing. It was from Angela as he had suspected, the address - RAF Cranwell, Sleaford, Lincolnshire - in her neat script. He glanced at his watch; just time to nip up to his room and read it in private before he had to meet the engineer chap. He was puzzled though: why was she writing to him now? He had received a letter from her not long ago.

Holding the letter in one hand, he took the stairs two at a time – there were advantages in being tall. His thoughts were of Angela and whether there was a problem. She was four years younger than him and he had always been the protective older brother. That had intensified when their parents had been killed in a German raid on Newcastle. He and Angela had by then left home – he was in the RAF and she was training as a nurse. It was bad enough losing your parents but if anything happened to her, he would be devastated.

Like all the rooms, his was spartan, just the basic furniture. He did have some pictures of aircraft and of course a few of his parents and Angela. It was all the family he had. Both his parents had been only children so there were no uncles and aunts. The day of the double funeral roared back into his mind, the utter loneliness he felt, his arm around Angela as if the two of them were marooned on a desert island far from other human life. They watched in numbed horror the coffins being lowered into the grave.

He swore silently then that he would protect her at all costs, never allow anything or anyone to harm her.

The bed springs creaked when he sat down and carefully opened the envelope. He withdrew the letter and read it slowly, at first disbelief and then anger flooding through him. "Bastard." Laying the letter beside him on the bed, he stared across the room at nothing, a picture forming in his mind, his fists clenched. He was shaking. After some minutes, he picked up the letter and read it again slowly.

28th February 1943

Dear Bert,

I'm so sorry that this letter will bring you bad news. I need to tell you though because I need your help. I don't know what to do.

You'll remember I told you about Michael and how we were getting on very well. On his last leave, we became much closer. I was very fond of him and thought he was of me too. I'm afraid I discovered a while later I'd fallen pregnant. Please don't be angry with me. I know it was stupid, I know we shouldn't have...you know...but I think I must have miscalculated my time of the month. Anyway it happened.

I felt sure Michael would stand by me and do the right thing. I wrote to him and yesterday I received a reply. I have spent the time since then in torment, wondering what I should do and whether to tell you. Anyway, in his letter, he said the baby was my problem and he certainly would not marry me. He said I should get rid of it. Just like that, get rid of it.

I can't believe he could be so callous, so unfeeling for a little baby that is after all half his and so cruel to me. He was happy enough with me when he took me to bed.

I'm so sorry to load this on you but I don't know what to do. You know how it is for unmarried mothers. Should I do what he said? Please write to me as soon as you can and please, please Bert don't reject me too. I couldn't bear to lose your love. You've always looked after me and I pray that you will do so now when I am most in need.

Your loving though foolish sister,

> Angela
>
> xx

He'd had his doubts about Michael who seemed to be a bit of a jack-the-lad but this! It was appalling. Gnawing at him, however, was the knowledge that this delayed his own happiness. He had hoped that Michael would settle, marry Angela and that would mean he would be relieved of the responsibility for her. He could find a young woman himself, at last start to build a life after the devastation of his parents' death. He wanted that so badly. A wife, some children, a family of his own to replace what he and Angela had lost.

He stared out of the window at nothing for several minutes, trying to control the anger he could feel boiling inside and trying to focus on the practical issues. What should she do? The simple answer was of course to get rid of it as that cocky bastard had said but it was clear Angela felt differently and it was her feelings he must hold in mind. Slowly but surely he came to a decision. He sighed deeply as he stood and crossed to the desk in one corner of the room. The desk drawer stuck a little when he pulled it open to retrieve his leather writing case. It was a gift from his parents when he first joined up, his mother's way of making sure he had no excuse not to write.

His pen hovered over the paper for several minutes of careful thought. Firstly he would tell her that he was not angry with her but he knew he would not be able to stop himself saying how angry he was at Michael. He must though reassure her that he wanted whatever she wanted and if that was to keep the child, he would support her in whatever way was necessary.

A lone mother was not such an issue as it would once have been. How many women were bringing up children on their own as they had lost husbands in the war? Hundreds if not thousands. Some tongues would wag but he could arrange for her to move away to a new area where no one would know any different. He could and indeed would support her financially –

she would not need to go without. And if that meant his own life was put on hold for a while, so be it. He had sworn to protect her always and he would remain loyal to her when others had betrayed her.

After what seemed an age of thought, he stared at the blank sheet of paper. His mind was too troubled to think straight, too turbulent to write. Closing the writing case, he returned it to the drawer. The letter he left open on the desk to remind him he must write later. He stared out of the window. Why was it that, after the unhappiness of their parents untimely deaths, she should have to deal with such betrayal?

CHAPTER 4

The flight from White Waltham to Brockworth had been uneventful and, as Alice had estimated, they approached the airfield ten minutes before ten hundred hours. Lizzie lined up the Anson with the runway and descended, adjusting the angle of approach slightly to correct for the wind direction. The aircraft bumped softly on the runway and Lizzie taxied to the buildings.

"Nice to have a hard runway. It was unpaved until last year according to our notes."

"Lots more flights I suppose and heavier aircraft."

They had hoped to have time for a cup of tea and to stretch their legs but Mr Healey was waiting for them inside the main building by some seats where his suitcase nestled. He was pacing back and forth, and had a look of anxiety on his face. Nervous about flying? Surely not, being an aircraft engineer. When he saw the three of them approach, he stood up but he didn't offer his hand.

"Mr Healey? Your transport to Cranwell. My name's Grainger – from the Ministry." The two men shook hands, Healey vigorously but on Grainger's part without warmth; he seemed embarrassed by it.

Lizzie saw that Grainger had no intention of introducing them so she stepped forward with her hand extended. "Second Officer Lizzie Barnes, Sir, your pilot, and this is Alice Frobisher our navigator."

Healey took Lizzie's outstretched hand, shook it warmly and did the same to Alice. "So pleased to meet you." He bent to pick up his suitcase, grunting a little as he did so. "Right. I'm ready."

He and Grainger walked out of the building side by side. "A perfect gentleman," Lizzie remarked.

Alice smiled. "Very friendly. I'm not sure how many gentlemen are left these days."

"I've met a few. It's not that I want to be treated as something fragile but it is nice to be acknowledged as a person."

"I guess most think we're not worth taking notice of. I mean we are just women and we don't have important jobs."

Lizzie looked at Alice. The irony in her voice was tinted with some bitterness. "You've obviously experienced similar things to me."

"Probably. We'd better go."

The aircraft left the runway almost exactly at ten hundred hours and Alice gave a flight time of thirty-eight minutes. Lizzie flicked the intercom switch on the panel and gave that information to their two passengers.

After a minute or two, Alice added, "We should add a few minutes to that for landing and maybe a bit more for finding the place."

A moment later, Grainger's head appeared in the cockpit doorway. "What do you mean 'to find the place'? I thought you were trained people. Trueman assured me you know what you're doing. Doesn't sound like it."

Lizzie looked guiltily at the panel and reached forward to flick the intercom switch off. "Damn," she muttered to herself, "should have turned that off."

As she did so, Alice turned in her seat to half face Grainger. "The airfield at Northolt is heavily camouflaged, Sir, so it's difficult to spot."

"It's a bloody airfield for God's sake. It's got runways and buildings and ...why should a bit of camouflage make it hard to spot?"

"Apparently, they've painted houses and gardens on the roofs of the buildings, Sir. It makes it look like a park set amongst a housing estate. The whole point is to disguise it."

"I know what camouflage is supposed to do. Just make sure you get us there. I do not want to be flying around over London when we have a very important man to pick up."

"I'm sure there'll be no problem, Sir. We've both found more obscure places in the past." Lizzie found it hard to remove the anger from her voice.

"Well our passenger is looking very nervous."

Lizzie leaned forward and flicked the intercom switch again. "Just to clarify, Mr Healey, there's no need for anxiety about finding the airfield. It's just that it is heavily camouflaged. We'll get you there on time."

Grainger grunted and returned to his seat; the two women exchanged a look.

After much agonising, Bert Swallow set aside the letter to his sister, Angela, and packed away his writing case. He sighed heavily as he slipped on his jacket. He now had to wait for the engine designer...or at least assistant designer, William Butler, who was due to arrive by car at about ten hundred hours. Before he closed the door to his room, he looked back. The letter from Angela was still on the desk, the envelope already in the bin. He knew he must put her out of his mind, prepare a face to meet the visitor, go through the motions, but he felt weary. He would much rather go to Turner and ask for compassionate leave, get himself up to Newcastle so he could be with her, put his arm around her, reassure her.

He trudged down the stairs and out of the building, walking slowly to the gatehouse to make sure Butler had not arrived early.

"Morning, Sir." The airman saluted smartly and Bert returned it.

"All quiet Sanders?"

"All quiet, Sir."

"I'm expecting a Mr Butler who should arrive at zero nine thirty. I assume he's not early."

"No visitors through the gate so far this morning, Sir."

"Direct him to the main accommodation building when he does come. I don't know if he's driving himself or being driven but, if the former, have him park over there."

"Will do, Sir."

Bert walked back to the main building and stood in the foyer, waiting. His mind was still churning over the letter. What should he do about that? He wanted to call him all sorts of names but, even in thought, he was restrained. Some fifteen minutes later, he was brought back to the present by the sound of a car driving past the entrance to the building. He watched a black Vauxhall 12 park in one of the visitor spaces and a small, wiry man step out. His movements were brisk, business-like. He took a suitcase from the boot and walked purposefully towards the entrance.

There was something severe about Mr Butler's greeting. The handshake was firm enough but his eyes betrayed no warmth. "Shall I show you to your quarters, Sir?"

"Not just yet, Sergeant." He raised the suitcase. "If I could leave this here, I'd like to check the engines straightaway. If there are any problems, they can be sorted in good time."

"As you wish but I'm sure there will be no problems. I've had my two best men check everything according to the manual and I'm very confident..."

"All the same. I'd like to check them myself."

Bert nodded. He took Butler's suitcase and tucked it in the housekeeper's office before leading the way out of the building. It was some way to Hangar Three where the aircraft was housed and, despite the shock he had endured that morning, Bert tried to make conversation but had little success. When they entered the hangar and stood in front of the aircraft, however, William Butler's demeanour changed.

He looked lovingly at the sleek lines of the aircraft from its nose to its tail, the letters DG206/G emblazoned on the fuselage just in front of the rudder. When Bert lifted the panels covering the engines, he looked really thrilled.

"I helped Frank Halford design the engine you know," said Butler unable to keep the pride from his voice.

"I'm impressed." Bert Swallow disliked this arrogant little man who clearly did not think he was worthy of friendship and made little attempt at civility.

"That's right. Shame we can't start them up in here but they may blow out the end of the hangar."

"That powerful then?"

"Ooh yes."

Butler worked on each engine in turn, checking the fuel pipes were properly tightened and running his eagle eye over every part. A born engineer and designer. Bert knew the type – completely obsessed with what he did.

"I always get a thrill of excitement when I see an impressive piece of machinery. That's why I love motor cycles: you can see the engine and gear box and how the power is transmitted. Not like a car where everything is concealed. A motorbike takes pride in its propulsion, not hiding it and trying to make it a mystery."

As he worked, William Butler talked to Bert Swallow, explaining the importance of the checks he was making and the beauty of the engine. Bert took little notice. He was an engineer himself but for him it was a job not a vocation. Instead he spoke briefly with the armed guard who hovered nearby, rifle slung over his arm. Group Captain Andrew Turner, the base commander had said the guard was essential and a decree from the ministry. 'The aircraft has a G after its number; that signifies an armed guard at all times it's on the ground,' he had said.

At last, Butler finished his checks and stood back. "Ok, the panels can go back on." The two men swung the engine cowlings back into position and turned the latches that secured them. William Butler slapped an engine gently. "Such a beauty. All ready for tomorrow."

"Let's get some tea," Swallow said. Towards the rear of

the hangar, a large tarpaulin covered what looked like another aircraft but Butler took no notice. The two men left the hangar and strolled towards the mess. "Where are you normally based?"

"Hatfield...the de Havilland factory."

"Wasn't that blown up a couple of months ago? I read about it in the newspaper, the Express I think it was. Had pictures too."

"It was sabotaged but actually not much damage was done. Looked a lot worse than it was. Didn't stop production of the Mosquito."

"Now that's a fine aircraft."

"Certainly is."

As they neared the mess, Albert Swallow looked sideways at William Butler. His face was austere, betraying nothing. His small frame was athletic, probably stronger than he looked. An interrogator would have a job getting anything out of him. Bert did not warm to him even though, as an engineer himself, they should have had plenty in common.

In the mess, the two men sat at a table with mugs of tea. "Big day for you t'morrow then?" Bert felt a need to fill the silence; it was clear that Butler would not initiate any conversation.

"Yes, a big day Sergeant."

"My name's Albert but most people call me Bert – please feel free. Sergeant seems very formal unless one's talking to the senior ranks."

William Butler smiled, a strange steely affair without warmth. "As you wish, Bert."

"Yep we've got some top brass coming apparently. Air Chief Marshall Stanley himself – you know – top man in Fighter Command. No doubt be good for you if it goes well t'morrow."

"It won't make any difference to me. I do my job that's all. It will go well anyway. No reason why not. The engines were fine and I'm sure the plane itself is A1."

"You can count on that. I've had my guys check every last rivet."

◆ ◆ ◆

Robbie McBane stood as soon as the door opened. He snapped to attention and saluted when he saw the officer enter the room, shown in by the corporal who had met him earlier. The thick band and three narrower bands on his sleeve meant he was an Air Chief Marshall, the second highest rank in the RAF.

"Morning, Sir. Sergeant McBane, RAF Police Special Investigation Branch."

The officer returned the salute. "At ease McBane. Air Chief Marshall Stanley." Stanley's lips puffed out a little. "In charge of Fighter Command. Are you flying to Cranwell too?"

"Yes, Sir."

"And what's your role?"

"As I understand it, Sir, it is to provide some security for yourself and another passenger and I've been asked to check security arrangements at RAF Cranwell."

"Good. Can't have too much security on this job." Stanley looked full into Robbie McBane's eyes for several seconds. "Keep it to yourself, McBane, but we think we might have a mole... someone feeding info to Jerry. Keep your eyes peeled, ear to the ground, that sort of thing. But not a word to anyone. Report to me."

"Understood, Sir." Robbie McBane stood awkwardly while Stanley strutted around the room. He was a short man, stocky, and his steps were small rather like a penguin but Robbie knew he was no fool; the penetrating look in his eye declared that unequivocally.

Suddenly he turned and walked closer to Robbie, fixing him with his eyes. "You know McBane, you're going to have to trust me on this assignment. Things may seem odd and I may not be able to tell you everything initially, so...trust me."

"Sir."

The sound of an aircraft flying over the base stopped

the conversation. Both men went to the window and looked out. "Anson Mk 1 if I'm not mistaken. Probably our transport." Stanley turned away. "I'll brief everyone later today when we get to Cranwell. What you'll see there is top secret and we need it to stay that way."

"Of course, Sir."

"It could win us the war, or at the very least shorten it considerably. That's the problem with war: you have to keep ahead of your enemy. They develop something better than you've got and you've got to find something even better."

" Yes Sir. But we've got good scientists and engineers I think."

"The best McBane, the best." Stanley fell silent and stared out of the window.

Robbie McBane watched the aircraft land and taxi towards the main building. Four people alighted, two passengers and two in flight clothes. As they walked towards the mess building, Robbie's brow furrowed. He was concentrating on one figure. Surely there was something familiar, the gait confident and... perhaps feminine? As if in answer, both aircrew removed their helmets and the one he had been watching shook her head, releasing long fair hair. His heart thumped in his chest. It was her, Lizzie. What a coincidence so soon after their last meeting!

CHAPTER 5

Checking his tie was straight, Bert Swallow approached Group Captain Turner's office door. Was this summons to his commanding officer some sort of act of fate, giving him an opportunity to ask for compassionate leave? But he didn't know if that is what Turner wanted. The next day would be perhaps the most important in Cranwell's history and he wanted to be a part of it. He was part of it…a very important part, charged with ensuring the security of the aircraft and its being in tip-top condition. And yet, when he thought of Angela, alone up North, his loyalties were torn between his duty and the one remaining member of his family.

He tapped on the door and grasped the handle firmly when he heard the instruction to enter. He stepped in smartly, closed the door and came briskly to attention, saluting. The very act brought him firmly back to his role in the RAF. He hoped that would last throughout the coming discussion whatever it might be about.

"At ease Swallow. Thanks for dropping by. Just wanted to run through things for tomorrow and make sure everything is in hand."

"Sir. I have already met Mr William Butler, the assistant engine designer who arrived this morning from Hatfield. He wanted to check the engines immediately so I took him over there. He seems happy with everything."

"Good. What did you make of him?"

Bert Swallow paused just for a moment which caused Turner to look up from his desk. "Seems to know his stuff, Sir."

"But…?"

Bert Swallow smiled. "Bit of a strange man, Sir. Very focused on his job, you might even say obsessed. Difficult to relate to…says little, doesn't really engage in conversation."

Group Captain Turner's lips tightened and he turned to look out of the window. "Often the way with people who have an element of genius. On the other hand…" he paused, "keep an eye on him Swallow. We think there may be someone supplying the Germans with information. No one is above suspicion."

"Will do, Sir." As Turner shuffled some papers on his desk, Bert Swallow felt again his sister's situation pulling at his heart. But the conversation had just confirmed how important he was to the smooth running of this event.

"Did he notice anything else in the hangar…you know what I mean?"

"I'm pretty sure he didn't, Sir, seemed totally focused on the engines."

"Good. I'm just wondering how he'll react when….you know…"

"Difficult to predict, Sir, but I'll be there to forestall anything."

"Good man, Swallow. I knew I could depend on you. Air Chief Marshall Sir George Stanley no less will be joining us later this morning. He's being flown up by ATA along with a Mr Healey who is a senior engineer on the aircraft design team. There's also a Sergeant McBane from the RAF Police Special Investigation Branch. I want you to meet him and make sure he's settled. Extra security for Sir George and of course to assist with the operation."

"Sir. I assume the visitors have been assigned quarters in the main accommodation building?"

"Correct. And see that the pilot and so on are made to feel welcome. You've sorted a rota for guarding the aircraft already I'm sure."

"I have, Sir, yes. Four hour stints, one guard always on right through until ten hundred hours tomorrow morning." Turner was reading through a document that summarised arrangements. His head was lowered and Bert Swallow again wondered if this was a good moment to ask for leave. He cleared his throat but Turner did not look up. Bert backed away like a horse shying at a fence. If he were to ask now and explain the situation, Turner would think that his mind was not on the job. Better to wait until after the whole test was over. It would only delay things by another day or two. He could leave on Saturday morning and be with Angela by late afternoon.

"Will that be all, Sir?"

Turner looked up briefly. "Yes, yes, thank you Swallow."

"Sir." Bert came to attention, saluted and turned smartly to leave the room

A corporal met them at the door to the building and showed them into a meeting room. Two men in RAF uniforms were standing inside. One was tall, powerful and had red hair. Lizzie's mouth opened in surprise and she broke into a huge smile. "Robbie McBane." She took a step forward but he did not move. Was it a reluctance to greet her in the way they had parted or was he maintaining formality because of the situation?

Robbie McBane smiled briefly and looked towards the other man. The corporal coughed. "Air Chief Marshal Sir George Stanley, Sergeant McBane from the RAF Police Special Investigation Branch. I'm sorry, I don't know your names."

Grainger stepped forward and held out his hand to Stanley. "Ian Grainger from the Ministry."

Stanley took the proffered hand. "Ah yes." His eyes narrowed slightly.

"And this is Mr Arthur Healey, the senior engineer with the aircraft's design team." Stanley shook his hand looking him in the eye but Healey did not meet the look.

Lizzie stepped forward with her hand out. "Second Officer

Lizzie Barnes, Sir. I will be flying you to Cranwell."

"You're the pilot?" Stanley did not take her hand.

"That's right, Sir. And this is Navigator Alice Frobisher."

"So we are in the hands of ladies?"

"No need to worry, Sir. I've flown an aircraft before...once or twice." Lizzie grinned without humour ready for any put-down that might come.

"Quite."

As the corporal poured coffee from a silver pot, Robbie McBane stepped close to Lizzie, took her hand and smiled warmly into her eyes.

"I thought you were ignoring me," she said with arched eyebrows.

"Not at all...just the formality of the situation...you know...very senior officer present."

Stanley noticed the interchange. "It looks as though you know each other."

"Aye, Sir. We worked together at RAF Silverstone last month...a murdered civilian girl, Sir, you may have heard. Miss Barnes was very important in the investigation. We both attended the funeral on Monday."

"Yes, I did hear something. Useful to know you're acquainted." He turned his eyes on Lizzie and she felt the intensity of his scrutiny. This was a man who was used to making judgements about people.

He turned away, coffee cup in hand and listened to the stilted conversation between Healey and Grainger about the weather, the state of the war. Lizzie was itching to ask Stanley what the mission was about but knew she had to contain her curiosity a little longer. After coffee, they filed out to the aircraft and the luggage of the new passengers was stowed.

The flight was uneventful. Through some breaks in the cloud, Alice pointed out the de Havilland factory as they flew over Hatfield and the distant spires of Cambridge to the East. Lizzie flicked the intercom switch each time and pointed out the landmarks to the passengers.

They were flying over the flat fens North of Cambridge when Lizzie spotted the small dot in the distance approaching from the East over the coast. She tensed. Although distant, she had her suspicions. They were above the cloud cover; she made her decision. "I'm going to drop below the cloud."

Alice turned at the tension in Lizzie's voice. "Copy that." She followed the direction of Lizzie's finger and saw the tiny black shape in the distance.

Lizzie pushed the joystick forward and the plane dived, gaining speed rapidly, the wind screaming in the wires. The cloud lay beneath them, fluffy like cotton wool that would soften their fall.

Lizzie flicked the intercom switch. "Possible enemy aircraft approaching from the East. Taking avoiding action – we'll hide beneath the cloud...hopefully."

Soon they were enveloped in an impenetrable grey mist and Lizzie started to level the aircraft. They were still dropping however; she was determined to fly beneath the cloud not through it. At last, at about 4,000 feet, she was able to maintain level flight. She hoped the enemy aircraft would not spot them through one of the occasional gaps in the stratocumulus cloud cover.

"What was it?" Alice asked when she judged Lizzie was able to answer.

"A Shrike I suspect...a Focke Wulf 190. I encountered one last month. The Germans are using them as day raiders, lone wolves that fly over, do what damage they can and then disappear. They're fast, faster than our Spitfires, and so are hard to catch. Coming alone like that, they can avoid radar too. We're a sitting duck in this thing; we haven't got anything like the speed nor manoeuvrability."

A face suddenly appeared in the cockpit doorway. "For God's sake what are you doing? Mr Healey is convinced he's going to die. Did you have to dive so dramatically?" Grainger was spitting with fury.

"Yes, Sir...unless of course you wanted to be shot up by an

enemy fighter."

"I'll certainly have words to say to Trueman when I get him on the phone." With that he disappeared and Lizzie's lips set into a hard straight line.

"That man really wants to get me into trouble."

"You did what you had to do. If they don't like it, that's their problem," said Alice.

They had followed the Lincoln road a short way before turning left onto the road that led to RAF Cranwell. After passing through the small village of Cranwell, they turned left again onto Raunceby Lane which Bob had realised from the map would take them past the end of the runways, running along the airfield perimeter.

"God, look at it. No cover anywhere. I forgot that they don't have trees up here."

But Hans did spot a small clump of trees some way off the road and they found a farm track that took them there. It was not perfect but it would have to do. Hans reached into his coat pocket and withdrew a pistol. A silencer was already attached, extending the barrel.

"Don't use that whatever you do. We need to be in and out without leaving any trace."

"Only if I have to. Must be prepared." Hans smiled grimly. "I can of course just use my hands…much quieter."

They left the van and walked back to the road that ran along the air base perimeter, tracking slowly along the high fence looking for the best place to climb over. A coil of barbed wire decorated the top of the fence along its length.

"Probably the best place to get on the airfield out here. We're a long way from any buildings or observers," said Bob. "We'll have quite a walk to the buildings though. Our information is that it's in Hangar Three. We just need the stills camera tonight. We need to be closer tomorrow; probably best on the road from Sleaford to Leadenham - it runs on the South side of the airfield and quite close to it. Hopefully we can shoot from the roadside."

As they talked, Hans pointed to a vehicle on the base driving slowly along the perimeter fence. It was a considerable distance from them. "Patrol," he said and pulled Bob's sleeve. They moved swiftly back crouching in a gap in the hedge on the far side of the road and watched as the Land Rover crawled around the perimeter. "Regular inspection I guess."

Bob looked at his wristwatch. "We need to check how often. I bet it's every hour."

An aircraft approached from the East and flew over their heads before touching down on the runway. They watched it taxi over to the buildings and a few people alight.

"Maybe that's the visitors arriving for tomorrow's show. Hope they enjoy it as much as we will." Bob chuckled and rubbed his hands together.

As they came into land, Lizzie braced herself for a dressing down from at least one of her passengers. She and Alice stood by the aircraft while two airmen from the base took off the luggage and loaded it into the back of a Land Rover. The shorter of the two seemed to struggle with one case which was clearly heavier than the others.

Group Captain Turner was on hand to welcome Air Chief Marshal Stanley. After the formalities, Stanley turned to Lizzie and Alice. He was gruff. "Thank you both. A Shrike you say? Bloody Germans. Well maybe we've got something better." He raised his voice and Lizzie thought he looked pointedly at Grainger. "Very smart move that, ducking below the cloud cover. Well done." Grainger scowled. "Perhaps we should have women flying combat missions."

"Very happy to do so, Sir."

"Yeees…though I think the World is not quite ready for that yet."

He turned away and addressed the assembled group. "Briefing at seventeen hundred hours. Does that suit Turner?"

"Absolutely, Sir. I suggest we use our Briefing Hut if that's ok with you."

"Fine. I need everyone there. That includes you Healey and McBane. Is Butler here already?"

"He is, Sir. I'm Sergeant Swallow, Sir, from Cranwell. I was with him earlier checking the engines."

"Good. Make sure he gets the message." Stanley turned back to Lizzie and Alice. "You ladies will need to be there too. You're going to see things tomorrow and you need to know how important they are." Without a further word, Stanley climbed into the Land Rover followed by Grainger, Healey and Group Captain Turner.

Lizzie, Alice and Robbie McBane were left by the aircraft. Sergeant Swallow strolled over to them. He had thick black eyebrows and dark hair smoothed back with pomade. He was powerfully built but there was something slightly neanderthal about him – arms a little too long, the slightest stoop in his posture - though he seemed friendly and cheerful.

"Sergeant Swallow, Bert if you please. I've got to look after you. I'll take you to your accommodation first and then we can get some lunch."

They climbed into a second Land Rover, slinging their bags into the back, and Swallow revved the engine. The car crossed a road that seemed to bisect the base before stopping at an imposing, palladian-style building.

"It looks very impressive," said Alice softly.

"Certainly does. We're not used to such luxurious accommodation."

"Don't get excited. Inside it's quite functional." Swallow grabbed their overnight bags. "Come on. Let's get you settled."

CHAPTER 6

It was a pretty dull job but he felt he had to do it. Robbie McBane strode around the perimeter fence of the airfield, looking for any possible security breach. Sergeant Swallow had said there was no need, that it was patrolled every hour, but Robbie was not going to take any chances. He'd been asked by Stanley to check security and he certainly did not want to upset someone of that rank – it would finish his career in the RAF Police and possibly the RAF itself if a hole in the wire was found later.

A few training flights had taken off as he walked but he made sure he kept his eyes on the fence. He estimated it would take him the best part of two hours to check the whole thing and then he would check the gate log and procedures for vetting visitors. The regular patrols certainly were in place; twice a Land Rover passed him. It seemed to be a tightly run ship. You developed a nose for sloppiness in this job; he had certainly smelt something wrong at RAF Silverstone last month.

His thoughts turned to the briefing later that afternoon. What would Stanley reveal that was top secret? Would he reveal anything or just keep everyone guessing? It was surprising that he had insisted Lizzie and her navigator should attend but then, if there was something top secret on the base that they might see, they would have to be informed and briefed to keep it secret. Seeing Lizzie again so soon was a joy but also a concern. In his breast, he felt stirrings which he feared would give him no peace.

A line of starlings suddenly lifted from the coil of barbed wire on the fence ahead of him and flew chattering and screeching into the air, wheeling around in crazy confusion until he had walked further on. Gradually they settled. "It's the effect I have on people as well," he said cheerfully over his shoulder.

As he approached the buildings again and the main gate having completed his circuit, Bert Swallow walked over to him. Had he been looking out for him, McBane wondered? Swallow was a large man like himself but not so athletic. He was a similar age he guessed, late twenties but already carried some excess pounds around his middle.

"Sergeant McBane. How goes it? Long walk all the way round."

"Aye it is but it has to be done."

"Of course. Find anything untoward?"

The question put Robbie on his guard. Was it a little bit too searching? "Nothing," he said, "all in order."

"Great. D'you fancy a cup of tea?"

"No thanks. Still got plenty to do." Robbie had paused only briefly; he now resumed his walk keeping his eye on the fence. Swallow hovered, as if disappointed. Was he trying to distract me, Robbie wondered? Is there something he doesna' want me to see?

When he reached the gatehouse, Robbie returned the salutes of the two guards and spoke lightly to put them at ease. "Just carrying out some additional security, chaps. I'd like to see the gate log please."

One of the men smartly turned, went into the gatehouse and brought out a log book. "Here y'are, Sir. All in order."

Robbie looked at the entries. "You do log every entrance and exit I assume."

"Course, Sir. That's our job."

Robbie scanned the entries for that day and the day before. He noticed a visitor, a William Butler, aero engineer from de Havilland, had arrived earlier that day. "This gentleman here, Mr Butler, he's still on the base?"

"Must be Sir if he hasn't been signed out. Came by car this morning, Sir. We were expecting him."

The other airman was standing close by. "So what's all this about, Sir. I mean I don't mean to be nosey but why the extra security checks?"

"Something important is happening on the base - I don't even know myself what it is but I've been asked to double check all security arrangements."

"Right, Sir. We did have a big truck come in, must be two, three days ago, you know a low loader with something on it that was all covered up. Looked like a plane but don't know if that would be secret."

"No idea I'm afraid. Anyway, thanks for that. All seems to be in order. Just keep your eyes peeled and report it straightaway if you see something unusual."

"Will do, Sir."

Bob slowly came to. He had slept in an uncomfortable position and felt groggy. The piece of carpet he had found in the van offered little comfort. He stretched as best he could in the confined space and looked at Hans whose eyes met his own.

"Blimey, I needed a couple of hours kip. Did you sleep?"

"Why would I sleep when you make so much noise snoring?"

"Me! Snoring! I don't think I snore."

Hans's voice was full of self-righteous indignation. "I can assure you that you do and loudly. I'm surprised someone didn't alert the Police."

"Don't exaggerate." Bob stretched again. "I tell you what, I'm looking forward to a big feed tonight."

"Let's hope there is something good to eat."

"Yep, let's hope." Bob looked at his watch. Four-thirty. I reckon we could head back by now. By the time we get to the pub it'll be nearly five. You can't work on a roof when it's getting dark – it's dangerous. We can have a wash and freshen up and then a beer or two before tucking in. I really fancy a nice steak and kidney pie me, with some veg and lashings of gravy."

"Do you ever think about anything else except food?"

"Well there is something else, yeah." Bob grinned and described an hour glass shape in the air with his hands.

"You'd better leave that out tonight. Can't afford to risk giving ourselves away."

"No that's where you're wrong again. That would make us more credible. I mean what could be more convincing for two roofers staying over to pick up a bit of how's your father?"

Hans was unimpressed. "Sometimes I wonder whether you speak English at all."

Lizzie took a large breath and looked out over the sea. The cloud cover was thinning and the fleeting early March sunshine provided little warmth. It was not a cold wind but she was grateful for her flying jacket.

"Let's walk along the embankment to the point over there."

Alice fell into step beside Lizzie. "This is very welcome. A whole afternoon hanging around the base was not an attractive prospect."

"It was fortunate that Bert was coming out to RAF Wainfleet. It's quite a landmark that tower in such flat countryside." Lizzie looked back at the tower that dominated the landscape.

"Certainly is. What are the barges for out at sea?"

"It's a range. They use it for bombing practice. I commanded a Wellington from RAF Silverstone with a trainee crew last month. Quite exciting to be doing something like that."

With the wind at their backs, it was very pleasant walking. There was a good stone track on the sea defence so no muddy shoes. Gulls wheeled overhead by the point and the fresh smells of the sea, even the rich aroma of weed on the beach, were invigorating. The two young women walked in silence for a while until Lizzie asked Alice about herself.

"I'm from Northamptonshire. Parents still live there..." Alice's voice faded and then she changed the subject. "I always liked Maths and Sciences at school though we didn't have as many lessons as I would have liked – not the thing for girls is it? They only need to learn to cook, sew and be the perfect hostess."

"I know what you mean. Same for me really. How did you become a navigator?"

"I did an evening class for a while but that was in nautical navigation. My father's very interested in sailing. He has a small boat on the Norfolk Broads. Not much need for navigation there but I was interested in it. Then I saw an advert for the ATA – looking for navigators and engineers, training provided and I thought, why not?"

"Good for you. Did they ask you how you thought you would do the job being a woman?" Lizzie assumed the clipped voice of a stereotypical male. "And what happens when we train you my dear and you go and get yourself pregnant? Bit of a waste of time then."

"No they didn't. I have to say the ATA were excellent. They didn't question my gender at all. I did the tests that everyone else did and passed them. I guess they're so desperate."

"I don't think it's that. You would have impressed them with your calmness. What did your parents make of it?"

"My Dad was fine. My mother...well she's not interested in us, only herself."

Lizzie looked at Alice. Her face betrayed nothing but there was bitterness in her voice. "I'm sorry to hear that."

"I'm used to it."

Lizzie pondered that. Her own mother had been baffled by her decision to join the ATA as a pilot but it was not, she thought, lack of interest in her, just an inability to understand why any young lady would want to do such a thing even in wartime. They fell silent again and after walking another half mile reached the corner of land that projected out to sea. Bert Swallow had said it was Gibraltar Point. It was no higher than the sea defence on which they had been walking but they stopped to gaze over the sea.

"Across there is Germany."

Lizzie could not read any expression in Alice's voice. Was it fear, fascination...even longing?"

To reach the point itself, they left the embankment and followed tracks across the scrub until they were standing on the line where grass gave way to sand. Lizzie scanned the horizon and then brought her gaze closer. The tide seemed to be receding from its highest point, leaving beautiful swirls and ripples in the sand. Then she noticed what appeared to be footsteps a short way north of where they stood.

"Footsteps in the sand. Let's go and investigate."

They followed a path through the grass until they were closer. There were two sets of prints and between them a gouge in the sand which led up to the long grass near where they were standing. Lizzie's brow furrowed.

"Anything strike you about those footprints?"

"They disappear where the tide was earlier – the sea has washed them away."

"Yes but surely they are coming from the sea? Look at the way the sand has been pushed into a little pile on the seaward side of each step. That would happen if you were walking from the sea to the beach. And what's that long groove in the sand between them?"

"Probably some people who've been out in a boat. Why is that strange?"

"Because if you took a boat down to the water recently, went out to sea for a while and came back, there would be a set of prints going down towards the sea as well."

"Perhaps they put the boat in further along the beach."

"Could be I suppose. Let's just go and look."

Lizzie led the way along the path in the scrub until they

reached the point where the footsteps met the grass. They could just make out boot prints continuing in places into the longer grass though they were not so distinct. Something, however, had pushed aside the grass recently; several stems were broken and flattened. Lizzie followed the trail until she came to a canoe upside down.

"A canoe. What's that doing in the middle of nowhere?"

"I expect it belongs to someone who goes out on the sea occasionally."

"But why leave it here? I mean it's miles to walk to the nearest house – it's way up there. Look you can see houses in the distance. Why would you leave your canoe here and have to walk all that way back home?"

"Perhaps they got tired paddling and came ashore here. I really don't think there's anything strange about it Lizzie."

Lizzie did not reply but put her hand under one side of the canoe. She lifted it and let it roll over against the long grass. The two paddles stored inside clattered against the wooden frame.

"It's a kayak." Alice said.

"What's the difference?"

"A canoe is open topped. A Kayak is covered except for the holes where people get in."

Lizzie looked at the craft carefully. There seemed to be nothing that might indicate its owner or its purpose. Then she leaned over and examined each seating position. In the one closest to the bow, there was something crumpled lying on the canvas floor. She lifted it out and began to unravel it. It was a piece of foil with a paper wrapper covering it. When she spread it out, her heart thumped. She held it out for Alice to see. The two women looked at each other in horror.

"Now I'd say that *is* strange," Lizzie whispered.

CHAPTER 7

"Robbie, Robbie." Lizzie tugged gently at Robbie McBane's sleeve. "I need to tell you about something we found on our walk this afternoon."

Air Chief Marshal Stanley was already on his feet at the front of the briefing room with Group Captain Turner standing beside him, waiting to give the introduction.

"Afterwards, Lizzie, not now."

Lizzie and Alice took seats next to Robbie towards the back of the briefing room. Lizzie surveyed the assembled group. All were men apart from herself and Alice. She wondered why they had been allowed to be part of such a male enclave but remembered what Stanley had said – they'd see something secret so needed to be part of the briefing. She smiled grimly to herself. They really do not trust women. Probably think we can't keep it to ourselves. Lizzie shook her head. Always the same.

Senior officers from the base sat near the front with the more junior further back. Sergeant Swallow was there and Mr Healey, the engineer from Brockworth, as well of course as Mr Grainger from the ministry who sat at the back in the row behind them. Lizzie wondered what exactly his job was – probably keeping an eye on the budget or making sure the RAF did what the Ministry wanted. Trueman had not even said what ministry he was from – the War Office, Ministry of Defence, the Treasury? He lolled back in his chair as if the whole thing bored him with the same amused look in his eye she had noticed that morning when he had been introduced.

She turned to Alice. "That man Grainger looks as though he thinks it's all a game."

"Probably is to him. I mean he's not getting shot at in an aeroplane is he?"

Group Captain Turner stood a little more erect and surveyed the room. He coughed loudly and the hubbub of voices faded. "I'd like to welcome all our visitors but in particular, we are very honoured to have Air Chief Marshal Sir George Stanley, head of Fighter Command with us. He will introduce our other visitors as necessary. Sir George."

There was a ripple of polite applause and Stanley took a pace forward. He began with the usual pleasantries about it being a well run base and what a super chap Turner was. Lizzie switched off for a moment, looking around the briefing room. It was, as were so many parts of RAF bases, functional, a hut with a space to pin large maps at the front and a blackboard. Lizzie focused her attention back on Stanley when he got to the point.

"You'll all be wondering what is happening that brings me to this base. Tomorrow, we will be having the first test flight of a new aircraft. We all admire the Spitfire and Hurricane and rightly so because they saved our skins in the Battle of Britain. The Mosquito is also a great aircraft, speedy, manoeuvrable and quick to build. That's why the Germans tried to blow up the factory. They think they did but actually they failed to do much damage at all. But, gentlemen, we are losing the war in the air over France because the Germans have an aircraft that is faster than our fighters. The Focke Wulf 190. As you know, Hitler is also sending them across often singly to carry out daytime raids. In fact, had it not been for the sharp eyes and quick response of the pilot who flew me up here this morning, I may not have made it."

Stanley paused and located Lizzie and Alice at the back of the room. "Miss Barnes and her navigator Miss Frobisher, Gentlemen." Stanley raised a hand in their direction and surprised faces turned to look.

"Our fighters also do not have sufficient range to fly to France, engage in an air battle and fly home again. We are losing too many. I would like now to introduce Mr William Butler. Mr

Butler is the assistant designer of a new type of engine. Mr Butler."

Butler stood up and faced the meeting. He was clearly not used to speaking in public and he struggled to look up from the notes he held with a shaking hand in front of him. "In 1936, Frank Whittle designed a new type of engine which we call the turbo jet. It does not have propellers but has combustion cylinders inside which suck air from the front and force it with great thrust out of the back. This has the potential to allow an aircraft to travel much more quickly than the propellers we are used to. I won't bore you with the detail but Mr Whittle's engine was simplified by my boss Frank Halford and I to produce an engine that is powerful and efficient. One of these engines has been mounted on each wing of a new aircraft designed by a team at Brockworth. A senior engineer with that team is Mr Arthur Healey. Mr Healey."

Butler sat down abruptly, clearly relieved to have completed his bit of the briefing. Healey took his place; he was nervous but in a different way – restless, eyes flicking about the room but not making contact with anyone. It was what Lizzie had noticed about him that morning when he was waiting for them.

"Gentlemen, my team has designed an aircraft that will take your breath away. It has only been possible by the development of the turbojet engine so I wish to acknowledge the debt we have to the Franks… Whittle and Halford…not the French!" He laughed at his own joke. A few tittered but the joke fell flat, perhaps the seriousness of the briefing deterring laughter from most.

"We have been calling this new aircraft, the Rampage but the Americans are developing something similar with that name so we are calling it the Meteor. Like its namesake, it will streak across the sky. We expect it to reach a speed of 400 to 430 miles per hour at sea level and up to 470 miles per hour at 30,000 feet. As you know, the Spitfire which has served us well, can only fly at about 300 miles per hour and the Focke Wulf mentioned by Sir Stanley has a maximum speed of a little over 400 miles per hour. Our new aircraft will not only be faster, it can climb more steeply. Tomorrow you will see that for yourselves."

Healey gave a short bow and enthusiastic applause filled the room. Stanley stood again. He looked around the room with a degree of belligerence. "So gentlemen, we have the chance of stealing an advantage over Hitler and his cronies and we cannot afford to lose that by word of this development leaking out. Our sources tell us that the Germans have developed a Messerschmitt with turbojet engines. It made its first flight in July last year. That is bad news for us except that they've had problems with the engines, the construction and Hitler changing his mind about what he wanted. If we can develop our own aircraft quickly, we can be ready for them and maybe even beat them to it." There was a quiet cheer at this point.

Stanley's face broke into a rather grim smile. "We can't afford for the Germans to find out about our aircraft nor to steal our technology. So, not a word to anyone. It will be exciting tomorrow and you will want to share the information with loved ones and so on. But don't." He glared at the audience, his face set in a passing imitation of a bulldog. "The first test flight will be at ten hundred hours tomorrow morning. Group Captain Turner has made arrangements for everyone to be in a viewing area. That is important as if you get behind this aircraft, you will be blown away...I mean that literally. Group Captain Turner."

Sir George Stanley resumed his seat, bolt upright, his squat figure looking solid and unshakeable. Lizzie understood how he could command people. He had a certainty, perhaps a simplicity in his approach: things were right or wrong, good or bad. But that was probably a useful characteristic in wartime. She had to acknowledge to herself that she had warm feelings towards him as he had congratulated herself and Alice in front of a room full of men. Perhaps that would avert any of the snide remarks she tended to hear about women's alleged shortcomings.

Group Captain Turner took over. "As Air Chief Marshal

Stanley has said, secrecy is critical. This test must not reach German ears. You are to find an opportunity this evening to brief all those in your command about the secrecy of what we will witness tomorrow. I would now like to introduce our test pilot for tomorrow, Flight Lieutenant Roger Dakin." Dakin stood up, faced the room and nodded his head in acknowledgement. He said nothing. Turner continued. "And now Mr Grainger from the Ministry."

Grainger ambled to the front of the room. He was tall, about six feet lizzie estimated, had well groomed hair and maintained his supercilious, amused expression. "Gentlemen … and ladies of course…" he looked in their direction with an ironic smile, "I have to inform you that our intelligence people believe the Germans may already know something about this aircraft."

Lizzie could feel the chill spread around the room at these words.

"I say it is possible. It is not definite. But even if they know we are developing a new, faster plane, we do not think they have any details about it. They don't know how it works or indeed if it does work. We need to keep it that way. As has already been said, any word leaking out about this test tomorrow could find its way back to Jerry. That could alter the course of the war in their favour. There really is that much at stake."

He stopped abruptly and walked back to his seat. Before chatter could break out, Group Captain Turner concluded the briefing. Lizzie and Alice looked at each other and Alice raised her eyebrows. "Well they certainly laid it on the line about secrecy." She paused. "You know, there's something about Mr Grainger that I don't like."

"You and me both. I do wonder exactly what ministry he works for. I wouldn't trust him to walk my dog…if I had a dog that is." They both laughed.

"What's so funny?" Robbie McBane had stood and was looking down at them with a quizzical expression.

"Nothing actually, Robbie. Can I talk to you now?"

"Of course."

"Let's go somewhere more private."

They left the still crowded briefing room and stood in a corner of the foyer. Lizzie pulled from her pocket the foil and paper wrapper she had taken from the kayak that afternoon. She held it out for Robbie so he could see the printing on it. He took it from her and looked at it carefully.

The name *Vauen* was printed in large letters on the paper wrapper that enclosed the foil and underneath it *Nuremberg.* Robbie McBane looked into Lizzie's face. "Where did you get it?"

"We were walking along the coast this afternoon and came across a kayak pulled into the long grass. This was inside."

"The kayak was in a remote location with footsteps leading from the sea and a gouge in the sand where it had been dragged up the beach," Alice added.

"It must be Germans who've landed from the sea."

"Now Lizzie, we mustn't jump to conclusions but I do need to report this to Stanley. Come with me both of you."

Sir George Stanley's head revolved slowly on a thick neck when the three of them approached. Group Captain Turner was with him as was Grainger. Their eyes followed the direction of Stanley's.

"Sir, I wonder if I could have a word, please?" Lizzie had noticed when she had last worked with Robbie that his Scottish accent was softened considerably when speaking in formal situations and to superiors.

"What is it?"

"Perhaps in private, Sir."

Stanley shot a quick glance to Turner and Grainger. "What you have to say can be said to Group Captain Turner and Mr Grainger."

"Well Sir, you asked me to report to you directly if I came across anything untoward. I've not found anything of concern on the base but, this afternoon, Miss Barnes and Miss Frobisher went for a walk along the coast, by RAF Wainfleet, Sir, and came across something that does cause me concern." Robbie McBane turned to Lizzie. "Perhaps you should tell Sir George what you saw."

The gaze of the three men switched to Lizzie but before she could speak, Stanley shot a question. "How did you get to the coast?"

"Sergeant Swallow was going to RAF Wainfleet, Sir, and offered us a lift. As we had nothing else to do, we thought we'd walk by the sea."

Sir George Stanley humphed and nodded his head. "Do go on."

"We walked along the sea defence to Gibraltar point and stood on the edge of the grass to look out – you know at the barges on the range, Sir. A bit further north, Sir, there were two sets of footprints leading from the high tide mark to the long grass and between them a gouge in the sand that looked as though a boat had been pulled up."

"So someone had been fishing." Grainger's voice was loaded with derision.

"Perhaps, Sir, but it was a long way from Skegness or any other habitation and seemed a strange place to land a boat."

Grainger shrugged. "Could be any number of explanations for that. I really don't think we need to worry about some fishermen. We've got plenty else to think about."

Lizzie was not going to be intimidated. She turned to Stanley again. "We took a closer look, Sir, and found a kayak in the long grass. That's not a fishing vessel, Sir. It was upside down and when we turned it over, I found this inside."

Robbie McBane held out the foil wrapping and pointed to the lettering on it. "It's an empty packet of tobacco, Sir, clearly originating from Germany."

The three men stared at it in silence.

CHAPTER 8

Bob heaved a satisfied sigh as he relaxed onto the chair. A pint of good beer in front of him, a nice meal to come and maybe a few hours kip before they had to go out again. Hans was looking around the pub, his sharp eyes picking up every detail. Just a few men were sitting at the bar having a drink after work no doubt before going home for a meal. Bob had to hand it to him, he was good at his job was Hans but he was rather a humourless bastard!

A young barmaid appeared at their table. She had brown hair in a large curl on the top of her head and hanging in soft undulations on her shoulders. Her eyes were bright, the lashes large and black with mascara and her lips were crimson. Bob's eyes travelled down her body, taking in the shapely bosom, hips and legs. He smiled and she returned it, her eyelids fluttering with apparent innocence.

"Not seen you gentlemen in here before. Nice to have some new faces. Are you eating?"

"We certainly are...especially if you're on the menu."

She tittered. "I've never heard that one before."

"Sorry. Same old lines. What're you going to tempt us with?"

"We've got a nice rabbit stew with spuds and veg followed by apple crumble and custard. That'll cost you nine pence...each o'course."

"Sounds delicious." Bob and the waitress exchanged a long smile. He smoothed the small moustache on his upper lip. He knew he was handsome and definitely attractive to women. He could sense disapproval from Hans.

When the waitress had walked away from the table, swinging her hips more than necessary, Hans leaned forward. "You should not be flirting with that girl, Bob. You're drawing attention to us."

Bob took a long swig of beer. "Keep yer 'air on 'Arry. I keep tellin' you. We've got to act normal. If we sit in a corner skulking that's what will draw attention to us. Just relax for God's sake. Leave it to me. Remember, I come from this country."

Hans leaned back and sat in hostile silence occasionally sipping his beer. Bob finished his and went to the bar for another. He had not been seated long when the waitress came back, carrying two steaming plates held with a tea towel. She placed them on the table.

"There y'are, gentlemen. I'll just get you some cutlery and salt and pepper." She swung away again and Bob's eyes followed her bottom until she disappeared. Hans shook his head and sighed. When she came back, Bob smiled up at her.

"This smells gorgeous. Did you cook it yourself?"

"No silly. It's me Mum does the cooking. Me Dad runs the bar, I do the waiting at tables."

"Sounds like a well-run ship. So what time do you finish work tonight?"

She pouted her lips. "Now why would you want to know that?"

"I'm making enquiries about the working conditions of staff in pubs." He grinned. "Now why d'you think?"

"It'll be late tonight. When the food's finished, I'll have to help behind the bar. We've got a band on tonight. There's usually a bit of dancing as well."

"Dancing? I love to dance. Can yer Dad spare you for a dance?"

"Maybe," she said arching her eyebrows. "We'll have t' see."

"I don't even know your name."

"Molly. What's yours?"

Bob stood up and held out his hand. "Mr Robert Edwards

at your service Miss Molly." She had placed her hand in his and Bob lifted it to his lips. Molly giggled and blushed. "But my friends, my special friends, call me Bob."

"I'll see you in a bit then, Bob...to collect your plates." She began to walk away but half turned. "So nice to see some new faces. It's so dull around here...I could do with some excitement." She smiled and gave a little wave.

When she was at a safe distance, Hans looked daggers at Bob. "No dancing, absolutely not."

"Look Harry. You're not my keeper. We don't have to worry. Now eat your grub and shut up."

The mess was already crowded when Bert Swallow led Lizzie, Alice and Robbie in. A warm smell of hot food added to the sense of cheer and camaraderie. Plates of steaming stew and vegetables or a dessert of stewed prunes were being devoured enthusiastically by the ranks. The clatter of cutlery and chatter of numerous voices bounced around the hard walls of the mess hut, the windows of which were covered with blackout curtains as darkness was already creeping over the airfield, a weak sun departing below the horizon.

They collected trays of food from the serving hatch and sat at a table that was empty except for Mr Healey and Mr Butler. Healey was enthusiastically explaining something to Butler who seemed to be concentrating on chewing each mouthful of stew.

"Big day for you both tomorrow then?" Robbie McBane said when there was a break in Healey's flow.

"Not really," replied Healey, waving his knife in the air. "The plane and the engines have been tested thoroughly. We've even had taxiing tests so we're confident it will fly well."

"It's not been off the ground as yet then?" There was something not quite right about Healey's confidence, Lizzie thought. He seemed overly enthusiastic.

"No true it hasn't but all the tests we've done and theoretical calculations suggest it will perform well. I expect you'd like to fly it." Healey smiled at Lizzie.

"Maybe one day…when I'm sure it's safe and I've had some training. Is it very different to fly from a normal plane."

"Not really. Just the speed. Things happen much more quickly at 450 miles per hour than they do at 150. The rate of climb should be much better. You see, a conventional aircraft uses its speed through the air to generate lift from the wings. This aircraft will do that as well but the engines are so powerful, it can climb very steeply as if it has rockets propelling it. That's thanks to Mr Butler's engines of course."

Having given his fellow engineer an entrée into the conversation, Healey put a piece of meat in his mouth and chewed it energetically. Butler did not take the cue, however, continuing to eat his meal morosely. Lizzie wondered if he was just very shy, perhaps in the company of women.

Bert Swallow asked Robbie McBane about his career in the RAF. "I was an aircraftman up in Glasgow," he said, his Scottish accent re-asserting itself, "but decided to join the RAF Police so I came down south. I'm based at Burnham Beeches."

"And what's life like in the Police? Don't you miss being part of the action?"

"Being an airman doesn't enable you to be a direct part of the action. I get more interest and excitement in this job than I did before."

"Is checking up on the rest of us that interesting?"

"I do lots more than that. Last month, I was at RAF Silverstone where we had to deal with the murder of a young woman. Lizzie was there as it happens and was a great help."

Bert Swallow looked at Lizzie and smiled, admiration perhaps in his eyes? "Changing the subject, I don't know what you folks fancy doing this evening but there's a pub in Leasingham, a couple of miles down the road where they have a band on a Thursday night. It's a great atmosphere. I could take us there in a Land Rover. There's even a bit of space to dance though it is quite, as you'd say, cosy."

The prospect of some life and enjoyment was very welcome to Lizzie. Alice seemed less sure but Lizzie persuaded her. Robbie McBane at first said he ought to stay on the base and keep an eye on things but Lizzie also persuaded him that an hour or two off would do no harm. Both Healy and Butler were adamant that they had some calculations to check for the test next day so declined the invitation. The two engineers then started a quiet, private conversation.

Bert swallow picked up his empty plates noisily. "I'll just go and organise a vehicle and permission. See you outside the Hall at..." he consulted his watch, "... say, nineteen thirty hours?"

They agreed and when he had left, Lizzie leaned over the table to Robbie McBane and Alice. "What did you make of the way Stanley dealt with the information we gave him after the briefing?" Her voice was low, making sure the two engineers did not hear.

"Difficult to say. None of them seemed to think it was anything to worry about...and perhaps it isna."

Alice looked thoughtful. "I felt that Grainger seemed very keen to dismiss it."

"Aye he did. Did you notice the looks that went between them when we were telling them. Was that concern? If it was, they wanted to hide it...pretend it was nothing."

"It's almost as though we found something they already knew about," said Lizzie.

William Butler drank the remainder of his coffee. He was beginning to tire of Arthur Healy who seemed to be unable to sit still and quiet. He chattered constantly about nothing of consequence, frequently looking around the now empty mess room as if expecting someone to join them. He twitched in his chair, unable to sit still for any length of time.

Unable to deal any longer with Healey's restlessness, Butler suggested they go and check the aircraft again. Healey seemed unwilling at first but then agreed, saying he must make sure he did some calculations for his next project before turning in for the night.

It was quite a walk to Hangar Three where the aircraft was housed. The airfield was quiet, arc lights mounted high on the buildings washing the apron with yellow light. In the West, a few streaks of pale yellow showed between the clouds where the daylight was retreating.

"The weather looks good for tomorrow," Healey offered as they made their way.

"Let's hope it stays that way."

"The Meteor will be able to cope with a lot heavier weather than a conventional propeller driven aircraft but wind and rain would not be ideal for a first test flight."

"Agreed. Looks as though it'll hold though."

They entered the personnel door at the side of the hangar and were immediately confronted by the barrel of a rifle. "Halt. Who are you?"

Arthur Healey jumped at the sudden confrontation. "We've come to check the aircraft. I helped design it and Mr Butler here designed the engines."

"Likely story. Are you journalists?"

"No. It's as Mr Healey said."

"Show your passes."

Butler calmly reached into his coat pocket and withdrew his pass. Healey fumbled around, muttering and mumbling until he at last found the pass. His hand was shaking as he presented it.

The airman took each pass in turn in one hand, holding his rifle in the other. "Ok, they look in order," he said begrudgingly. "What do you want to do?"

"We just want to have a final check of the aircraft before the test tomorrow." Healey tried to assume a casual air but failed. Suspicion settled on the airman's face but he motioned with his rifle towards the plane.

The hangar was lit by a single, large light suspended from the ceiling which cast a huge shadow of the aircraft onto the concrete floor. It looked beautiful, mysterious, the engine pods with their air intakes like mouths were devoid of the propellers that a conventional aircraft would have. Both engineers began a thorough examination of the plane, making sure all panels were secure, running hands over the sleek lines. Healey reached up and moved the rudder, then walking forwards, moved the flaps on the rear of the starboard wing.

"Everything in order I think," he said. Butler grunted his agreement.

The guard sounded defensive. "No reason why it shouldn't be. I mean it's been guarded all the time it's been here…at Cranwell, I mean."

"Yes, quite so. Do you have a long stint on guard?" Healey sounded sympathetic.

"I've just come on…twenty hundred. Just four hours 'til midnight then I get relieved. I'll be happy to get to me bed, I can tell you. I hate guard duty. It's so boring."

"Well I hope the time passes quickly for you, um… Airman…"

"Sinclair, Sir."

"We'll wish you goodnight then, Sinclair."

"Rightio. Goodnight." Sinclair's voice was friendly enough but he watched from the personnel door as the two engineers walked away from the hangar towards the accommodation building. His eyes narrowed and he pursed his lips. Something odd about those two.

CHAPTER 9

Swing music greeted them when they tumbled from the Land Rover in high spirits at the prospect of an evening out and maybe some dancing. Bert Swallow waltzed his way across to the door of the pub, earlier gravity dispelled

"Here we go, folks. I'm definitely in the mood."

The night was dark, no moon, no stars and of course no artificial light showing outside because of blackout regulations. Inside, however, there was light, warmth, excited chatter and the smoke from numerous cigarettes. Several other men in uniform stood in the area in front of the bar, talking loudly and laughing; some of the locals eyed them suspiciously, no doubt resenting the invasion of the RAF. At one end of the room, a fire crackled vigorously in a large fireplace. At the other end, the band was already playing. Bert Swallow bought the first round of drinks and they eased their way through the crowd to a table that gave a good view of the band and the tiny area in front of it which was the dance floor.

An older gentleman with a large shaggy beard and white hair reaching at the back well past his collar was playing the trumpet, blowing vigorously, the instrument pointed upwards and almost touching the low ceiling. His band mates were all of similar age, a saxophonist who weaved notes around the trumpet part unerringly, a double base player whose face was an expressionless mask but whose left hand travelled the length of the long neck with impressive accuracy and a banjo player whose head was bowed over his instrument as he plucked rapid but delicate notes from the strings. A sign at the front proclaimed it to be The Bill Bailey Band.

Lizzie leaned towards Alice. "I thought they would have a drummer."

Bert Swallow heard the remark. "The place is too small for a drumkit and it would deafen everyone. These guys do fine wi'out drums."

The atmosphere of excited camaraderie was infectious. No one was dancing as yet but Lizzie wanted to. She looked at Robbie McBane and, when she caught his eye, inclined her head towards the floor. He shuffled uneasily in his seat and made a face but Lizzie was not going to be denied. She reached her hand across the table so that he could not resist the invitation.

There was a brief smatter of applause when Robbie took her in his arms and they began to sway around the floor. He spoke very close to her ear. "This is the first time I've danced since...you know...since I lost..."

Lizzie squeezed his hand and pulled him a little closer. "Sorry, I had forgotten Catriona." Robbie's eyes looked distant for a few moments and then he seemed to snap out of his reverie.

"It's okay. I must move on. And who better to dance with than you?"

"Bit of a smooth talker then?" Lizzie felt a little more pressure on her back, drawing her closer.

"I'm trying."

They were soon joined by Bert and Alice though Alice looked reluctant. She forced a smile when she met Lizzie's eye but, otherwise, her gaze was on the floor. At the end of the song, she thanked Bert Swallow and returned to their table. He looked surprised, almost shocked in fact but followed her. Lizzie could see Bert watching her and Robbie; the expression on his face was hard to read but was a mixture of disappointment and anger, his dark brows drawn together in a frown. After the next dance, she led Robbie by the hand back to the table.

As soon as she had sat down, Alice leaned close to Lizzie. "Don't look right away," she hissed, "but at the next table, there's a couple of men. One of them is lighting a pipe. I just saw him fill it from a packet that looked exactly the same as the one we found in the boat."

Lizzie watched the band for a short while and then turned back to look at the men. The smoker, tall, fair-haired with strong cheek bones, was sitting erect in his seat and pulling meditatively on his pipe, sending thick clouds into the smoky air. The smaller one, cropped dark hair, a little moustache and a face that was sharply defined with alert eyes that seemed to dart to and fro was more hunched and seemed to be restless. He was looking over towards the bar and taking occasional gulps from a pint of beer.

Lizzie smiled at Robbie. "Come on let's dance again."

"You'll wear me out."

"Nonsense. We don't get much chance to dance and have a good time. We should take it while it's available."

Grumbling but secretly pleased, Robbie McBane stood and took Lizzie's hand. As soon as they were in hold and moving to the rhythm, Lizzie turned Robbie so that he was facing the table with the two men. "Alice told me that the chap smoking the pipe just filled it from a packet of tobacco that looked exactly the same as the one we found in the boat."

"They seem harmless enough. Nothing that might suggest they're Germans."

"They may not be German. Hitler recruits British people as spies."

Just then, the shorter man walked across to the bar. With a broad smile, he said something to the young barmaid. She returned the smile, had a word with the burly gentleman Lizzie took to be the landlord, and then came out from behind the bar. She had a pretty face, heavy with make-up, bright red lips full and sensuous. She took the man's hand and sashayed onto the dance floor. Lizzie noticed the way she danced so closely and the teasing smile that shone in her eyes. She had all the art of a girl practised in male attraction. As for him, he held her very close and his hand strayed down her back, sliding slowly over her body.

The two danced for a while in silence and then Lizzie

could see them talking. As she and Robbie revolved slowly, Lizzie manoeuvred them closer in the hope of hearing what was being said.

"What time will you finish then?"

"About eleven, by the time I've cleared glasses and what not."

"I've got to go out for a bit later."

"What, at night? You can't work on a roof at night."

"No, just got to check something. But I could come to your room when I get back."

She pulled away from him a little. "Don't be daft. My Mum and Dad might hear." Her voice suggested shock though whether it was genuine Lizzie did not know.

"Well you can't come to mine 'cos I'm sharing."

She said nothing for a while, pulled closer to him and then said, "That's your van outside isn't it? The one with the ladders on. I bet that's cosy."

He chuckled. "Not exactly cosy, but we won't be worrying about the décor will we?"

She tossed her head back and laughed, her rich brown hair swinging from her shoulders. "You're a right one ain't you? But thank God you've come here. Nothing ever happens…I'm dying of boredom. I need some excitement."

The song ended and both couples left the floor, the barmaid's hand lingering in her partner's before, smiling at him, she returned to her duties.

Lizzie whispered into Robbie McBane's ear. The proximity felt good. "It's suspicious, I'm sure. Why would he need to go out later on? Let's take a look at his van before we leave. Do you think we should tackle them?"

Robbie turned to face her. "Of course not. We have no evidence of anything and besides it would be the job of the Police to deal with civilians. There's probably a perfectly innocent explanation for the tobacco packet and they are probably just two working men out for a good evening."

"But we could ask the landlord about them – he'd probably

know who they are."

"Why would he tell us anything?"

"Well you're in the Police aren't you? I know it's the RAF Police but it's the same kind of thing."

"You are nothing if not persistent, Lizzie."

"That's because I know there's something suspicious."

Robbie McBane looked at her. "You mean, like you knew that it was Dearing who murdered that girl at Silverstone even though it turned out to be someone else entirely."

"Yes but he was involved…and he was or is a thoroughly unpleasant man."

Robbie sighed. "I'll see if I can have a word with the Landlord but I need to make sure the girl's not listening." He lifted his drink and walked slowly through the standing drinkers to the bar. Lizzie was watching keenly. He had not been gone more than a few seconds when the shorter man from the next table was at her side.

"Hello…Bob Edwards." He held his hand out which Lizzie took automatically, giving her name. He was standing beside her and smiling down. "May I have the pleasure of this dance?"

Lizzie didn't really want to dance but she was so taken aback, she stood and allowed herself to be led back onto the dance floor. And so it is that reluctance is often overcome by surprise. She did not allow him to pull her too close, though she could feel constant pressure on her back. She had to hand it to him, he was a good dancer, balanced and nimble on his feet. Then it occurred to her she might be able to achieve something.

"Are you from the Base?" He asked.

She turned her head and smiled at him. "I am, sort of. I'm staying there but I'm not RAF. I'm ATA…Air Transport Auxiliary. We deliver planes and people to air bases and so on."

"Ah yes, an Atta girl." He smiled at her, his eyes frank and genuine, no sign of anything secretive or hidden.

"And you? Are you local?"

"Me, no. We come from Skegness on the coast. We've got a little roofing job to do but we couldn't do it in one day and, with the petrol rationing, we needed to stay over for the night. We're staying here tonight and it's back home after work tomorrow."

"Did you grow up around here?"

"No, no. I'm a Londoner."

"And what about your mate?"

"No, he's not local neither. Not sure where he comes from actually. Anyway, you ask a lot of questions."

"Just like to know about the man I'm dancing with that's all."

"What d'you do in the ATA?"

"Fly planes."

"What actually fly them?"

Lizzie laughed. Yet another man who was surprised that a woman could be flying a plane. "Yes...I actually fly them."

"Blimey. That's impressive. What got you into doing that?"

"I learnt to fly when I was eighteen. My grandmother left me money in her will. My elder brother is a pilot in the RAF and I'd always wanted to try it. Then in 1940, I saw an advertisement for the ATA so I applied."

"Good for you. And what planes do you fly?"

"On this trip, I flew an Avro Anson Mark 1. We use it to transport people. I had a couple of important passengers."

"And who might they be?"

"Whose asking a lot of questions now? Top secret that."

They danced in silence for the remainder of the song. Bob escorted her back to her seat in a very gentlemanly way. She thanked him politely and he resumed his seat by his friend. Robbie McBane was still at the bar talking to the Landlord. The pub door opened and a familiar figure walked in.

"Isn't that Grainger?" Lizzie asked Alice.

"Yes."

The two women watched him walk to the bar and order a drink – whisky – interrupting Robbie in his conversation with the landlord. He nodded a greeting to Robbie and then mingled in the crowd. Although he stood amongst the drinkers in the middle of the floor, he gradually moved closer to the table next to Lizzie and Alice, the table at which Bob and his friend sat. Alice and Lizzie sipped their drinks and watched him with lowered heads. He held his glass in his left hand with his right in his jacket pocket. They watched as he withdrew it and saw, despite his attempts to hide it, a folded piece of paper between his fingers. That hand seemed to flop onto the table, was withdrawn and returned to the pocket. Quickly, Bob's hand covered the paper and slid it off the table into his own pocket.

It was very subtly done and unnoticed apparently even by Bob's mate.

Lizzie and Alice exchanged a glance. Robbie McBane came back from the bar. "They're roofers from Skegness staying over to do a job."

"Yes. I've discovered that. He asked me to dance."

"Happy now? He's not a German spy."

Lizzie's face was serious. "Perhaps not but that tobacco packet *is* suspicious and there's something else."

Lizzie leaned over the table and Robbie leaned towards her. "Grainger has just come in and surreptitiously passed a piece of paper to Bob...the short one. It's not just me, Alice saw it as well. What connection can Grainger possibly have with two roofers from Skegness?"

CHAPTER 10

Sir George Stanley relaxed into the leather armchair and, leaning his head against the high back, took a sip from his brandy glass. He looked approvingly around the room, the lounge of the Officers Mess. The walls were panelled with oak and in each section hung a portrait of a high ranking RAF Officer from the past. In pride of place of course was his boss's portrait, Marshal of the Royal Air Force. One day, he mused, his own portrait would perhaps hang there.

He turned to his left where Group Captain Turner sat. "Everything's in place for tomorrow, Turner, I hope."

"Of course, Sir. I have assigned two engineers who are absolutely trustworthy to work on the aircraft early tomorrow morning. The hangar is designated an exclusion zone so there will be no interference. We have one guard on duty at all times. There's a telephone in the hangar in case reinforcements are needed but all the other security around the base should not require that. "

The two men sat at an angle to each other with a coffee table in front of them. They had enjoyed a very good meal and the brandy was a welcome 'digestif'. Stanley had been very complimentary about all the arrangements and his room so Turner was feeling confident. One had to make sure that the most senior members of the RAF went away with a good impression and this visit was of huge significance. He had been honoured to have had his base chosen for the test flight.

"What about spectators? Presumably you'll keep everyone in an area that is tightly controlled? We don't want anyone straying too close and getting hurt or seeing too much for that matter."

"All in hand, Sir."

"And the perimeter?"

"That Sergeant McBane from the RAF Police who came with you, Sir, checked the perimeter fence this afternoon and checked all security arrangements. I'm confident the fence is secure and our position in the countryside means that we don't get onlookers. The fence is patrolled constantly, once per hour in a Land Rover, day and night."

"Is someone briefed to deal with anything outside the perimeter, any onlookers as you call them? Someone who knows what to deal with and what to ignore?"

"Absolutely, Sir. That's all arranged. We'll ask McBane to stay with the spectators to make sure no one is taking pictures."

"Good. You know, what amazes me is how Jerry found out about this aircraft. We must have a mole somewhere."

"They have definitely found out about it have they?"

"Definitely. Grainger was a little circumspect at the briefing but we had hard intelligence that Jerry knows we've developed a new plane. How much detail they have, we don't know."

"If there is a mole, tomorrow will confirm their suspicions."

"Yes…but will make them wonder…." Stanley stopped abruptly and the two men exchanged a long look. Stanley's mouth slowly broke into a smile and Turner reciprocated.

Robbie McBane looked worried. Were the two women seeing things they wanted to see? What significance could a piece of paper have? It could have been anything. It might have been a bit of rubbish which Grainger dropped on the table though Lizzie was very clear that he had tried to hide it and that

Bob, the shorter roofer, had slid his hand over it immediately without his mate seeing. Grainger had since slipped away.

"D'you think we should be getting back?" Robbie's question was directed at Bert Swallow.

"I guess so. Things seem to be finishing early tonight. Ah well. Hope you enjoyed it like." Bert looked knowingly at Robbie though Robbie did not understand the meaning of it.

"Lizzie, Alice, we'd better hit the road."

"Ok but we need to talk."

Bert Swallow was helping Alice on with her coat. Robbie McBane helped Lizzie with her flying jacket and as he did so, spoke very quietly in her ear. "Not here. Not with Bert about. We don't know anything about him."

"Right. When we get back we need to find somewhere."

"Agreed."

The four of them called 'Goodnight' to the Landlord and Lizzie managed a smile at Bob still seated at the adjacent table.

He responded and said, "Thanks for the dance. I wish we could dance again next week but we're only here the one night."

"I'm only here tonight and tomorrow. Bye."

Outside, Lizzie walked close beside Robbie. "Do you have a torch?"

"Aye…a little one."

"Let's take a look at their van."

"We'll not see much even with the torch." Robbie did however shine it on the van as they passed, keeping his hand over the top to prevent light escaping upwards. The van was black or a very dark colour with the name Allen Roofing on the side. Two ladders were tied to a roof rack "All seems to be as it should for a pair of roofers.

"Shine the torch in the back window."

Robbie did so. There was nothing to be seen, just a couple of metal boxes probably for tools. "Satisfied now?"

"Not really." They caught up with Bert and Alice and climbed into the Land Rover.

Bert seemed to be angry. He swung the Land Rover

around the corners and put his foot down as they sped along the straight piece of road to the base. The vehicle swayed drunkenly when he turned into the entrance and braked hard at the gate. He showed his pass and was nodded through. Again he revved hard when the gate was opened and the car shot forward up the drive.

"You ok?" Robbie said quietly to him when they had screeched to a halt outside the great pillars of the main building and had jumped out. Lizzie and Alice had started to walk in.

"You'd think that a young woman would want a bit o' fun when a chap's gone out of his way to provide it." His Geordie accent seemed more pronounced than before.

"Alice?"

"You're obviously alright with Lizzie. Special she is. I thought it would be a tidy foursome."

"I guess she's just shy. Maybe feeling out of her depth in a strange place. Tired...time of the month. It could be anything... nothing to do with you."

"Mebbe. There's precious little chance of meetin' young women stuck out here like. Probably need to go to Boston. Might be more chance there."

"Aye it's difficult. It's the War. Creates all kinds of problems."

Bert Swallow climbed slowly back into the Land Rover and drove off around the building presumably to park it. Robbie walked into the impressive lobby, pondering Bert Swallow's anger...loneliness that's what it was. He felt a different kind of loneliness, the loss of Catriona, but Lizzie certainly lifted his mood. He must try to unravel this thing about the two men in the pub and Grainger. Lizzie was bright and very observant but he had found when they worked together the previous month that she did let ideas run away with her.

She was waiting on a sofa in the lobby. "Alice has gone up. Tired."

"I think Bert Swallow was hoping for some romance...or at least something else."

"The latter I should think knowing men! Let's go somewhere private."

Lizzie stood up and Robbie McBane followed her, unsure of where they were going. She led him along a corridor and through a door marked "Library". When she flicked on the lights, a beautiful room lined with full bookshelves was revealed. It was not large but everything about it spoke of comfort, relaxation, quiet. No fire was lit in the grate and it was a little cool but they sat on a wing-backed settee that faced the fireplace.

"This is where they drink brandy I expect," Lizzie grinned.

"Aye, but I don't see any around."

"So what do you make of it all, Robbie. We find a German packet of tobacco in a kayak hidden in the long grass by the sea. We see a man in the pub filling his pipe from the same brand of tobacco. We see Mr Grainger surreptitiously slipping a note to that man's mate, Bob Edwards. It all adds up to something very suspicious to me."

"We mustn't jump to conclusions, Lizzie. In the morning, I'll report what you have seen to Stanley and see what he thinks."

"Huh! He'll just dismiss it as female nonsense."

"You have to admit there's nothing very concrete about it. We can't ask the police to arrest a man because he's got hold of a German brand of tobacco."

"But Grainger can be tackled about that note. What possible, legitimate connection could there be between Grainger, a man from the ministry – whatever ministry that is – and a roofer?"

Robbie McBane looked hard at Lizzie, remembering Stanley's words to him when they had met at Northolt that morning. "It's not hard evidence, Lizzie. Let's be careful about jumping to conclusions. If Grainger is involved, we need something more definite. I don't want to alert him before we're ready. Stanley was happy for Grainger to be in on the conversation about the tobacco packet. You can't suspect Stanley of being complicit with German spying surely? I'll report to Stanley in the morning."

"I just hope that's not too late." Lizzie stood up. Robbie stood and stepped close to her. His hand moved to her waist and his head began to lower but she did not respond. "Goodnight Robbie. Sleep tight." She turned away and left the room.

Robbie was disappointed. Her departure felt like a rebuke and he had so wanted to share a brief time of intimacy with her. He felt Catriona slipping further from him. Lizzie was lovely, bright, attractive if, perhaps, a little headstrong.

◆ ◆ ◆

"You are risking the mission. It's bad enough dancing with that girl but you cannot, you must not have sex with her."

"For God's sake stop worrying Hans. It's ten-thirty. We'll go out very soon, do what we have to do, be back before midnight and then I'll meet her. What can possibly be wrong with that?"

"You must not give anything away. Plenty of secrets have accidently been communicated between the bed sheets. She could be planted to find out what we are doing."

"When I'm with a woman, mate, there's no time for talking – it's all action." Bob laughed. "Besides which, there's no way she's been planted. I mean, they'd have had to know we were coming wouldn't they?" Bob patted Hans on the back. "Stop fretting. It'll be ok." He looked over towards the bar. "She is very tasty," he muttered to himself.

"You have the whisky?"

"Yep, bought it already. Landlord was pleased. See that's what I mean. He just thinks we're good guys, having a nice evening, spending money at his pub. Act natural that's what we've got to do."

Molly, the barmaid, had been around collecting glasses. At their table, she leaned over as she picked up their empties, her ample bosom plainly visible. "Let's say midnight. We're going out for a bit now and we'll be back by then. Can you let us in?"

"I'll leave the back door unlocked. You can come in that way."

"Lovely job. Meet me down here and we can decide where to go."

Molly looked around. The pub had almost cleared and the band we're putting their instruments back in cases. "I'll be ready well before then, if you want to meet up sooner."

"I'd love to but we've got to go."

"I'd like to know where you're going at this time of night - sounds exciting."

"Ask no questions, and I'll tell no lies." Bob laid a hand on her back and let it slide downwards. Molly giggled and whisked away with the empty glasses tinkling in her hand.

Bob nodded at Hans. "Let's give it another ten minutes then we'll do it."

The two men sat at the table watching the last few customers draining glasses, issuing cheery farewells and leaving the pub. Bob missed pubs. They were places where you could always find comradeship, laughter, a good feeling. A bit of alcohol made the World a better place or rather made it look a better place. Your cares slipped away, you felt on top of things, you felt anything was possible. The beer had warmed him thoroughly and put him in a confident mood. He felt the half bottle of whisky nestling in his coat pocket and tapped it affectionately.

After ten minutes had elapsed, Hans looked at his watch. He was restless, eager to get on with it. Bob would have liked to wait a little longer but Molly had disappeared out the back and there was now no one else in the bar. He stood up. "Ok. Let's do it."

The night was dark and felt chilly after leaving the warmth of the pub. Bob shivered but Hans seemed to take no notice. He was impervious to anything that one. They clambered into the van and Bob started the engine. The gear clunked into position and he let in the clutch. Shame it wasn't a bit less noisy but you can't have everything he consoled himself.

"So, I tap him on the head and put some whisky into his mouth while you make a start in the hangar."

"That's it Hans, but it's got to look like he was drinking and fell over, hitting his head. Don't kill him for God's sake. Leave no trace remember."

They parked away from the airfield initially, watching for the patrol. Bob had judged the time well. After only a few minutes, the lights of a vehicle skirting the airfield came into view. On top of the cab was a bright light directed at the fence. After it was safely past, Bob started the van and drove to the designated spot.

They didn't need to say anything. Bob stood on the running board on his side, stretching upward to untie the ropes and lifting off the ladder. Hans did likewise on his side. They put both ladders up against the fence. "Let's get the stuff then," Bob whispered even though, in that remote spot there was no need to keep their voices down. Bob went to the back door of the van and yanked it open.

"Surprise." Molly - grinning in the weak light cast from the interior lamp that had illuminated with the door opening.

"Bleeding, bloody hell! What are you doing here?"

"Come to see what you're up to. We can have a bit of fun in here."

Hans, hearing the voices, appeared at Bob's side. "I told you, idiot" he hissed. "Now what are we supposed to do?"

CHAPTER 11

Lizzie tapped softly on Alice's door. "It's me…Lizzie."

The door was opened, cautiously, Alice peering around it through the small gap. "Oh, hello."

"I just wondered if you're alright."

"Yes," but Alice looked down at her feet, her unfastened hair falling in front of her face. "Well…not really."

"Can I come in? I won't keep you up late…promise."

The door opened wider and Lizzie walked in. Alice closed it quietly behind her. The room was identical to her own next door, the emphasis on function rather than comfort. A single bed was against the wall with a little cabinet beside it, a wardrobe at its foot and a small chest of drawers in the corner opposite the bed. A chair stood forlornly beside it.

Alice watched Lizzie take in the room. "Not exactly a posh hotel but it will do."

Lizzie smiled. "I wonder if Bert Swallow bothered you at all, I mean did he, you know, try it on?"

"No…but he clearly hoped for something. I'm sure he's a perfectly nice man, Lizzie, but I'm not in the mood for anything like that tonight."

"I know what you mean."

Alice looked up. "Do you? How can you?"

"What I mean is that we're here to do a job and somehow romantic attachments don't seem appropriate. It's so difficult anyway…being based elsewhere and you know…"

Alice motioned Lizzie to the chair and she sat down whilst Alice herself sat heavily on the bed. "It's not that Lizzie." She came to a decision. "Today is my birthday…"

"Alice, I wish you'd said. We could have made this evening more special...given you the bumps or something."

Alice smiled. "In that case, I'm glad I said nothing." The smile faded. "I'm not bothered about celebrating my birthday. What's to celebrate about having lived another year?"

"It could be regarded as quite an achievement with Hitler's lot trying to kill us all."

"I telephoned my parents just before dinner...felt I should, you know... they let me use the telephone in the lobby downstairs. Not very private but that was fine. My Father had not arrived back from work so I spoke just with my Mother. All she could talk about was what she'd been doing, the WI this, the charity that...just a constant stream of how wonderful she is doing all these things. Not once did she ask me how I was or what I was doing. She never even mentioned my birthday. It obviously just doesn't feature in her thinking."

Alice stopped abruptly and Lizzie noted the bitterness with which she had spoken, especially towards the end. Her own voice was gentle. "Has she always been like that?"

"Yes. Oh she's remembered birthdays in the past but it's as if I'm out of sight and hence out of mind. I can't make her out, Lizzie. I mean she did all the things that mothers are supposed to do when we were children but as soon as I became a teenager, it was as if she didn't want anything to do with me. You'd think a parent would do anything for a child...anything to save a child from harm or distress." Alice's voice became an appeal, a plea. "What is it about me, Lizzie? Am I just not worth knowing?"

And then she hung her head and her shoulders were shaking. Lizzie was up and sitting next to her on the bed in an instant, her arm around her shoulders, pulling her close. It seemed as if Alice had finally shattered like a glass vase, brilliant, dazzling in some lights, but brittle and vulnerable. Her sobs seemed uncontrollable.

With close physical proximity and gentle shushing sounds, however, Lizzie was able to calm the flood of unhappiness. "Tell me about her, from the beginning. Say all the things you need to say but tell me first how she treats your Father."

With a handkerchief dabbing her eyes, Alice explained how her Mother treated her Father with contempt, using him as a convenient earner and handyman but showing him no affection. "My Father is a lovely man...he was always kind and loving towards us when we were children, always supportive when we grew up. He encouraged me to become a navigator and join the ATA and I have absolutely no doubt of his love for me and his pride in me."

"So it's not just you that your Mother overlooks."

"No, but she seems to reserve a special hostility for me. For some reason she seems to blame my father for her life. I don't know whether that's because my brothers and I didn't turn out as she wanted or because my Father didn't push himself to rise to more senior positions in his firm."

"Perhaps both. It's unnatural though isn't it for a Mother to treat her children like that? I understand that marriages break down but you'd think her children would be the most important thing in life for a mother."

"I think she perhaps dislikes us because we are the product of my Father. I don't know. I try to be civil, I ask her about what she's doing, I always give her something on her birthday but nothing seems good enough for her." Alice lifted her head and looked at Lizzie, her eyes pleading. "Is it me Lizzie?"

"I think you've had the misfortune of being born to someone who is governed by self-interest and has no real capacity for love. I'm so sorry Alice. You seem to me to be a truly lovely person. You're intelligent, attractive and present yourself as being very capable. It's not your fault Alice, I'm sure."

That provoked another brief tumble of sobs and Lizzie pulled Alice close again. "Now, come, come. That'll never do. We can't have these men here thinking all we do is cry."

Alice managed a brief laugh and wiped her eyes. She blew her nose. "Thank you so much for listening, Lizzie. I know compared to what other people are suffering, it's nothing, but all the same…you know." She paused for a few seconds and then turned to Lizzie. "You seem to understand. I wonder if you've had the same thing?"

"No, no. My Mother and Father are rather pre-occupied with what they do. They don't really understand why I want to be a pilot instead of just getting married to some rich accountant or something but they haven't stopped me. I wouldn't let them. And you mustn't let your Mother erode your self-confidence, Alice. You must hold on to your sense of self-worth. There are too many people in this World too ready to belittle us women."

The intensity with which Lizzie spoke caused Alice to look keenly into her eyes. "There is something, isn't there Lizzie?"

"There is but I used it to make me stronger, more determined and you must do the same. We have as much right to have fulfilled working lives as anyone else."

Alice managed a weak smile. "I'll try to hold on to that. Thanks."

"Do." The two young women hugged sitting on the bed then Lizzie stood up. "I'd better get my teeth cleaned and get to bed. Do you want to use the bathroom first?"

"No…it's fine…you go ahead."

Lizzie left Alice in rather better spirits than when she had arrived at her room but wondered at the unnatural behaviour of her mother. How could she treat such a lovely young woman as Alice as she did?

◆ ◆ ◆

"Just wait in there a moment, sweetheart, while we sort something out." Bob closed the rear door of the van and motioned to Hans to move away. "God knows what she's doing in there. I said I'd meet her when we got back," he hissed.

"If you had not been carrying on with her, she would not

have done this."

"Ok, ok. We need to think quickly."

"No need to think." Hans pulled the pistol from his coat pocket. "We need to get rid of her."

Bob stared at the long barrel of the silencer, horrified. "We can't do that. It'll give the game away."

"By the time her body is discovered, we'll be gone."

"But we don't want them to know that we've been here at all...ever."

The conversation was interrupted by a banging on the side of the van and Molly's plaintive voice. "Oi, let me out."

"We'll tell her we're playing a prank and say she's got to stay in the van."

Bob opened the rear door of the van and Molly climbed out before he could stop her. She ran her fingers over her hair, smoothed down her black coat and then stood with one hand on her hip. "So what are you up to, naughty boys?"

"Look we're just going to play a prank on a mate of ours who works on the base. So you just stay in the van and we'll be back in ten minutes or so."

"What stay in there on me own? You must be joking. There could be all kinds of madmen about." Her voice changed. "Why doesn't Harry go play the prank and you and me can stay in the van." Her hand slid onto Bob's shoulder.

He put his hands on her waist and held her back. "No, no sweetheart. This is not the right place for a lovely lady like you. You just stay here."

"I ain't staying here on me own and that's final. Besides, I like a prank so count me in."

Bob put his arm around her and pulled her close to him. He kissed her softly on the cheek and then brushed his lips over hers. She did not resist.

"I hope you won't drop us in it about this prank. We happen to know our mate is on duty tonight in one of the hangars. It's his birthday; his name is Micky Sinclair."

"Ooh I do like a practical joke. What're we gonna do?"

"The plan is that we climb over the fence here, and creep along till we reach the hangar – number three it is. Then we were going to make ghost noises round the back so he'd come out and we'd keep doing it to get him really wound up. Then we'd leap out and give 'im a drink of whisky. See I've got the bottle." Bob pulled the half bottle from his coat pocket. "Bought it from yer dad earlier see."

"Well that sounds like fun." Molly giggled. "What d'you want me to do?"

"If you're sure you want to come with us, when we get him out, you could sidle up to him and, you know, come on to him a bit, give him a drink and…" Bob paused to think, "…we'll then jump out and give him another surprise."

"What if I don't want to kiss him. I mean I only kiss good-looking blokes…like yerself."

"Just give him a cuddle if you don't want to kiss him. Main thing is to keep him occupied for about ten minutes so we can give him a good shock."

"Ok. I can do that."

"I knew you'd be up for a laugh. Come on then."

Bob and Molly joined Hans at the fence but he pulled Bob aside and gestured to Molly to stay where she was. "Are you mad?" he hissed. "She'll give us away."

"She's better off with us; she ain't going' to go blabbing about it if she knows she could be in trouble herself. We're stuck with her now."

Hans swore quietly and turned back to the fence. He had placed one ladder up against it and thrown the carpet from the van carefully over the barbed wire, squashing the coil. He picked up the second ladder and climbed with it until his waist was level with the top of the fence. He lowered the second ladder over it onto the other side, climbed a couple of steps higher and swung his leg over onto a rung of the inner ladder. He descended with swift strong steps and was quickly on the ground inside the airfield.

"Are you expecting me to climb that…in a skirt… with

these shoes?"

"You'll be alright. Those shoes are flat. It's not like you're wearing heels."

"I don't want him or you for that matter looking up my skirt."

"We won't. Scout's honour. Anyway, it's too dark to see anything…unless I shine me torch up there."

"You'd better not, you dirty sod." Molly put one foot on the bottom rung and looked back at Bob. "Look away then."

Bob dutifully turned away but when she had climbed about halfway, he turned back and looked up. Sadly there was nowhere near enough light to see anything interesting. He did consider getting out his torch but that might draw attention. He sighed and comforted himself with the thought that he may be able to get a much closer look later.

Molly reached the top of the first ladder and gingerly lifted one leg. She returned it without stepping onto the second ladder. "I can't do this. You need to steady me."

Bob was up the ladder in a flash. Molly tried again. "I need to pull me skirt up. Don't you dare look."

She held on with one hand and, lifting one knee, slid her skirt right up past the top of her stockings. She was able to step over then but had to repeat the procedure with the other leg. Bob made no attempt to look away and, even in the dim light, saw the white, naked flesh above the top of her stockings. It was all he could do not to reach out and run his hands over that sleek thigh. Then the moment had passed, her skirt was back where it should be and she was safely on the ground. Bob followed swiftly carrying a small metal box.

"Bloody hell. I've done some things in me time but nothing like this. I hope you're friend appreciates it."

"Oh he will alright." Bob gave Molly a brief hug. "You're a trooper you are. A real good'un."

Hans took hold of the inner ladder and laid it on the ground. "We just have to risk the other ladder. But then, the van is more visible. Come let's go."

Bob consulted his watch, shining his torch on the face but inside his coat. "Forty-five minutes max we've got. Let's get going."

Molly giggled as they set off, stooping, along the fence towards the hangars. Bob, smiling, shushed her though he must keep up the appearance of it being a game.

CHAPTER 12

Robbie McBane let out his breath slowly. It had been a long day and he was grateful to sink into bed. Not the most comfortable in the World but it would be sufficient. He was dog tired and he was sure he would sleep well – provided Lizzie didn't appear in his dreams telling him that everyone was a spy. He smiled to himself. She'd suspect Sir George Stanley if she saw anything unusual.

He looked at the picture by his bedside. How much longer would Catriona stay with him? Already he felt her slipping. The photograph helped, refreshed his memory but sometimes, during the day, when he called her to mind, her face would not fully form. Her voice was there, bringing a warm glow to his breast, but she seemed to be increasingly a ghost, an ever more distant memory. Would Lizzie replace her? He had to admit to himself that Lizzie had all the qualities he admired in a woman: she was intelligent, attractive and full of spirit, at times playful and at times infuriatingly persistent.

Caught between the living and the dead.

He turned on one side and switched off the bedside lamp. Tomorrow, he must be alert, watching for anything that might suggest a spy or a saboteur. Tonight he must sleep. He closed his eyes and formed a picture of Catriona's face, except he could not quite complete it. Sometimes her eyes were not there, sometimes her lips, but he sensed her smiling at him, teasing him but loving him. It would almost certainly prove the biggest tragedy of his life. To lose a wife after many years together must be awful; to lose one's girlfriend before one could even marry was just as bad. It was the loss of the future, of hope, as devastating as any other loss.

He was on the verge of sleep when a knocking at the door brought him immediately alert and sitting up. He listened. There it was again. He had not been mistaken. Quickly, he swung his legs out of bed and grabbed his greatcoat for he had no dressing-gown with him. He walked quietly to the door and spoke.

"Who is it?"

A hiss came from outside the door. "It's me…Lizzie."

Robbie opened the door. Lizzie was standing in her nightdress with her flying jacket on, casting swift glances down the corridor. "Sorry, but can I come in?"

He opened the door wider and she glided into the room, her bare feet making no sound. Robbie closed the door behind her. "I assume this is not a social call?"

"No. Sorry to disturb you Robbie. Were you asleep?"

"Almost. Just in the blissful state of knowing I would very soon be."

"I'll get to the point."

"Would you care to sit? I can't offer you any refreshment after your long journey down the corridor but if I had some whisky, I'd offer you a wee dram."

Lizzie grimaced. "Ooh, no thanks. Can't stand the stuff."

"No Scottish blood then. What is it?"

"Our bathroom is further along the corridor and there are rooms beyond that with another bathroom I assume. I'd used the facilities and, when I came out, I heard a tapping sound. It was mechanical, like metal touching metal. It seemed very odd at this time of night."

"Lizzie, there could be all kinds of explanations for that. It could just be the water pipes expanding and contracting as they heat up or cool down. It could be someone tapping a pencil, it could…"

"Okay, okay. I know you'll think I'm over-reacting but I think you should check it out."

"What now?"

"Well of course now. It may not be there if we leave it."

Robbie was about to protest but decided that acquiescence was an easier path. "Come on then. Show me." He closed the door quietly behind them and they walked softly along the corridor both in bare feet. The boards were smooth but cold. Lizzie stopped outside a door and listened. No sound came from it. Robbie McBane looked at her quizzically and she held up her hand as a signal to wait. They leaned closer to the door.

After a minute or so, a tapping sound started, very short bursts of it, a tiny pause, then another little burst. Each burst was not identical in length. After listening for a couple of minutes, Robbie McBane pointed back down the corridor and they walked as quietly as before to his room.

Once inside with the door closed Robbie spoke. "If anyone had seen us then, they would have regarded it as very suspicious – listening outside someone's door."

"Agreed. But what of the sound?"

"It's not pipes expanding and contracting certainly."

"Nor a pencil tapping."

"No." he thought for a moment. "Could be a typewriter."

Lizzie shook her head. "When people type there is usually a long burst of tapping and occasionally the bell will ring when the carriage reaches the end of the line. Besides which a typewriter makes a very distinct clacking sound. What we heard was not like that."

"So what do you think it was?"

"Morse Code. Do you know Morse Code?"

"I did a bit as a boy but I don't think I'll remember it now."

"Same here, but maybe we could write it down and look it up later. Do you know whose room that was?"

"No, but we can find out easily enough tomorrow. Room six."

"I'll get some paper and a pencil. Are you coming?"

"I think it's unnecessary and unwise but I'm not letting you do that alone. God knows what you'll do next!" He grinned at her and once again they left his room and crept along the corridor.

They crept along the fence, keeping as low as possible. No lights shone directly where they walked but there was some spill from those on the apron in front of the giant hangars. Hans led the way followed by Molly and Bob. At the edge of the apron, they paused and huddled together.

"Right. Here's the plan. Molly, you take the whisky and, when I tell you, walk down between the hangars. No light shines down there as far as I can see. I suspect the personnel door at the side of the hangar will be open. That's near the front so you'll need to slip past that quickly. You wait near the back. We'll be close to the door. Then you make an owl sound – can you do that?"

"An owl? What you mean like tuwhit tuwhoo?"

"Nah, that's not convincing I'm afraid. How about you sing a song? What's your favourite? One he'll know."

Molly thought for a moment. Bob could see in the light escaping from the apron lamps her eyes brightening. "How about 'We'll Meet Again'?"

"Perfect. Don't sing it too loud unless he doesn't hear. But he's bound to come out. You then walk forward tell him you're his birthday present and lead him back to the place you were so he's well out of the way when we give him his surprise. We'll leave it a good five minutes maybe more so don't be in any hurry."

Molly began to sing softly, "We'll meet again…"

"Not here. It is him we want to hear it no one else," Hans snapped.

"Alright. Keep yer 'air on."

"Now, you need to get him a bit excited – know what I mean." Bob chuckled softly. "If you can get his trousers off that would be great."

"Oh I can do that no problem. You wait and see."

"When it's time to go, I'll make an owl noise. Make sure he's had some whisky and can't follow you quickly...on account of not having his trousers on...and then run back to us."

Bob scanned the apron carefully. There seemed to be no guards on it or outside any of the hangars. "Now remember. His name's Micky Sinclair. Let's go." Still crouching, with his hand on Molly's back he moved forward and Hans brought up the rear. When they reached the gap between Hangars Two and Three, Bob pointed between them and nodded at Molly. She moved ghostlike between the hangars, briefly seen by the light spilling from the open doorway, until the darkness enveloped her. Bob and Hans waited. Then the song reached their ears, a clear, beautiful voice, the sound made ethereal by the metal walls of the hangars. Hans looked doubtful but Bob was entranced.

"God she's got a good voice. How could anyone resist that?"

A figure appeared in the hangar doorway, silhouetted against the inside light. It stepped out and took shape. The airman held his rifle across his body, two hands, ready to bring it to the firing position.

"Who's there?"

There was no answer but the song continued. Slowly, he took a step towards the sound and then another. "Who's there?" he called again, his voice betraying some fear. "Show yourself. Come forward slowly." He stood ready, waiting for some apparition.

Molly emerged from the darkness, still singing, walking slowly towards him. She stopped some three yards from him and finished the verse. "I know we'll meet again some sunny day. Happy birthday Micky."

"What's going on? It ain't me birthday." Micky spoke in a rich Newcastle accent.

"Oh yes it is and I'm your present...from your friends. So why don't you come and spend a little time with me. I've even got some refreshment." She lifted the bottle of whisky from her coat and held it up between thumb and fingers.

Micky Sinclair did not move. Slowly, Molly walked towards him until she was very close, close enough for him to feel her breath on his cheek. She kissed him lightly and put her free hand under the lapel of his greatcoat pulling him towards her. His lips found hers and he let his rifle dangle in one hand, slipping the other around her waist. After a long embrace, she wriggled free and, taking his hand, led him back into the darkness.

"Ok. We go now." Hans was already moving and Bob, clutching the small metal case, was right behind him. They were in the hangar in seconds and looking at Britain's latest secret weapon in the war with Germany. Working without speaking, Bob put the metal case on the floor, took out a light and a small camera. Hans meanwhile went to one wing and unclipped the engine cowlings, exposing the new engine. He whistled silently at its neat construction.

Carrying the camera to the engine, Bob handed the battery operated light to Hans who switched it on and shone it on the bright metal. Bob took several pictures from different angles, once or twice twisting Hans's arm so that the light fell on particular features. That done, Hans closed down the cowlings and Bob stood back to take some pictures of the whole aircraft. The equipment was packed away and within four minutes of entering the hangar, they were leaving.

Bob whispered close to Hans' ear. "Right. This is the tricky bit. We need to get her back." Bob put down the metal case and cupped his hands around his mouth. He made the sound of an owl, even fluttering his hands a little to add vibrato. The sound floated in the space between the hangars. They waited. He tried again and again they waited.

"Shit," Bob breathed. "What do we do now?"

"You've got all the answers. You tell me. You told her we'd surprise him. She's waiting for that."

"Okay, leave it to me. Be ready to grab Sinclair if he follows her but join us immediately if he don't. I'll run with Molly." Bob stood up and crossed to the door of the hangar. He stood in the doorway and, assuming the clipped accent of an English public school, called out. "Sinclair. Sinclair. Where the devil are you?"

There was a commotion from the darkness. "Right here, Sir. Just checking a noise I heard."

"Alright man. No problem. I was just passing and thought I'd check. Can't be too careful you know."

Suddenly Molly laughed. "It's alright Micky. It's your mates. They're playing a practical joke on you. It's Bob and Harry, the roofers."

"Practical joke? Bob and Harry? I don't know any Bob and Harry."

Molly emerged from the darkness and Bob moved swiftly to where Hans was lurking in the shadow by the wall of Hangar Two. He grabbed the metal case. "I'll get her away. Wait only a few seconds then follow."

From the darkness, Micky could be heard cursing and stumbling around. "Where's me fucking trousers?"

Bob clutched Molly's hand and shouted in his normal voice. "What's that Micky? You don't remember your old mates Bob and Harry. It's been a while I grant you. Hope you enjoyed your little treat. I've got to get this young lady home before her Dad finds out. He's a wild one is her Dad. Enjoy the whisky. Come on then gel, let's get you home."

Bob and Molly crouched by the end of the hangar waiting for Hans. In a matter of seconds, he appeared moving stealthily along the hangar wall to join them.

"Let's go. Quick," hissed Bob.

"But what about…?" Micky's plaintive voice was still audible from the darkness.

Bob yanked her arm and almost dragged her away. They had only just passed the second hangar, when Hans suddenly pulled Bob and Molly into the space between it and the first. He tugged Bob's sleeve until they had reached the darkness near the back of the hangars.

"Someone coming," Hans whispered urgently.

They listened intently. The sound of steel-tipped heels on concrete grew, echoing in the dark silence. The sound stopped.

"Shit," breathed Bob.

CHAPTER 13

The smell of toast was a welcome scent in the dining room. Lizzie and Alice walked into the hubbub of voices. There was a palpable air of excitement in the room, created, Lizzie was sure, by the test of the new aircraft later that morning. They stood at the serving hatch with trays, hot food steaming in large metal dishes on the counter. An airman in chef's clothing gave them a broad smile.

"Nice bright morning for the test ladies. What can I tempt you with? Got some lovely scrambled egg – substitute of course but it's very tasty, tinned tomatoes, sausages and of course toast...always lots of toast. Tea and coffee is at the end of the counter; help yourselves to that."

Alice took only some toast and a mug of tea but Lizzie had everything on offer. They sat down at an empty table. Lizzie looked around the room. Several tables away, the two engineers, Butler and Healey were eating in silence. Was one of them the night telegrapher? Perhaps she should ask them if either knew Morse Code but that would only produce a denial.

"Did you sleep well last night?"

Alice nodded her head as she chewed a mouthful of toast. "Yes thank you. I wouldn't have done had you not be so kind to talk with me."

"Us girls have got to help each other. I'm damn sure no one else will."

"And what about you?"

"Not really. Too many things flying around my brain."
Lizzie looked at Alice, her hair once more tied neatly in a bun at
the back of her head. "Do you know Morse Code, Alice?"

"Yes, I do as it happens. Why?"

"Last night, after I'd done my teeth, I heard a tapping from
one of the rooms further along the corridor. I'm going to try to
find out who is in there. I went and got Robbie and he agreed
it was probably someone using Morse. So I wrote down the dots
and dashes but it means nothing to me. I wonder if…"

"I'll happily look at it. Nothing much else to do."

"That's great. Here's Robbie now."

Robbie McBane had collected food from the serving hatch
and joined them at their table. "Ach, nae porridge to be had
today," he said in his richest Scottish accent.

"Well you're in a civilised part of the World now Robbie."

"Civilised? Is that what you call it? Doesna seem very
civilised to me."

"Robbie, Alice knows Morse Code and said she'd look at
what I wrote down last night."

"That's great. It'll probably be someone sending a
message home. 'Be back soon. Keep my slippers by the fire.'
That's if you managed to write it down accurately."

"I did my best."

Robbie smiled at her. "Aye. That's all any of us can do."

An airman marched smartly up to their table and saluted
in front of Robbie. "Sir, Group Captain Turner would like to see
you in his office as soon as you've finished your breakfast."

"Very well. I'll not be long. It's in the same building as the
Officers Mess I suppose."

"Correct, Sir." The young airman saluted again and
walked smartly away.

Robbie finished his breakfast speedily and bid Lizzie and
Alice farewell. Not long afterwards, they left the dining room.
The route to their rooms took them through the lobby and Lizzie
noticed a door off it marked 'Housekeeping'. A young woman
was inside, dressed in a chamber maid's uniform, briskly folding

laundry. Lizzie knocked on the door which was ajar but did not wait for an answer before entering.

"Hello. We're staying here at the moment, upstairs, and I wondered if you could tell me who's staying in Room 6 on the front corridor. It's just that I don't want to knock on the wrong door."

"Of course, Miss." She picked up a list from the small desk. "Room 5, Room 6. Here we are. That'll be Mr William Butler. Visiting us for two nights."

"Oh good, it is Mr Butler. Thank you so much. I won't make an embarrassing blunder now." The two young women crossed to the big staircase and ascended. "Butler. What on earth would he be doing sending Morse Code messages?"

"When you show me the message, I may be able to tell you."

They went to Lizzie's room and she handed the piece of paper to Alice.

--- / --.. / -..- / --- / -..-. / ... / .-. / -..-. / -.- / --. / ...- /

.. / .. / --.. / -.-- / -..-. / -.. / -..-. / .-. / -.. / --. / --. /

-..-. / -.-- / .--- / -..-. / .. / .--- / -..-. / .... / .--- / -- / --.. /

"Do you have a pen or pencil?" Lizzie picked one off the dressing table and handed it to her. "Well the first letters are O, Z, X, O then a word break, then V, N, word break."

"So I've clearly written down gobbledegook."

Alice smiled. "Not necessarily. It's probably a cipher. That may take a little longer to unravel but I'm happy to have a go."

"That would be great Alice. Why would our friend Mr Butler be wanting to send a message in Morse Code at all? Why use a cipher unless it had to be kept secret? I mean who can he possibly be sending it to? He must have equipment in the room." A recent memory popped into Lizzie's mind and her eyes lit up. "I remember when the airman lifted a suitcase from the Anson, he nearly dropped it because of the weight. Healey must have brought a transmitter with him. I wonder if Healey and Butler are working together? Unless of course that suitcase was Grainger's."

◆ ◆ ◆

Robbie McBane walked more or less in step with Group Captain Turner from the latter's office in the main building to the Sick Bay. It was a strange situation, Turner had said. A young airman, Sinclair, had been on guard duty in Hangar Three the night before and was relieved at mid-night. However, when his relief came, he had found Sinclair on the ground outside the hangar, unconscious and smelling strongly of whisky. An almost empty bottle was still in his hand.

"I'm told he is awake now but has a very sore head. He came out with some ridiculous story about a young woman singing outside the hangar. He went to investigate and she lured him away with a half bottle of whisky, started to seduce him and then he was hit on the head by someone. It looks to me like he got plastered on the whisky, had a fantasy about the young woman and fell over hitting his head."

"Strange story, Sir."

"Very strange. See if you can get to the bottom of it will you? I mean the only young women we have on the base at the moment are the two who flew you up here. You'll see that our nurses could not be described as young! The housekeeper does not stay overnight."

"I'm certain neither Lizzie nor Alice would have been involved. Was the aircraft damaged?"

"No. That's the thing. Nothing touched at all." Turner

spread his hands. They had arrived at the Sick Bay and Turner showed Robbie in. "I must go and brief Sir George so I'll leave you here."

"I'll report back to you and Air Chief Marshal Stanley when I've got what I can from him, Sir."

"Very good, McBane." Turner turned on his heel and walked swiftly away, his heels clacking on the concrete floor, head held high, shoulders back. A military man through and through.

Robbie was shown into the main ward by a nurse, a rather sullen woman probably in her late thirties. Not the kind to seduce someone in the middle of the night! Sinclair was sitting up on a bed, looking fragile.

"Morning AC Sinclair. May I call you Micky?"

Dull eyes were lifted to meet his. "If you want."

Robbie pulled a chair to the bedside. "My name's Sergeant McBane. I'm with the RAF Police Special Investigation Branch. I happened to be here to support security on the base during the test flight this morning. I gather you had a strange experience last night."

"You can say that again."

"Tell me about it."

"I already told Sergeant Swallow but I don't think he believed a word of it. He thinks I drank most of a half bottle of whisky whilst on duty, fell over and hit my head."

"And did you?"

Sinclair's brows knitted in anger but he spoke slowly, occasionally putting a hand to his head.. "No I did not. I was in the hangar guarding the plane. Was about eleven I'd say, so I only had an hour to go. The personnel door is open and I hear a woman's voice, singing a song, 'We'll Meet Again', you know, Vera Lynn. Nice voice. Sounded a bit eerie to be honest, a bit ghostly." Robbie could see that Sinclair thought he would not believe the story either. "No, don't get me wrong. I'm not saying it was a ghost. I don't believe in stuff like that."

"Go on."

"So I goes outside and call her to come forward. The singing carries on for a bit then she walks slowly forward. She was pretty, I give you that. She comes right up close and holds up the bottle of whisky. It was full at that point. She said, 'Happy birthday' and said *she* was a present from my friends. Well that was weird cos it wasn't my birthday but I thought maybe it was my mates having a laugh. I'm standing still, like, me rifle in both hands ready for anything. She comes real close then, stands on tip-toe and kisses me on the cheek. Next thing I know she's snogging me, you know, real passionate like."

"Tell me a little about the girl... age, hair colour and style, what she was wearing."

"It was difficult to see much in that light but she was wearing a dark coat and a creamy skirt but you could only see a bit of it beneath the coat. I'd say her hair was brown but I could be wrong cos there's not much light between the hangars."

"Then what happened?"

"Well I know I was well out of order. Should have just arrested her and sounded the alarm. But, you know, it was cold, I'd been on watch for several hours, she was very pretty and... and..."

"She took you somewhere?"

"Yeah, just further towards the back of the hangars where there really is no light. Anyway, things started to get quite cosy for a few minutes. She opened the bottle and I had a few swigs. She didn't drink any though. So after a bit of cuddling she was getting really...you know... I hear this noise like an owl hooting. I didn't take much notice but then it came again. She giggled but I don't know why. Then there's this voice like an officer asking where I am. So I shouts back that I'm just checking a noise and I try to get up to sort mesen out but she pushes me back down."

"And could you see the person whose voice you heard?"

"Yeah. Well I could see the figure but the light was behind him so it was just a silhouette. Not tall...I couldn't recognise him from that. Then she says quite loudly like, that it's ok, it's just me mates Bob and Harry playing a practical joke. But I can't think of any mates called Bob and Harry. Then she says they're roofers but that don't mean nothing neither."

"Roofers?" Robbie McBane sat forward on his chair.

"Then this voice says, 'Don't you remember your old mates?' Well I never had mates called that."

"The same voice as you heard to start with…the officer's voice?"

"Nah. Completely different. Sounded like a London accent but I was still thinking this was my mates having a laugh so I guess I didn't take too much notice. Anyway, next thing, she giggles and runs off but I can't follow 'cos she's taken me trousers off. I'm stumbling about amongst all the plants and stuff looking for me trousers. There's hardly any light down there so it took me a few minutes to find 'em and when I got back to the personnel door, there's no sign of anyone. Then suddenly I feel a blow on me head and I'm passing out." Sinclair's brow furrowed. "I think I heard someone say, 'That's far more sinister' but I can't be sure. I remember thinking what's he on about? Anyway, I don't know anything after that till I woke up in here. My God, I've got a sore head though."

"What does that mean? 'That's far more sinister'." Robbie McBane spoke softly, to himself. "Perhaps something a spy would say?"

"What's that you said, Sir?

"Oh nothing. You're sure you had only a few swigs of whisky?"

"Yessir."

"Do you think you'd recognise the girl if you were to see her again?"

"Might recognise the woman but definitely not the bloke – I never actually saw him. But you know how it is with women, they change their hairstyle, even colour, put different make-up on and they look different."

"Aye some do. What about her voice, her accent? Was she from around these parts?"

"I'd say she was, Sir."

"But the man was perhaps from London."

"I'd say so but...you know...my head, Sir. It hurts."

"Is there anything you can remember that might be important, anything that might help corroborate your story?"

Sinclair shook his head slowly, sadly. He knew this was not going to be good for him. "The last thing I saw was the ground coming up towards me. Sorry, Sir." He smiled weakly and slumped back exhausted.

CHAPTER 14

"You have jeopardised the mission. The Sturmbanfuhrer will hear about your antics." Hans was leaning across the table, his voice an urgent hiss.

"Calm down mate. I keep telling you. We have to blend in."

"But she could have ruined the mission, may still do so."

"Trust me. She won't." Bob smiled, an irritatingly smug smile. "I've got her exactly where I need her... round here." He held up his little finger.

Hans fumed silently for a while. "It's just as well that guard did not look between the hangars."

Bob chuckled. "Yeah, that was a close shave."

"What time did you leave her last night?"

"Ohh,.. about two o'clock I guess. Did you hear me come in?"

"Of course. Where were you?"

"In the van." Bob grinned boyishly. "We grabbed some cushions from the bar and we were very comfortable. My God she was ready for it. Amazing what a bit of excitement, a bit of intrigue does for a girl."

"The guard will talk...probably has already."

"Did you kill him?"

"I did not touch him. I did what you said, though if I had my way, he would not be alive to tell the story."

"Then they'll think he had too much whisky and imagined everything. No problem."

"What if he recognises the girl?"

"I doubt if he was looking at her face." Bob laughed. "He was a bit of an animal apparently. She thought she'd have to fight

99

him off. Mind you, she is tasty."

The two men sat in silence for a while until Molly came through from the back with two plates of cooked breakfast. She was looking as bright and perky as she had the previous evening and approached the table with a broad smile. She laid the plates in front of each but only looked at Bob. After setting the plate down, her hand rested lightly on his forearm and lingered there.

"Hope you're hungry this morning. Probably will be after all that activity last night."

"I'm ravenous. Really looking forward to something tasty." Bob looked up at her and her eyes sparkled as they met his. "Ooh you certainly know how to use the charm don't you?"

"That's me. Silver tongue Bob they call me."

She giggled. "What've you got on today then boys?"

"Just got to finish off the job we started yesterday," Bob said as he lifted his fork to his mouth. "Then we'll be off back home to Skegness."

"You could stay tonight as well. Go home tomorrow."

Bob finished his mouthful. "Now that is very tempting but I don't think we'd be able to answer the questions that would arise. I mean think about it. 'Why did you stay another night?' 'Cos I fell in love with a beautiful woman.' Don't think that'd go down too well."

"You could at least drop in for some dinner before you go. I mean working hard all day, you'll be hungry."

"That is a very good idea." Hans looked up sharply and stared ferociously at Bob but the latter ignored him. "Around five or five thirty. Would that suit?"

"Perfectly Sir. Molly gave a mock curtsy and left them, turning to blow a kiss to Bob as she went.

"What did you say that for? We'll be finished by eleven o'clock this morning. Now we have to hang around all day."

"Mate, we've got to hang around either here or at Skegness. May as well break it up a bit, have a decent meal before we go back." Bob tapped his nose. "Just leave it to me Harry."

◆ ◆ ◆

Robbie McBane tapped on Turner's office door. There was no immediate response and he was about to tap again when he heard the command to enter. Turner was standing at one end of his heavy and highly-polished wooden desk, Stanley in the middle of the room and Grainger lounging against the windowsill. The room was very comfortable with upright chairs and padded armchairs. Some matching cabinets were against the wall opposite the window. As everywhere in this building, the slightly cloying smell of furniture polish hung in the air.

Turner spoke first. "Ah McBane." He turned to Stanley to explain. "McBane has been interviewing Sinclair the guard. Did you get anything from him, Sergeant?"

"Well, Sir, he repeated what you had told me though perhaps in more detail. I have to say that I was convinced by him. It didn't sound like a story to me."

Grainger snorted. "Not like a story? I think you and he have been reading too many spy novels Sergeant. Who was this mystery woman? There are only four women on the base apparently."

"She may have come in from outside, Sir, with the two men he talked about."

"How would she do that? The gate is guarded every hour of the day and night and the airfield is protected with a six feet high wire fence which you yourself inspected yesterday afternoon."

"A wire fence can be cut, Sir. I'd like to have it inspected again. Perhaps I could have a couple of men?"

"Certainly. See Sergeant Swallow and he'll assign you a couple," said Turner.

Robbie McBane hesitated. He looked directly at Stanley. "Sir, the guard, Sinclair, mentioned that the girl said the whole thing was a practical joke by his friends, Bob and Harry the roofers." From the corner of his eye, Robbie could see Grainger stand up fully. "Last night, Sergeant Swallow took us to a local pub where there was a band playing. There were two roofers staying there from Skegness. They had a van with 'Allen Roofing' on the side and they had ladders on top of it. One of them was definitely called Bob."

"This is going into the realms of fantasy. Why on earth would two roofers be interested in coming onto the airfield and pulling a stunt like that unless of course they are friends of Sinclair?" Grainger was becoming heated.

"He denies any knowledge of people called Bob and Harry, friends or otherwise, Sir."

"I really think we are wasting time with this. No damage was done, nothing was taken and all we have is the word of a man who had consumed a considerable amount of whisky."

"Two swigs he claims, Sir."

"Two swigs? Of course he'd say that. He's trying to avoid a charge for dereliction of duty."

Sir George Stanley looked from Grainger to McBane and then addressed Turner. "What do you think Cyril? Is Sinclair's story feasible?"

"Well, Sir, as Grainger says, no damage was done and nothing taken. Unless evidence is found of an incursion through the fence, I think we must assume Sinclair is making it up. I'll have him put on a charge."

Again Robbie McBane hesitated but this time decided not to say anything for the moment. Grainger must know about Bob and Harry. He had slipped a note to Bob last night. He must be in on it – whatever *it* was. Robbie decided to keep his powder dry until he could be more certain about what was going on. But Grainger, he was now sure, was trying to cover it up. Could it be that he was the mole, the German spy?

Lizzie sat on Alice's bed trying not to interrupt her. Alice was sitting by the cabinet that doubled as a dressing table, a piece of paper in front of her and a pencil poised in her hand.

"Ah. I think I've got it. An elementary cipher and a very simple blunder in the message. Here, take a look."

Lizzie looked at the piece of paper on which she had written the message in Morse Code the previous night. "What am I looking at?"

O	Z	X	O	end	V	N	End	K	G	V
--- /	--.. /	-..- /	--- /	-..-. /	...- /	-. /	-..-. /	-.- /	--. /	...- /

I	I	Z	Y	End	D	End	R	D	G	G
.. /	.. /	--.. /	-.-- /	-..-. /	-.. /	-..-. /	.-. /	-.. /	--. /	--. /

End	Y	J	End	I	J	End	H	J	M	Z
-..-. /	-.-- /	.--- /	-..-. /	.. /	.--- /	-..-. /	.... /	.--- /	-- /	--..

"A man who thinks no one is going to hear this message and try to decipher it. Look at the words – you can tell where each ends by the code dash, dot, dot, dash, dot; I've written 'end' above the code each time. I've also written the letters above the code for each.

"It makes no sense at all."

Alice smiled. "No, not until you start to unpick the cipher. Look on the middle line. There is a letter on its own. What letters appear on their own in normal writing?"

"Well…I and A."

"Correct. So the letter D in this message is either an A or an I. Now an elementary cipher would simply move letters on by a certain number. So if that D represents an A, it probably means that the letters that we need have been shuffled back by four places. A letter B would be represented by the letter E in the code."

"I'm glad you've got a mathematical brain, Alice. I think my head is going to explode."

"I have my uses. However, that doesn't work. The message is still nonsense. However, if we move the letters forward five spaces, the letter I is represented in the code by the letter D. Now the message makes sense."

"Brilliant."

"Hardly. It is a very crude cipher, the sort of thing a schoolboy would come up with. It raises the question as to whether the message is really going to someone who is working with the Germans."

"But what does it say?"

"It says: 'Test as planned I will do no more.' Presumably there was more of the message before the bit you managed to write down but of course we do not have that."

"But even that little bit tells us that Butler is communicating with an enemy agent about the test today?"

"Not necessarily, Lizzie. He might be communicating with his people back at the factory and confirming that it's all going ahead and he doesn't need to do more checks."

"Oh come on Alice. He'd pick up a telephone surely and wouldn't be doing it in the middle of the night."

"Granted. It is a bit suspicious."

Lizzie looked at her watch. "Zero nine thirty hours. We need to go out for the test, Alice. Bring the piece of paper and we can up-date Robbie McBane."

The two young women put on their coats, tripped lightly down the stairs and out of the magnificent frontage of the building. They headed across to the section of the airfield designated for spectators. It was already fairly crowded with all personnel wanting to witness this historic occasion. The air was full of excited voices, calling, laughing and talking animatedly about what they were going to see. Lizzie and Alice wandered through the crowd looking for Robbie MacBane. They found him near the front of the roped-off area, facing away from the runway and scanning the crowds in front of him.

"Robbie, Robbie."

He turned in their direction and smiled. "Looking forward to the show?"

"We certainly are. But Alice has worked out the cipher for that message I wrote down last night."

Alice stepped forward and handed the piece of paper to Robbie which he read. "Not exactly incriminating is it?"

"That's what I thought," said Alice, "but Lizzie pointed out that it was being sent in the middle of the night. Why do that if there was nothing suspicious about it?"

"True. I'll brief Stanley after the test flight and then I'll speak to Mr Butler and see what he has to say for himself. By the way, Sinclair, the airman who was found unconscious last night, says he was lured out by a young woman, given whisky and then hit on the head. Grainger and the others think he's making that up to avoid a charge but he mentioned two men called Bob and Harry."

"I told you. Those two aren't roofers."

Just then, two airmen strode up to Robbie, saluted and, rather breathlessly, said they needed to report to him. He told them to go ahead.

One looked nervously at Lizzie and Alice. "Sir, we haven't finished doing the perimeter fence inspection but, like you said, we did find a place where the grass had been flattened on both sides of the fence and we could make out indentations in the soil, the sort that a ladder would make. The barbed wire had been flattened and there was a couple of tufts of fabric caught in it."

Robbie nodded at Lizzie to acknowledge the look of satisfaction on her face. He turned to the airmen. "Anything else? Nothing dropped on the ground?"

"No, Sir. Nothing that we could see."

"Well done chaps. I think there is no need to complete the inspection. Stay here and enjoy the action. Oh and, by the way, better to say nothing about this to anyone. I'll inform Group Captain Turner and Sir George Stanley."

"Very well, Sir. Mum's the word."

CHAPTER 15

"This is not looking good," Bob muttered half to himself. He was driving the van along the main road on the south of the airfield. "We'll be too far away if we're on the road. We need to get over the fence again."

"In broad daylight. That's madness."

"No it's not. They'll all be watching the show. We can whip up and over with the gear and be off afterwards smartish. But, let's go up that lane we were on yesterday and see if there's a way of getting on without the ladders."

Bob found a turning into a field and reversed the van into it, pulling away again in the opposite direction. It took only a few minutes to reach the left hand turn into Raunceby Lane. He swung the van into it and drove along slowly looking for somewhere suitable. "There are some trees and shrubs down this end at least." He saw an opening on the left, a made up road. When they reached it, there was a large heavy gate across it – lower than the fence but with barbed wire on the top. He pulled in but did not switch off. "I'll do a little recce."

"You'll be seen."

"It won't matter if I am. They won't think anything of it – just wait!" He rolled out of the van, hitched up his trousers and started whistling. He appeared to be very casual as he walked over towards the gate but his eyes were strafing the area beyond. There was a small hut that looked disused, grass growing around the edges and some old, dead leaves piled against the door. He stood by the gate with his hands by the fly of his trousers, whistling cheerfully. No sign of anyone. No guard appeared. Sloppy.

He returned to the van and climbed into the driver's seat. "Looks all clear. They obviously don't guard this entrance. We'll just wait for the patrol to pass, I'll pull the van in tight, then we can climb that gate and see how close we can get to the runway. Get your pipe out and I'll have a fag. Nothing strange about a pair of roofers stopping for a smoke."

They smoked in silence, eyes searching the airfield perimeter for the patrol. At last it came into sight, travelling slowly along the fence. "If they stop and ask questions, leave the talking to me." Bob climbed out of the van and leaned nonchalantly against the bonnet. As the Land Rover drew close, he raised his free hand lazily in a wave. The vehicle did not stop.

When it had travelled well beyond them, the two men took the large metal case from the back of the van and the piece of carpet. Throwing the latter over the barbed wire, Hans hoisted himself over the gate; Bob passed the case to him and then followed, wobbling with one leg either side as he climbed over. Cautiously, they walked towards the hut keeping it between them and the main airfield buildings which were some way off in the distance. The outer reaches of the airfield were clothed in long, dead grass which bent slightly under the light wind, seeming to whisper.

Crouching low, they ran through the grass until they were close to the intersecting runway which was oriented north-south and crossed the main runway at the end of the airfield closest to them. "D'you reckon this is near enough? It'll take off from this end into the wind so we should get good shots of it until it gets up speed. Or we could go round this runway and further onto the field."

"Stay here. The further we go onto the airfield, the more risk of being seen."

They squatted in the long grass and Hans opened the case. From it, he took a small tripod stand and erected it, lifting it enough so that the top was just a little higher than the stems of grass. He took from the case another, bulkier piece of equipment and fitted it to the top of the tripod. He swung it from left to right checking that it moved freely, then opened a door on the side. Something much smaller was lifted from the metal case and passed through the little door, which was then clicked into place. He looked through a sight and adjusted a mechanism on a projection at the front.

Hans knelt behind the tripod "Ok. Ready."

Bob lay on his stomach beside him, his head raised and a pair of binoculars held in his two hands in front of his face. He put his eyes to the sights and adjusted the focus. "Just opening the hangar now." He held his gaze for another minute. "Here it comes…being towed by a tractor. Have you got it?"

"Yes. Nice and clear. It looks much smaller than it did last night."

"It would do in the open and at this distance."

"I'll wait until they get it to the end of the runway before shooting."

"Good idea."

Robbie McBane looked worried. Lizzie could see him scanning the crowd. Sir George Stanley, Group Captain Turner and some other senior officers were at the front of the enclosure in chairs. Grainger, small binoculars in hand, was with them, Butler and Healey close by. Butler wore his usual, inscrutable and rather miserable expression whilst the latter was restless, unable to stand still. The crowd fell silent and all eyes were fixed on the hangar door which had been rolled open. A tractor appeared from it and behind that, on a long tow bar, the new aircraft.

There was a faint gasp which Lizzie took to be wonder and admiration. For the first time, she and most of the people around her were looking at the Meteor, the first jet powered aircraft to be tested in an Allied country. It was not like any aircraft she had seen before. There was a large pod on each wing but no propellers attached as one would expect. The underbelly was painted yellow; apparently that was usual for a test aircraft. But what was most surprising was that the Meteor was almost parallel with the ground. A conventional propeller powered aircraft sat up with its nose in the air to give the wings the lift they needed on take-off. Lizzie remembered what Healey had said about its power, its ability to ascend at a much steeper angle than other aircraft.

"Wonderful," she breathed to no one in particular but Alice caught her exclamation.

"It is, isn't it? You wonder how it can fly."

Bert Swallow had stepped close to them. "It hasn't done so yet!... But perhaps I'm being too cynical. I'm sure it will."

The aircraft was towed slowly along the taxiway, passing the spectator enclosure. The pilot's head in flying helmet, goggles and mouthpiece was clearly visible. In the plane's wake were two fire trucks and an ambulance with two airmen walking beside. It seemed to take a long time to get to the end of the taxiway and to line the aircraft up at the end of the runway. The tow bar was disconnected and the tractor drove slowly back towards the hangar.

Lizzie reached for Alice's hand and gently pulled her towards the group of senior officers. She did not know what she hoped to see but something compelled her to get closer. Grainger, Butler and Healey – she trusted none of them. Alice followed her without resistance and Bert Swallow tagged on behind Alice.

They seemed to wait an age before anything happened. Lizzie assumed the pilot was waiting for permission to take off. The aircraft began to move forward, slowly at first but then gaining speed rapidly but no sound reached their ears. It was ghostly, the silver body streaking forward with no obvious means of propulsion, it's metal surfaces reflecting a sudden shaft of sunlight that penetrated the cloud.

"Why can't we hear anything?" Lizzie said aloud.

"Because with jet engines, all the sound is thrust

backwards. You'll hear it when it passes us and then it'll be deafening when it takes off." Bert Swallow seemed unimpressed.

"Curious that the flags at the end of the runway are not being ripped off their masts...if the engines are as powerful as Healey was suggesting..."

"Perhaps not quite in line with the thrust." Bert Swallow sounded just a little irritated by Lizzie's observation.

Suddenly, the air was rocked with two huge explosions, the second following the first so closely they might have been one. Pieces of metal flew out from each engine. Two balls of orange flame burst from the wings and rolled into the air, dispersing in thick black smoke that drifted slowly away on the breeze. The aircraft had rolled to a stop. Immediately, siren bells were clanging; the two fire trucks and ambulance were racing down the runway towards the stricken plane.

"Oh my God." Alice's hand went to her mouth in shock and blended with the babble of voices from the enclosure.

"What were you saying about it not working Bert?" Lizzie turned away briefly from the scene of devastation to look at Bert Swallow.

His face was locked in an expression of shock, his mouth frozen open. "It was just a joke." There was something not quite right about his response.

When she turned back, she could see Butler gesticulating wildly and shouting. "What have you done to my engines?"

"More to the point, what have your engines done to my plane?" Healey shouted in response.

The two of them faced each other and both were shouting. "I checked those engines myself yesterday with Sergeant Swallow. They were absolutely fine."

"Well they weren't fine today. Let's hope the pilot is okay."

Scraps of metal littered the runway and adjacent grass. One fire truck was on each side of the aircraft dousing what was left of the engines and trying to stop the fire reaching the cockpit. Two ambulance crew bravely put a short ladder up to the cockpit, wrenched the canopy open and began to lift the pilot from the aircraft. His body was limp and they struggled with him. Once they had lifted him over the shoulder of one, he was carried down to the waiting ambulance.

The harsh jangling of the ambulance's bell intensified and then faded as the vehicle sped towards them and passed on its way to the sick bay. Lizzie felt a sickness in her stomach. He was a brave man to get into an untested aircraft.

Robbie McBane had walked close to them but went straight to Sir George Stanley who, with the other senior officers was standing, staring at the scene. "Excuse me, Sir."

Stanley seemed distant. "McBane?"

"I think we need to have a conversation about all the things I've picked up. There's more come to light since I spoke with you last."

Stanley stared at him as if he were mad. "Can't you see McBane that now is not a good time? We may have just witnessed the death of an experienced and valued pilot and you want to talk to me about tobacco packets again?"

Lizzie could see that Robbie McBane was fighting back anger. "It's more serious than that, Sir. This looks like sabotage and I think I know who is responsible."

"Sabotage, Sergeant? Why on earth do you think that? Surely it's just that the engines don't work?" Grainger slipped his binoculars into his overcoat pocket. He showed none of the shock that seemed to have frozen the others.

"What's that you said?" Butler strode towards him belligerently. "There's nothing wrong with those engines, They've been tested time and time again in the factory since the design was finalised and they've never given any problems. It must be sabotage, either deliberate or by incompetence from the technicians here."

Bert Swallow's voice was cold. "My technicians are the finest in the country. You checked the engines yourself yesterday."

Lizzie noticed that Grainger had slid away. Why was he so sure that it was not sabotage? Why was he so sure it was the engine design or manufacture that was at fault? She watched him walking casually towards the main buildings. He must be involved - he had slipped that piece of paper to Bob in the pub. Was it his case that was heavier than the others? He must be working with them and was now trying to divert attention. And what of Bert Swallow? He seemed to be ready for the aircraft to fail. What did he know? She must make sure Robbie reported everything to Stanley and convinced him that Bob and his mate had sabotaged the aircraft.

Then Lizzie had an idea. The guard at the Hangar, what was his name?...Sinclair... had said a young woman had given him whisky. Maybe that young woman was the barmaid from the pub. If she could establish that with some degree of certainty, she could be interviewed and might admit they had been on the base. She made a decision. She would talk to Sinclair herself...and take Alice as a witness.

CHAPTER 16

"Holy shit!" Bob stared at the smoking wreckage. "Keep that camera rolling."

Hans checked the cine camera was still running but his eyes were quickly dragged back to the carnage on the runway. "My God. So the British don't yet have a weapon to defeat us." He laughed. "They'll love this footage when we get it back to Berlin."

"They certainly will. Let's get packed up and get off the airfield. We've got what we came for. So much for their revolutionary new engine!"

"I don't suppose there's much fear of them discovering us. They'll all be too busy looking at the wreck. Shame about the pilot. I don't suppose he'll have survived that."

"No, poor sod. Still that's war for you." Bob watched Hans take the film out of the camera. "Make sure you don't expose that. We must get it back to Berlin."

"I'm not a fool, Bob."

Hans took the camera off the tripod and collapsed the latter, stowing everything neatly into the metal case. The two men walked back the way they had come, unconcerned about being seen.

"Just need to get back home tonight and that will be mission accomplished."

"Quite right, Hans. We need to hole up somewhere for the rest of the day and then we'll get a good feed in the pub before we go back to the coast."

Hans decided not to argue. They had achieved what they had come for and he could afford to be magnanimous, provided they did not stay too long. He would have to make sure that Bob did not become entangled with that young woman again.

"Come on Alice. We're going to pay a visit."

"Where?"

"Sick Bay. We're going to talk to that guard that passed out yesterday night. Sinclair."

"We can't just stroll in to sick bay and talk to him. Surely we would need to get permission."

Lizzie smiled. "Would anyone give us permission to talk to him?"

"No, I doubt it."

"Precisely. If you think the answer will be 'no', don't ask."

Lizzie strode ahead and Alice followed in her wake, protesting still but with an increasing sense of the futility of doing so. She was learning that Lizzie was quite headstrong; when she had made her mind up, she could not be dissuaded. They walked at speed over to the main buildings where they had seen the ambulance disappear. Lizzie had to ask for directions when they got there as the sick bay was tucked away behind the large building that housed the Officers Mess and associated rooms.

A rather fierce looking nurse in her late thirties confronted them in the corridor almost as soon as they had walked through the swinging doors. "Can I help you?" her face was severe, frowning.

"Oh yes please." Lizzie employed her full charm. "My name is Second Officer Lizzie Barnes and this is my navigator, Alice Frobisher. We're on the base as we flew up yesterday with Sir George Stanley, you know the Air Chief Marshal who's in charge of RAF Fighter Command. Well, you see, I've just spoken to my parents on the telephone and they said that the son of a friend of theirs had been taken into the sick bay here last night.

Apparently he's not well and they asked if I could drop in and see him…you know, check how he is, report back. His name is Airman Sinclair."

The eyes that scrutinised Lizzie's face were not convinced. "You need to wait along here for a few minutes." She sat them on some chairs further along the corridor and walked away.

Alice tittered quietly. "Well it certainly wasn't her who tried to seduce Sinclair last night."

Lizzie stifled a laugh. "She's a bit of a bulldog isn't she?"

They waited for several minutes. As with all hospitals, there was a lingering smell of ether or some such chemical. It was not unpleasant and contributed to the sense of a place that was rigorously cleaned, an impression reinforced by the shiny floor and blank walls. The sound of two pairs of shoes clacking towards them on the hard floor turned their heads and brought them to their feet.

The nurse was accompanied by an older woman who scowled at them with dark brows. "Miss Barnes and Miss Frobisher. You want to see Sinclair?"

"Yes please if that's possible. Just want to check how he is."

"How close are you to Sinclair?"

"Oh not close. He's the son of some friends of my parents but I do not know him directly…just by reputation as it were."

"You need to know that Airman Sinclair died an hour ago. We're waiting for a doctor to sign the death certificate and then there will have to be a post-mortem."

"He's dead?"

"That is what I said."

"But how? I thought he had just fallen and hit his head. He was alive this morning."

"I am certain that the post-mortem will reveal that the blow on the head caused internal bleeding which eventually killed him. Death is not always instant from a blow on the head. There was nothing we could do."

Lizzie looked at Alice, unsure of how to continue. Alice came to the rescue. "Would it be possible to see the body please? You can at least tell your parents that there is no mistake."

"Yes...yes please...if that is possible."

The Matron looked doubtful. "That is not regular if you're not a close relative."

"I could give some comfort to his parents perhaps."

The older woman nodded to the nurse who had first greeted them. She led them further into the sick bay and into a small ward off the main corridor. The contours of a body could clearly be seen beneath a sheet that covered a bed. The nurse stepped forward and pulled the top of the sheet back, revealing the dead man's face. It was pale, motionless, lifeless, unmistakably dead. The two young women looked at a face that seemed to have been carved from marble. Such a waste. Here was a young man in the prime of life doing his bit for the war effort and now he lay lifeless on this bed, all his thoughts, impulses, passions drained from him. In Lizzie's breast something stirred, a sense of injustice, a sense of a wrong to be righted. Bob and his accomplice must be brought to justice.

"Thank you," she said softly.

The nurse covered the face again and led the way out of the room. As they reached the doorway, a good-looking man with dark hair and mischievous eyes was walking past in what looked like flying gear. He waved cheerily to the nurse and sauntered along the corridor humming to himself.

"Was that Mr Dakin, the test pilot?"

"It was indeed. Do you know him as well?"

"No...except from the briefing we had yesterday. But surely, he must have been badly injured when the aircraft exploded?"

"As you can see, he was not. Some people are just lucky I suppose. They got him out quickly. We checked him over. Not a scratch on him."

"He could have been burnt alive." Alice's eyes followed the jaunty figure until he pushed through the outer doors and they swung closed behind him."

"We need to find Robbie McBane and Stanley," Lizzie said to her quietly.

◆ ◆ ◆

"But Sir, we cannot afford to leave it any longer. There is something very wrong here." Stanley, Turner, Grainger and McBane were standing in a rough circle in Turner's office though Grainger seemed keen to keep aloof.

"Look McBane, I know I told you to keep an eye on things but we've got a serious situation to deal with here and I don't have time for tittle tattle." Sir George Stanley lowered his head slightly like a bull threatening to charge and fixed Robbie McBane with a stare.

"Sir, this has all the appearance of sabotage and I am certain that Sinclair was right. A young woman and probably two men were on the base last night. The perimeter inspection found evidence – flattened grass and indentations probably from a ladder. I think I know who the men are and, if we act quickly, we may be able to arrest them before they leave the area."

Grainger, who had been lounging against the back of an armchair with his customary amused expression, stood up. "If these two men are saboteurs, do you really think they will be hanging around in this area? They'll have made themselves scarce long ago."

"Quite. Grainger's right."

Group Captain Turner spoke calmly. "I'm having the aircraft checked now. As Grainger says, it probably is simply that the engines are faulty though Mr Butler is creating hell about that."

"If he is so sure that the engines are fine, Sir, as he checked them himself yesterday, doesn't that suggest sabotage is the more likely explanation?"

"If it's sabotage, Sergeant, there will be evidence of it. Rest assured, we will find it." Sir George Stanley had decided this conversation had lasted long enough. "Thank you, Sergeant. Keep your eye open for anything untoward."

"Well, Sir. There is something else. Last night, Miss Barnes alerted me to a sound coming from Mr Butler's room. We listened carefully and it was definitely morse code. Miss Barnes wrote down a section which turned out to be in a cipher that was very easy to break. Miss Frobisher did so. The message being tapped out said, 'Test as planned I will do no more."

"Butler?" The smile had disappeared from Grainger's face. "Butler?"

"Yes, Sir. Miss Barnes checked the room number with the housekeeper. It can't be innocent can it? I mean why would he be sending a message by wire at night unless it was secretive?"

Sir George Stanley spoke slowly as if to himself. "Could our mole be Butler? Surely not? He was one of the engine designers. Could he really be a German spy?"

There was a commotion at the door to Turner's office. A knock, the slightest pause and the door was opened. A corporal entered apologetically. "Sir, I'm very sorry to disturb you but a Second Officer Barnes and Navigator Frobisher are here, Sir. They say it's very important."

Turner looked at McBane. "What's this about?"

"No idea at all, Sir. Shall we find out?"

"Show them in."

The corporal saluted, turned and opened the door. "Group Captain Turner will see you now…"

Before he had finished speaking, Lizzie strode into the room with Alice following shyly behind, keeping in her shadow. Lizzie faced Stanley. "He's dead."

All eyes had already been turned on her. Now there was a shocked silence. "Dead?" echoed Stanley.

"Yes Sir. Dead."

"But he can't be. Turner, this cannot be can it? Has

something gone wrong?"

Lizzie, Alice and McBane exchanged puzzled glances. Turner and Grainger seemed to share Stanley's shock.

"How did he die?" stammered Turner.

"Apparently, it was a delayed reaction to the blow on his head."

"But we were told he had no injuries at all. No one mentioned a blow on the head." Stanley's words added to the bewilderment Lizzie, and Alice had already experienced.

"The only question, Sir, is whether the blow was accidental from falling or deliberate having been made by an attacker."

Grainger realised the cause of the confusion before the others. "Miss Barnes, are you referring to the test pilot Squadron Leader Dakin or to…"

"No. I am not. Dakin is perfectly well and we just saw him walk quite happily and unaided out of the sick bay. He seemed very cheerful and none the worse for his ordeal in the Meteor. I am talking about Airman Sinclair who is now lying dead awaiting the doctor's confirmation and a post-mortem. The nurses believe that he died because of a bleed on the brain caused by the blow to his head. It was thus a delayed reaction"

"Sinclair?" The relief in Stanley's face was very evident. "I thought you meant Dakin."

"No Sir. Sinclair. I don't believe the blow to his head was an accident. A perfectly fit young man does not fall over after a couple of swigs of whisky and does not die even if he does bang his head. Someone hit him and hit him hard. I think we are looking at murder, gentlemen, and we think we know who is responsible."

CHAPTER 17

"We have our orders, Sir. No one, absolutely no one is to go near the aircraft." The Guard stood solidly by the roped off area around the runway where the stricken Meteor lay.

"But I designed the engines and Mr Healey is the senior engineer on the plane. We have to check it to find out what went wrong."

"Group Captain Turner has given strict orders that no one apart from the particular people he has assigned is to go near the aircraft. Sorry, Sir, but I'm sure you will be invited to look at it when the initial salvage has been carried out."

"This is outrageous," Butler fumed. "What kind of organisation does not make use of the experts immediately? Vital evidence could be lost."

"I'm sorry, Sir, but those are our orders." The young airman stared fixedly at Butler who eventually turned away.

Healey went with him, the two engineers walking slowly across the grass towards the main buildings. "Perhaps we should go to see Turner himself," Healey offered. "It's a ridiculous state of affairs."

Butler was quiet for a moment and then exploded again. "There is nothing wrong with those engines. It must be sabotage or complete incompetence on someone's part. I'm going to see Stanley. Coming?"

Without waiting for an answer, William Butler altered direction heading for the main office building and Officers Mess. All those who had watched the test flight or rather failed test flight were streaming off the airfield returning to their duties. They knew there would be no flying probably for the rest of the day or at least until the runway was cleared. The second runway could be used at a pinch but initial trainees would not fly from it as they would have to deal with a cross-wind albeit not a strong one. There were clusters of men gesticulating as they walked and talking animatedly to and over each other.

William Butler barged through the main swing doors of the office building. A corporal was sorting some papers at a desk and looked up, surprised.

"We need to see Stanley…now."

"I'm afraid Air Chief Marshal Stanley is with Group Captain Turner and cannot be disturbed."

Butler picked up the supercilious tone which enraged him further. "That's what you think." He strode past the table and, guessing where the office was, continued along a short corridor to the left of the foyer. Healey smiled apologetically at the corporal and followed. Butler had chosen well. At the end of the corridor was a door with 'Group Captain Turner' emblazoned in gold letters. Breathing heavily, Butler grasped the handle, flung it open and marched in. Stanley, Turner and Grainger stared at him from the chairs they occupied. Turner rose slowly from his chair about to remonstrate but Butler gave him no chance.

"It is outrageous that you are preventing Mr Healey and myself from checking the aircraft before any evidence gets destroyed by your clumsy personnel. I demand access to the aircraft now."

"I understand that you're upset Mr Healey but we must follow proper procedure." Turner spoke with stern gravity but Butler was not to be silenced.

"Procedure, procedure. Don't you understand that I am expert, expert on those engines and Mr Healey is expert on the aircraft. No one is in a better position than us to establish what went wrong."

Turner was about to reply when Stanley raised a hand to silence him. He rose from his chair slowly, his brows furrowed and looking at Butler with his characteristic lowered head. "You suggested I think Mr Butler that the explosions must have been sabotage. If that is the case...it is a possibility...there may be booby traps on the aircraft, other explosives which will be triggered by hands and feet that are inexpert in the field of sabotage. You are of course expert in engine design, Mr Healey in aircraft design, but not in explosives...unless of course you have an undisclosed past."

"Undisclosed past? Of course not. I've been security checked, I've signed the official secrets act."

"Quite. But you have not worked with explosives. You are not familiar with the way that booby traps are laid I think."

Butler blustered to a halt and Stanley smiled at him coldly, knowing he had no answer. Turner looked admiringly at Stanley but Grainger looked troubled. He spoke from his languid position in the chair, one leg propped over its arm.

"Of course, the Air Chief Marshal is not saying it is sabotage, merely that we need to eliminate any possible danger before investigating the cause."

"Quite so." Stanley resumed his seat.

"Now gentlemen, if you would kindly leave us to our deliberations, you will be informed as soon as we are ready for you to inspect the wreckage." Turner held out his hand towards the door in an invitation to leave. He smiled pleasantly as the two engineers left the office and closed the door behind them. "I'm so sorry Sir George. I'll have words with whoever is on duty outside. That should not have been allowed to happen."

Stanley waved it away. "It's not a problem. I just hope this whole thing works. It's causing quite a problem. How long can we leave it until we let Butler and Healey near the wreckage?"

"We need to clear it from the runway and we can take time doing that."

"As long as you need. Grainger, you need to get some photographs don't you?"

"I'll get some from ground level but we really need some shots from the air. They will show the extent of the damage more clearly and will look more like shots from a spy plane."

"Right. Can that be arranged before the runway is cleared

Turner?"

"We can probably get an aircraft up from the second runway. Wind's light. Shouldn't be a problem."

Grainger sat up. "I think gentlemen, we should ask Miss Barnes and her navigator to take us up. The Anson is ideal for that purpose but more to the point it'll keep them out of mischief. Miss Barnes in particular seems to have a mind that is disturbingly inquisitive." He smiled and the others responded.

"Good idea Grainger. Would you speak to her? I'm sure she'll be flattered to be asked."

◆ ◆ ◆

"For God's sake Hans, just relax. Go to sleep or something."

"Don't be foolish. How can I sleep? We should have gone far away. Waiting in this area is tempting fate. The van might be seen. Someone might put two and two together, think we've sabotaged the plane. If we are arrested and they find the film, the mission is a failure."

"We won't get arrested, they won't find the film. We're roofers doing a job. We're parked amongst trees so no one will see us from the road which is a good half a mile away. Just relax for God's sake. We'll just sit here, have a snooze in the van, then go back to the pub for a good feed and later we can drive back to Skegness in plenty of time for the rendezvous."

"If this mission fails, I will make sure our superiors know why and that you are responsible."

Bob's answer was an uncharacteristic spurt of anger. "And when it succeeds as it surely will, I wonder if you'll tell them who was responsible, who made sure we acted naturally, blended in, removed any suspicion from us? Will you tell them that?"

Both men glared at each other in hostile silence before turning away. Hans took the pistol from his coat pocket and caressed it gently. Bob hunched down and let his head rest against the cold steel of the van. He closed his eyes and let out a long breath. In twenty-four hours, they would be back in Germany handing over the film, explaining how Britain's new secret weapon had exploded before leaving the runway. They would be congratulated, perhaps recommended for an honour and then he would be able to return to his quarters and sleep.

It was not a life that would suit everyone but he loved the excitement. It was the same rush as he had experienced on the robberies. He smiled to himself, picturing the daring raids they had done - the Jelly Crew people called them – on account of the way they blew open the safe door with gelignite. He remembered the rush of seeing the cash or jewels and even once gold bars when the smoke cleared. They were untouchable. Poor old PC Plod could never pin anything on them. They were too clever that's why. It was ideal training for the life of a spy, a saboteur. Bob knew he was amongst the best. If there was any risk of getting caught, he knew he could talk his way out of it. He'd done it so many times before.

In some ways, he hoped the War would never end. But then again, he knew at the end of it, he would have a tidy sum of money to start a new life somewhere. Find a nice lady, live the life of Riley, cocktails before dinner in an expensive restaurant. He thought of Molly at the pub. She may do though he fancied someone with a bit more class. Maybe he'd have a yacht... now that would be special...in the Med...sunshine, warmth and no work in the morning. Going into nightclubs a classy bird on his arm. 'Good evening, Sir. The usual table?'

Hans saw that Bob was asleep. How could he sleep so easily?

Robbie McBane looked at the dead man lying on the bed,

his face ashen and immobile. Doctor Philips gently pulled the sheet over him again and turned to face Robbie.

"Seems doubly tragic doesn't it when a young man dies on an airfield with no enemy in sight?"

"Did he just fall as has been suggested?"

"That's for the pathologist to say. I am merely confirming death and suggesting the cause was internal bleeding on the brain." The doctor stepped over to the hand basin and washed his hands thoroughly. Robbie McBane waited for him to turn off the tap and start to dry his hands.

"Would he sustain an injury like that from falling, that's what I'm asking?"

"I know what you're asking Sergeant but I am not the person who should tell you. What I will say is that, in my experience, a fit young man, falling over after drinking would crumple, his knees buckling and his upper body rolling on the ground. His head would of course hit the ground but only in the last stage of the fall. It would have had to hit something with an edge, a large stone or the edge of the concrete base beneath the hangar. There is a wound, there would be blood."

"Is the wound consistent with such a fall?"

"Yes but it could also have been made by being hit on the head as he told you. Something like the butt of a pistol or a spanner."

"He said he had only drank a couple of swigs of whisky. Would that have been enough to make him so drunk he fell?"

"Is there any way of corroborating his story? Did someone see him drinking the whisky? How long before he was found did he drink it?"

"No one saw him drinking as far as I know. It must have been only half an hour or less between this young woman giving him the drink – if that did really happen of course – and him being found by the next person on guard duty."

"Even if he had drunk the whole half bottle, he would not have been rendered unconscious in that time but he would have been feeling the effects by then. Two swigs would not have that impact unless they were extremely large swigs."

"So you would be inclined to believe his story?"

"I cannot comment on that but I think you should start at the scene. If you find blood on a stone or piece of concrete in a suitable position, he may have fallen and hit his head."

"Thank you Doctor. Goodbye."

Before Doctor Philips could give his farewell, Robbie McBane was rushing out of the sick bay. He headed at speed across to Hangar Three, cursing himself for not examining the scene more carefully sooner. But then, he consoled himself, he had accepted Sinclair's version of events and had not long found out that he was dealing with a possible murder rather than an accident or assault.

Several people were still picking over the pieces of the wrecked aircraft in the centre of the airfield. He felt that events were overtaking him. The story that was now firmly in his mind was that the two roofers had got into the base last night with a woman, enticed Sinclair out of the hangar and then sabotaged the aircraft. They had hit him on the head perhaps supposing he had seen them and could identify them. He would search the area outside the hangar thoroughly. If there was no sign of blood on a stone or the edge of the concrete, he would know Sinclair's story had been right. If he found blood, Sinclair probably had hit his head when he fell.

CHAPTER 18

Lizzie opened the throttles and the Anson rolled forward. She knew as soon as they cleared the ground, she would need to turn to starboard to head more directly into the wind and hence gain more lift. She would make sure she had reached the highest speed she could by using the full length of the runway before pulling back on the stick and lifting into the air. She looked across at Alice who was sitting as calmly as usual.

"About seventy degrees to starboard should turn you into the wind." Alice smiled.

"Thanks. Let's hope we don't have to come down again."

"Not a lot of room for that but the hedge at the end of the airfield will catch us."

"Good to have someone so confident beside me."

The Anson was shaking as it gathered speed over the runway, the noise of the tyres on the concrete increasingly deafening. Lizzie wondered if it would bother her passenger. The answer came seconds later when Grainger's angry voice could just be heard above the engines.

"For God's sake get this thing in the air before I get shaken to pieces."

Lizzie ignored it and concentrated on the runway ahead disappearing with alarming speed beneath them. She glanced at the air speed indicator. She needed more. "Come on, come on," she muttered between clenched teeth.

Alice looked at her quickly and back to the disappearing runway. "I was only joking about the hedge by the way."

Lizzie said nothing, her concentration totally focused on the air speed and the runway. At last with just fifty yards of concrete left, she pulled back on the stick and the Anson lifted off the ground. Immediately she turned to starboard and only let out her breath when the aircraft started to turn into the wind. "Well done old girl." She grinned at Alice and whooped.

The ground fell slowly away under them. Lizzie held her course gaining some height. She flicked on the intercom. "What sort of height do you want us to maintain when we fly past the wreckage?" She deliberately did not add the 'Sir'. Such an unpleasant man and one she suspected of espionage did not deserve it.

Grainger appeared in the cockpit doorway, gripping the sides firmly. "I want some shots at fairly low level, say one hundred feet and then I'll want some much higher up. You'll need to make passes several times on both sides to make sure I get good pictures so I guess you'll circle the airfield. We need to be... probably about a hundred yards from the wreckage. I'll give you a shout when I'm ready for the higher altitude shots."

He disappeared back to the passenger cabin. Lizzie turned the aircraft to starboard and, when the Anson was facing the airfield again, began to line it up for her first pass parallel to the runway where the stricken aircraft lay. She dropped down to a hundred feet as they approached and she flew steadily almost due East until they had cleared the airfield and passed a clump of trees. It was then a matter of making a large loop to starboard and lining up the Anson with the runway again, flying almost due West.

Flying past again due East with more leisure to look around, she spotted the dark shape in the clump of trees on the far side of the airfield. Glancing from her instruments and back, she watched as they flew closer. Yes, she was sure of it. It was a van with two ladders on the roof.

"Alice, when we go around, take a good look at that clump of trees and tell me what you see there."

They flew on without talking further, the whine of the wind in the wires just audible above the drone of the engines. As they flew on the eastern leg again, Alice focused on the clump of trees. When it disappeared from view under the aircraft nose, Alice nodded. "A van with two ladders on the roof...just like the one we saw at the pub last night."

"They haven't made themselves scarce yet then."

Grainger appeared in the doorway. "Right you can go up to about five thousand feet now provided we're not in the cloud."

"Sure you wouldn't want just another couple of pass...?"

"No. Ascend now." Grainger snapped and returned to his section.

Lizzie looked at the intercom switch. She flicked it off. "Damn and blast. I've done it again. He must have heard us talking about the van. That just confirms my suspicions. He doesn't want us to know Bob and his sidekick are still nearby."

Robbie McBane walked very slowly, bent over and staring hard at the edge of the concrete base to the hangar. He walked its full length. Nothing. He then returned examining the base of Hangar Two. Nothing. The next bit was harder. He walked very slowly between the two hangars, back and forth, examining a strip of ground about a yard wide in front of him, his eyes sweeping the stony surface slowly and methodically. He was thankful that the weeds had only just started growing and did not obstruct his scrutiny.

Nothing.

He straightened, rubbing his back with both hands. No evidence of a fall that caused Sinclair's injury then. So the dead man's account of being hit on the head was more likely. What had he heard from the person he said had hit him? 'That's far more sinister.' It made no sense unless it was something to do with the German agents. But why would they say that?

He turned his attention back to the immediate task. A weapon was the next object to search for. If it had been the butt of a pistol, it would have been taken by the assailant. But it would be a good idea to check as something else may have wreaked havoc on the poor man's skull. He probed the shrubs that grew along a fence at the rear of the hangars, using his foot to push aside small branches that straggled to the ground.

After half an hour, he concluded nothing had been thrown there. A murder weapon could of course have been hurled over the fence to land God knows where or it may have been dropped elsewhere entirely. Needles and haystacks came to mind. Robbie McBane sighed. As he passed the personnel door into the hangar, he noticed a guard looking thoroughly bored inside. He walked in the door and coughed to alert him.

The airman jumped to his feet and, seeing the stripes on Robbie's arm, saluted.

"At ease. I guess you're having a quiet guard."

"You can say that again, Sir. Everyone's out on the field looking at the crash. Hope the pilot's ok."

"He is apparently. Why is a guard still needed. I mean now that the Meteor has exploded, there can't be any need to guard the hangar."

"Ours not to reason why, Sir. No idea…just carrying out orders."

Robbie McBane looked around the hangar. A large tarpaulin was draped over another aircraft further back but there was no obvious reason why it should need guarding. Probably just an oversight on someone's part – forgot to stand down the guard. "Mind if I look around?"

"Help yerself, Sir, though there's not much to see."

The hangar was as he had known when he was an aircraftman in Scotland. There were two sets of steps parked neatly at the side and a gantry used for maintaining aircraft. Beyond those, again tucked into the side of the hangar were heavy wooden benches with vices attached and above them racks of tools. He paused at a set of spanners hanging on a board in order of size. One end of each was a ring upon which it was hung. The other end was an open spanner and tilted slightly so that it hung inwards. A thought crossed his mind. Each one was subject to careful examination in turn without being removed from its position.

Robbie stopped at the last and largest one. It was hanging with the open end tilted outwards.

The slightest trace of darkness appeared on the edge of the hanging end. Grease or blood? Carefully taking it at the ring end, he brought it close to his eyes. The dark smear was definitely tinted red like congealed blood.

He walked slowly back to the sentry. "I'll need to take this with me."

"Something need fixing, Sir?"

"It certainly does but not in the way you mean." Robbie McBane left the hangar. Did that airman know Sinclair was dead. Did anyone else know he was dead? Did anyone care?

"Wake up, wake up." Hans shook Bob's shoulder.

"Whass up?" Bob sat forward. "What's 'appening?"

"You did not hear it? The plane?"

"I was fast asleep."

"I know. But we must go...now. There has been a plane flying backwards and forwards. They must be looking for us. We must get far away."

"But...but what about dinner?"

Hans lost his temper. "Dinner? Dinner? Forget about food for one minute can't you? There won't be any dinner if they find us here. We must get away."

"But...but...what makes you think the plane is looking for us?"

"It has flown overhead several times, backwards and forwards. That only happens when they are looking for something."

"How d'you know it's the same plane? I mean we are right next to an airfield."

"The sound was exactly the same and it's still up there though it sounds higher now."

"So they can't be looking for us can they if it's up higher. It's a training base so they're probably training pilots."

"We're leaving now. Give me the keys to the van."

"Gor blimey. You're such an old woman. There's the damn keys but we ain't going far and we are goin' to have dinner at the pub tonight…at least I am even if you want to starve."

Hans picked up the keys from the van floor and, hunched over, climbed in to the driver's seat. Stretching as best he could in the confined space of the van, Bob struggled into the passenger seat. Hans started the engine and revved it. The van lurched forward and bumped over the uneven ground before gaining the track.

"What if they see us leaving and follow us? We won't be able to escape them."

"We'll have to take that risk." Hans stared fixedly through the windscreen only moving his head when they reached the road. With swift glances each way, he revved the engine and swung out heading South.

"You're on the wrong side of the road you idiot. For God's sake let me drive. We won't get far with you at the wheel."

Hans took no notice at first but yanked the wheel so the van lurched onto the correct side of the road. Bob maintained a constant one way argument about why he should drive. He knew that Hans would take them miles away and they'd never get back for dinner. He was going to see Molly again whatever Hans thought. When they reached the junction at the end of Raunceby Lane, Hans hesitated, trying to ensure his tired brain enabled him to turn onto the correct side of the main road.

Bob saw his moment. "Look Hans, mate, you're too tired to drive when you're not used to this country. I'll drive."

Hans said nothing but he pulled the van to the side of the road, jumped out, slamming the door behind him and stormed round to the passenger side. Bob eased himself past the gearstick into the driver's seat. He drove off at a more sedate pace. Following his instinct as much as the map, he drove into Holdingham and on to Sleaford but the road was taking them South and further away from Leasingham and Molly. He pulled over briefly to consult the map and, when they had set off again, took the next left hand turn, following a road that should take them to Ruskington. After they left the buildings of Sleaford behind, he began looking to left and right for a suitable place to stop. A clump of trees would be ideal.

Some two miles out of Sleaford with flat, open fields either side of the road, having passed a couple of lanes on the right, he spotted a large copse some way off to the east of the road. A minor road looked as though it would take them in the right direction so he pulled the steering wheel and the van lumbered into it. It was straight and narrow and, disappointingly, they could see a gate across it in the distance. Bob eased the van to a halt in front of the gate. It was a railway line and a sign on the gate informed them it was private property beyond the track.

Hans clapped his hands slowly. "Very good Bob. You've taken us to a dead end."

"I've just about had enough of you. It's a bloody gate not an impenetrable obstacle." He flung the van door open and jumped out, slamming it behind him. He made no attempt at concealment. A house, presumably the gate-keeper's, stood silently beside the lane. No one appeared. If someone challenged him, he was a roofer who had a job to do at the big house.

Bob stamped over to the gate, trying to relieve his growing frustration with Hans. He unhitched the gate and swung it open, not bothering to latch it in its new position. It did not swing back. Marching over the railway track, he opened the gate on the other side. He returned to the van.

"Well don't just sit there. You'll need to close the bloody gates when I've driven through."

Hans turned a face of pure anger and hatred to Bob and,

with studied calm, opened the van door. When he was out of the van, Bob let in the clutch and it bumped over the crossing. He deliberately drove further than was strictly necessary on the other side. The miserable sod could walk!

CHAPTER 19

"Does it look like dried blood to you Matron?"

She turned the spanner in her hands, looking carefully at the open end. "It certainly does. That's the way blood looks when it's congealed."

"Thank you."

"Would this be to do with the young man who died this morning...Sinclair?"

"Perhaps, but I must ask you to tell no one about this conversation. I'm certain his death was no accident and that those responsible are not from Cranwell but, until I'm sure, let's keep it between ourselves."

"As you wish."

Matron turned away without a smile and clacked down the corridor. Robbie McBane had hoped Doctor Philips would still be in the sick bay so he could get his opinion but Matron would have seen plenty of blood at different stages of congealment in her career so her judgement was, he felt sure, sound. Holding the spanner at the clean end, he left the sick bay intending to take it to his room. He would need to show it to Stanley later to prove Sinclair's story was true. Then maybe Stanley would accept that the roofers, Bob and his mate, had been on the base and murdered Sinclair. If the aircraft had been sabotaged, they were almost certainly responsible.

It would perhaps be something for the young man's family too – that he had not been so drunk he had fallen and bashed his head. He thought of the grieving parents, perhaps a sweetheart at home who would never see him come back on leave. But how foolish he had been. Why were some men so easily tempted by the siren call of an attractive woman? But then, perhaps it was easy to condemn others when one had not experienced that same situation. The long hours of boredom on guard duty, the chill of the night, the unexpected diversion of a lovely young woman with a warming spirit – both within herself and in a bottle – would perhaps be too much for any man.

Deep in thought, Robbie walked slowly across to the main building. Even if he could solve the matter of Sinclair's death and the destruction of the Meteor, he still had to establish whether Butler was indeed a German spy. Confronting him with the evidence they had of the Morse Code message may be the only way. That would best be done with Stanley or Grainger. But was Grainger part of the spy network? The information about the piece of paper Grainger had slipped to Bob in the pub was known only to himself, Lizzie and Alice. He needed to confront Grainger with that but Stanley and Turner would have to be convinced first. What a mess this was. There were too many possibilities. Truth as ever was too elusive, a wisp of mist, intangible, drifting across open moorland.

Bert Swallow was about to leave the main building and the two men met in the middle of the foyer. Bert stopped suddenly, looked confused, pointed to the spanner. "What've you got that for?"

There was something odd in Swallow's demeanour. "Oh just something I'm looking in to. It's not a problem is it? I'll return it as soon as I've finished with it."

"No...oh no...no problem. It's just that we don't usually allow tools to leave the hangars. Too much risk of them going missing, you know. Plenty of our guys have motorbikes they work on. You know how it is."

"Of course. I'll put it back exactly where it came from as soon as I'm done with it."

"Thanks." Bert Swallow seemed restless, shifting his weight from one foot to the other and back. "So any news about...you know...last night or the explosions this morning?"

"I can't tell you about the Meteor as Turner has ordered

only specific people to examine the wreckage and I'm not one of them."

"No of course not...you wouldn't know anything. But last night?"

"Well you know, I suppose, that Sinclair is dead."

"Dead?" Bert Swallow's face went very pale and then flushed. "Dead?"

"Aye. Apparently it's not unusual to have a delayed death after a blow on the head. Bleeding on the brain the Doctor thinks but we have to wait for the post mortem for a definitive answer." Robbie McBane watched Bert Swallow's face carefully. The death of one of your men in combat would be bad enough and Sinclair's passing on the base had certainly shocked Bert Swallow.

"But surely that would not be caused by falling over and banging his head? I mean it can't have been that hard a blow."

"No one knows at the moment and perhaps we never will."

"No...perhaps not." Bert Swallow seemed to relax a little and then he said "Must get on. See you later."

Robbie McBane watched him walk swiftly out of the building. He could not quite put his finger on it but he thought Swallow knew more about events on the base than he was letting on.

At five thousand feet, Lizzie and Alice could not see whether the van with the ladders on the roof was still in the clump of trees. Lizzie was becoming impatient. They had flown over the airfield several times and she had already asked Grainger twice if he had taken enough photographs. Was he deliberately delaying their return to a lower altitude? If he was working with the two German spies – she was convinced that was what Bob and his mate were – he would want to delay their own return to the ground to let them get away.

At last, Grainger appeared in the doorway and said they could now land. Lizzie gave a thumbs up and headed due northeast ready to make her approach. This gave her and Alice a good view of the clump of trees as they approached. There was no sign of the van. Lizzie's eyes flicked to the intercom switch. Definitely off.

"I'm going to go round again Alice and a bit higher and wider to see if we can spot that van. It can't have got far away. Start to put the wheels down and stop. I'll tell him they're jammed." She grinned.

At the start of their approach to the runway, Alice started pumping to lower the undercarriage. She had not pumped for long when Lizzie held up a hand palm out as a signal to stop. "RAF Cranwell, this is Avro Anson Kilo six two nine five over."

A bored male voice came on the radio. "Anson Kilo six two nine five, this is RAF Cranwell. Over."

"We have a problem with the undercarriage. It seems to be jammed. I'm going to go round again and try to free it. Over.

"Roger that. I'll put the fire tenders on standby. Over."

"Thanks. Hope we won't need them. Out."

Lizzie flicked off the radio and switched the cabin intercom on. "We've got a slight problem with the undercarriage Mr Grainger so we'll have to fly round and see if we can get it sorted."

Seconds later, Grainger's face appeared in the doorway. He looked frightened. "What's the problem? I must get these cameras back intact. Can't you fix it?"

"That's what we'll be attempting to do as we fly around. Don't worry Mr Grainger, we have these sorts of situations frequently. We'll sort it out won't we Alice?"

"We'll certainly do our best. Anyway they've got the fire trucks on standby if we have to come down on our belly." Both women turned to look at Grainger. His eyes were wide with fear and he hurriedly returned to his seat.

Lizzie took the aircraft up to about five hundred feet so

it gave them a wide view of the ground. She and Alice scoured the landscape, tracing the roads away from the clump of trees, hoping to see the van. There was no sign of it.

"Can we risk another, larger circle d'you think?"

"Why not? The undercarriage still seems to be stuck."

The aircraft described a larger circle in the sky but still there was no sign of the van. Lizzie was cross. Perhaps she should have ignored Grainger and his photos and concentrated on that van. She could then have alerted Robbie McBane. She imagined the drama, Robbie in a Land Rover leading a couple of police cars with bells clanging and blue lights flashing. But now, Bob and his fellow spy had evaded capture. They could be miles away by now or they could be hidden somewhere else – a barn, a disused factory, who knew?

"We may as well head back, Alice. Finish dropping the wheels please."

Lizzie radioed the tower and landed without incident. No sooner had the aircraft slowed to taxi-ing speed than Grainger was in the doorway. "What are you playing at? Trying to be a master spy-catcher are you? What on earth do you think that van has got to do with anything? I can tell you now, Miss Barnes, that your career is effectively over. I'm going straight to Stanley now and then I'll telephone Trueman. You can go back to being a typist or whatever it was you were before some damn fool let you near an aeroplane."

"We'll see about that Mr Grainger. It may not be my job that's about to end."

"How dare you speak to me like that. I am a very senior civil servant and I have a great deal of influence over such things as the operation of the Air Transport Auxiliary."

The aircraft came to a stop and Lizzie shut down the engines. The cabin door was opened and steps presented by the ground crew. Grainger took his camera and stomped down the steps without a word.

"I don't think he's very happy," said Alice.

◆ ◆ ◆

"Why on Earth do they need to take high altitude photos of the wreckage. I mean what is that going to tell them?" William Butler, craning his neck, looked upwards where the Anson had been flying..

"I don't know...I don't know at all but there's definitely something strange going on here. That test didn't ring true to me. They've done nothing about clearing the runway. All they've been doing is poking around amongst the wreckage. I can understand taking some low-level aerial shots of it but not from the altitude they were flying at." Arthur Healey's eyes flicked from the forlorn sight of the shattered Meteor to the sky above them.

"If there were any booby traps, they must have found them now. I wonder if for some reason they're trying to discredit your design or perhaps more likely our engines. Perhaps there's a rival engine that they prefer and they want us out of the way. It's these ministry types, the likes of Grainger, I don't trust."

"I agree. They never come out and say anything directly. Addicted to secrets. I wouldn't mind betting he's a Nazi spy."

William Butler looked around sharply. "What makes you say that?"

Arthur Healey looked at the ground. "Well you know... he said last night that the Germans had got wind of the Meteor. How does he know unless he's told them?"

"That's a bit of a stretch but you could be right."

The two men fell silent, looking out over the airfield at the activity or rather inactivity on the runway in front of them. They stood for a long time as if their continued attention would shame someone into letting them inspect the damaged aircraft.

They had watched the Anson descending and approaching the intersecting runway at almost sixteen hundred hours according to Butler's watch. Arthur Healey had pointed to the fact that the Anson's wheels were not fully down and they watched as it had begun to ascend again turning to port and heading East. Some ten minutes later, it was approaching again, this time with the undercarriage fully in place. That had prompted a brief discussion between the two engineers about maintenance at Cranwell.

"May well be an issue," Butler had offered, "though that Anson is not based here...arrived yesterday. It's an ATA plane apparently."

"Yes, I flew up here with Grainger. Both the pilot and navigator are young women. Did a good job as far as I can see. She certainly knows how to handle an aircraft."

Butler had looked dubious. "It's not a job for women really is it?"

"Necessity. We've lost too many pilots, especially in 1940. Some bad days. Nearly lost my son just before Dunkirk."

William Butler looked at Healey but there seemed to be no compassion in his eyes or voice. "Sorry to hear that."

"D'you have children?"

"No...no kids."

"Hard to understand then I suppose, what it means to a parent. You'd do anything for your children, anything."

CHAPTER 20

Lizzie, with Alice beside her, followed Robbie McBane into Group Captain Turner's office. She was nervous but determined not to be cowed by Grainger's bullying manner. He was there of course as was Sir George Stanley. Chairs had been arranged in a circle which surprised Lizzie. She thought she and Alice would be standing in front of the desk with Stanley or Turner formally charging them or at least telling them they were stood down.

Stanley waved vaguely at the chairs. "Do please sit." He paused until they had done so. "Miss Barnes, Mr Grainger tells me that you made use of this afternoon's flight, which was arranged to take photographs of the Meteor, to look for a van, a van which was supposedly used by saboteurs." He smiled indulgently.

"Yes Sir. It did not affect the mission to take photographs and I thought it would be useful for Sergeant McBane's investigations."

"Mr Grainger feels you should return to duties at White Waltham. In fact he thinks ground based duties might be more appropriate for you." Stanley, smiling, looked at Grainger whose brows were furrowed in anger, replacing the usual supercilious expression. "What do you say to that?"

"Mr Grainger seems to find it difficult to accept that the two men in that van are not just saboteurs but possible murderers. To come onto an RAF base and kill one of our men is a crime that should not go unpunished. I wonder why Mr Grainger is so keen to protect them."

Grainger said nothing but hostility radiated from him. Stanley and Turner seemed untroubled by it. Perhaps they shared her own suspicion of ministry types.

"Perhaps before we go any further Sir, I should update you on where I've got to with the death of Sinclair." Without waiting for an invitation, McBane continued. "I spoke with the doctor who signed the death certificate. He is confident that the post mortem will confirm Sinclair died from a bleed on the brain caused by a significant blow to the head. His view is that a fit young man falling as a result of intoxication would crumple and so not bang his head with sufficient force to cause death. However, he said it was possible if his head hit something very hard such as the edge of concrete. In such a case, traces of blood would be evident. I have inspected the site very, very carefully. I could find no traces of blood anywhere. What I did find though, was a spanner in the hangar which had some dried blood on it. The probability is that the spanner is the murder weapon...I say 'murder' because I am certain that is what it is."

Robbie McBane stopped to let that sink in. Stanley looked at Grainger who said nothing. Lizzie decided to spell out the connection. "The most likely people to have murdered Sinclair are the two roofers who came onto the base last night. We know one of them uses a German brand of tobacco, impressions of a ladder were found on both sides of the fence and we believe that they brought the young woman from the pub where they stayed last night."

Suddenly Grainger was on his feet. "This is not evidence. Someone who has a grudge against Sinclair may have gone to the hangar last night, had an argument with him and hit him on the head with the spanner. It does happen. People get angry."

There was a shocked silence at this outburst. "What is interesting, Mr Grainger, is that you should become so angry at what is a reasonable supposition." Alice's quiet voice surprised them all.

"I'm fed up with wasting time on this."

"Investigating a murder is not a waste of time Mr Grainger." Robbie McBane's eyes were burning into Grainger.

"What about the spy we might have? What are you doing

about that?"

"Grainger is right, that is very important McBane," Stanley said. "It's about national security and the war effort. Of course the death of one of our men is important but we must stem the leak we might have. Please get on to that."

"That is another line of investigation. We need to pursue what we heard last night from Mr Butler's room but we need to act quickly if we are to apprehend the two roofers. If they are innocent and indeed roofers, we can easily establish that can't we? I believe that is the most important thing to do right now before they disappear."

"If they haven't already," added Lizzie.

Robbie McBane addressed Group Captain Turner who had said nothing so far. "Is there any news about the Meteor, Sir. Was it sabotage or faulty engines?"

"Um…ah…nothing as yet McBane. My chaps are still looking into it but we think sabotage is unlikely. No evidence of explosives."

"So the explosions may have nothing to do with anything else. It is rather a coincidence though that people should come onto the base at night and then an aircraft blows up." Lizzie was pleased that Robbie was so determined not to be diverted from the van and its occupants.

"You cannot be sure that any intruders were on the base last night. The so-called evidence Miss Sleuth Barnes has presented is purely circumstantial. I think we are dealing with completely unconnected events and I advise you to concentrate on establishing what enemies Sinclair might have had on the base. And who might be giving secrets to the Germans."

Robbie McBane stood up. "Thank you for your advice Mr Grainger but I think I will decide how to conduct my investigation." He turned to Stanley. "If that will be all Sir, I would like to get on. Time is of the essence."

"Grainger is right, McBane. You need to pursue the mole. Remember what I said to you."

"I do remember, Sir. But I must be able to investigate these issues as I see fit."

Stanley's eyes narrowed; he stood up and for a moment looked as though he was going to explode at Robbie. His mouth opened but he turned to Lizzie and mildly said, "Miss Barnes, do please try not to upset Mr Grainger. We are supposed to be on the same side."

"Yes Sir. We are *supposed* to be."

Grainger looked furious again but said nothing while Robbie, Lizzie and Alice filed out.

◆ ◆ ◆

"We will stay just long enough to eat. Then we go."

"Of course but we've a lot of time to kill before the rendezvous." Bob needed to pacify Hans but he was not going to miss out on a nice bit of flirtation with the lovely Molly.

"And you park away from the pub not next to it as before. If they are still looking for the van, it will tell them where we are if we park too close."

"Okay, okay but you're worrying about nothing. We're roofers remember from Skegness. Just hang onto that."

Bob started the van and drove it slowly from the cover of the trees onto the lane that led to the level crossing. They had to wait while a train rattled through the crossing, blowing smoke and cinders into the air. It was a goods train, high-sided wagons that might contain anything from coal to ammunition, heading perhaps to Lincoln or beyond.

Hans drummed his fingers on his knee impatiently. "Just as well it's not a passenger train...not many eyes to see us."

Bob said nothing but raised his eyes. Hans was a pain in the neck. Why couldn't he just relax. They'd achieved their mission and all they had to do now was kill a few hours, drive back to the coast and wait to be picked up. At last the train passed, its sound diminishing as it left the crossing behind.

Hans did not move.

"The gates have to be open for us to drive over, Hans."

"Your turn to open them."

"So you want me to get out, open the gates, drive over, get out again and close the gates while you just sit there?"

Hans shrugged and looked out of the side window.

"Fuck you." Bob shoved his door open and marched up to the first gate. He swung it open, crossed the line and opened the far gate. Returning to the van, he climbed in, revved the engine and drove over the crossing as fast as the van would accelerate, bouncing himself and Hans so their heads hit the roof. Neither spoke. Bob jumped out and, calling Hans all sorts of names under his breath, closed the two gates. He then drove in hostile silence, straight across the crossroads with the quickest glance in each direction onto the road that led to Leasingham.

"Your anger will get us killed. You need to control it."

"Sometimes, it's just not possible."

On the edge of Leasingham, they came to a right hand turn which Bob took. This road took them through the village past St Andrews Church and to the Prince of Wales pub. Bob's anger had subsided and he knew that Hans was right. They should take the precaution of parking away from the pub in case a search was on for the van. Beyond the pub, a road called The Square appeared on the right. Bob took it but it proved to be a dead end. He managed to turn the van in a driveway. He drove back to the road they had followed and turned right to go a little further.

The next turning on the right was Chapel Lane. A line of what looked like council houses stretched away on the left. Bob drove just beyond them and pulled in at the side of the road. "This is perfect. It's the sort of road where roofers would live. It'll be fine here and it's not far to walk back to the pub."

Hans did not argue and the two men climbed out of the van. They walked in silence, each longing to be back in Germany and out of each other's company.

◆ ◆ ◆

Lizzie had tried to persuade Robbie to borrow a vehicle and try to track down the van with Bob and his mate but he felt he should at least have a discussion with Bert Swallow about Sinclair if only to keep Grainger off his back.

"But every minute we delay going after the roofers, is a minute they can get further away."

"I know that Lizzie but it may be a wild goose chase." He glanced at his watch. "It's gone seventeen hundred hours. We'll have a discussion with Bert Swallow, get something to eat and then go back to the pub. You never know...Grainger could be right. Sinclair may have made enemies on the base."

"I feel it in my bones, Robbie, that Bob and his accomplice are responsible."

"Unfortunately, Lizzie, your bones, lovely as they no doubt are, will hold no weight in a court of law."

They did not have to wait long for Bert Swallow to return to the accommodation building. He was deep in thought, frowning, but managed a smile when they stepped forward.

"Ah. I hear you've been upsetting our man from the Ministry, Miss Barnes."

"News travels fast."

"I'm afraid it does on an RAF base."

"I'd like to have a word about Sinclair if you can spare me a few minutes."

"Sinclair? Why?" The smile faded from Bert Swallow's face.

"Shall we go somewhere more private?" Without waiting for an answer, Robbie McBane led the way to the Library that he and Lizzie had used the night before. Once inside and seated, Robbie asked Bert Swallow whether Sinclair was popular on the base, whether he may have made enemies.

Swallow hesitated before answering. "Enemies? I'm not aware of anything like that. He seemed to be popular, not the life and soul of the party but always ready to join in with a joke, that sort of thing."

"He didn't get himself into arguments, not involved in any bullying, one way or the other?"

Bert Swallow shook his head slowly. "No, no, can't think of anything like that. He was just like everyone else, got on with the job, seemed happy to do whatever he was ordered."

"Where did he come from...I mean where was his home."

Bert thought for a few moments, his eyes searching the carpet for the information. "That 'was' is so final isn't it? Hard to grasp that he's dead. I think he came from the North East somewhere."

"Aye that was obvious from his accent. You can't be more precise?"

"Not without checking the records." He hesitated again. "I can do so, if you want..."

"No, it's fine for the moment. So you are not aware of anyone on the base with a grudge against Sinclair?"

"No, I'm not."

"Thanks Sergeant. Now we plan to go back to that pub after dinner. Any chance of borrowing a vehicle?"

Bert Swallow seemed to brighten. "I'll arrange it."

There was something that did not seem quite right to Lizzie about Swallow's answers. It was not what he said but the way he spoke, the slight pauses, the hesitations as if he was thinking of the right thing to say. Probably, it was just that he was very troubled by Sinclair's death. She must not let her imagination run away with her as she knew she was prone to do.

CHAPTER 21

William Butler and Arthur Healey had eaten their meal without conversation. They sat on their own table, ignoring as best they could the hubbub around them. Snatches of conversation reached them, much of it about the events of the morning. When Butler had finished his pudding – rice with a splodge of jam – he put his spoon into the bowl and looked up.

"Let's not wait for permission. Let's just go over to the hangar and take a look at the plane. It's ridiculous. They finished clearing the runway an hour ago. There cannot be any danger of booby traps...that was just nonsense anyway...so we can take a look."

Arthur Healey nodded. "We can try but it will be guarded."

"We'll talk our way in. Leave it to me."

The two men left the mess hut and walked towards the hangar. They were not hurrying and they wore no facial expressions that might suggest the determination they were both feeling. About a hundred yards from Hangar Three, they could see two guards had been stationed outside, one at the main door which was firmly locked and one outside the personnel door which was closed. Butler paused and looked up into the sky, pretending to assess the weather.

Healey followed his lead. "What's the plan?"

"Not sure. We could just say that Turner had authorised us to inspect the wreckage but..."

"If the guard does not buy it, we're a bit stymied."

"One of us could distract the guard by the personnel door and the other slip inside to take a look."

"Might work but we both need to take a look really."

William Butler thought for a moment. "Let's stick with Plan A. If it works, it means we can both get inside."

The two men continued towards the hangar. Healey smiled at the guard by the huge main doors and called a greeting. The guard replied cheerfully but his eyes followed them as they walked past. They turned the corner of the hangar and approached the guard by the personnel door at the side.

"Evening. William Butler and Arthur Healey. We're the designers of the Meteor. Group Captain Turner said it would be okay for us to inspect the wreckage now."

"I'm not to let anyone in without signed authorisation from Group Captain Turner. So if I could inspect that please, Sir."

"He didn't give us anything in writing, just said it would be fine to inspect it now. I assume your orders apply to other people but not to us."

"They were very clear, Sir. No one comes in without written authorisation. Sorry Sir, but you'll have to go back to Group Captain Turner to get it."

Having failed with his first approach, Butler tried bluster, allowing the anger that always lurked within him some freedom. "Now look here. This is ridiculous. We know more about this aircraft than anyone else and I mean anyone. We are best placed to establish what went wrong this morning but we can only do that if we can inspect the wreckage. I mean Heaven's sake man, we're not spies or something."

The airman held his rifle firmly across his body both hands gripping it in readiness. But he tapped the door behind him with the barrel. He said nothing to Butler and Healey in reply but turned and faced them. After a few seconds, the door behind him opened and Sergeant Swallow appeared.

"These two gentlemen would like to inspect the wreckage of the Meteor, Sir, but they don't have signed authorisation."

Bert Swallow's voice was friendly. "I'm so sorry, gentlemen, but that is absolutely correct. You will need to get authorisation from Group Captain...."

William Butler exploded. "Dammit man he said we could look at it after dinner. Here we are, we've had our dinner. What more permission should we need? We designed the damned thing after all."

Healey laid a restraining hand on Butler's arm. "I'm sure there's just been a breakdown in communication Sergeant. Group Captain Turner perhaps thought we would not need written authorisation given who we are. We won't need long to see what happened and then we'll leave you in peace."

The conciliatory tone of Healey's voice, the reasonableness of his request might have swayed a weaker man. But Bert Swallow had his orders which he had given to the guards and he was not going to be persuaded to disobey them. "Sorry gentlemen. I canna let you in without that signed authorisation."

This produced another angry outburst from Butler. "Why on earth are you people being so secretive? Are you trying to protect your own reputations? You know that there was a failure in maintenance or fuelling the aircraft or some such thing and you're now covering it up."

It was a deliberate goad and Swallow responded in a low voice, his eyes narrowing. He hadn't liked Butler from the start, a weasel, a rat. "That is grossly offensive Mr Butler and I can assure you that my engineers prepared the aircraft exactly according to instructions. You are not coming in so I suggest you make your way back to the accommodation block and enjoy the rest of your evening."

"This doesn't end here, Swallow. You'll regret it." Butler turned on his heel and strode away with Healey in pursuit.

◆ ◆ ◆

"That was lovely, almost as lovely as the waitress."
Molly giggled. "You're such a smooth one you are."

"So can you get away for a few minutes...that's all we need?"

"Maybe...when all the dinners are finished and I've washed up. About an hour's time. I'll have to help in the bar after that. Friday night's usually busy."

"That'll do nicely. Outside...must be a quiet corner somewhere."

"What about your van? It worked yesterday."

"We're not parked right outside. We're up the road. Should be ok provided there are no prying eyes."

Molly smiled at him knowingly. "I'll take your plates, Sir."

She lifted the two pudding bowls and whisked away, swaying her hips as she did so. Bob's eyes followed her until she was lost from view. "Whoa...very tasty." He lifted his pint and took a long drink.

Hans leaned forward across the table. "I told you. No more nonsense with that girl. You are jeopardising the mission. It was already a mistake coming back here. We must leave now."

"I'm not going anywhere yet. You go if you want."

"I might just do that. If I do, I'll take the van."

Bob reached into his pocket and flung the keys on the table. They slid across towards Hans and dropped off the edge into his lap. "You probably won't get far 'cos the police'll stop you for driving on the wrong side of the road." His eyes twinkled with amusement. There was some pleasure in baiting Hans. He was so straight, so serious, so bloody boring.

"And how will you get to Skegness?"

"Don't you worry about me mate. I'll talk my way into a lift from someone. I'll be there at the rendezvous."

Hans stared straight into Bob's eyes. The stare was returned. "Never trust a Britisher. No wonder this is such a puny little country. Everyone is only interested in eating drinking and having sex. When we win this war, we will need to sort it out."

Bob said nothing. The two men sat in silence until Hans suddenly stood up.

◆ ◆ ◆

The three men sat around a coffee table in the lounge of the Officers Mess, sipping brandy and drawing on cigars. Unlike the previous evening, the mood was pensive, each lost in his own thoughts. Stanley broke the silence.

"This is becoming harder to maintain, gentlemen. Where have you got to with the mole Grainger? We must establish where the leak is before we can do anything else."

Grainger leaned forward and tapped his cigar on the ashtray. "I'm well aware of that, Sir George, but all we have is what that Barnes girl and McBane think they heard last night in Butler's room. It's not much to go on."

"Has Butler been tackled yet?"

"No. I thought I'd listen outside his room tonight and tackle him if I heard anything. Not sure we can rely on our Scottish Sergeant...probably not bright enough to trap him into an admission. But Butler? That surprised me."

"Can't you tackle him now? I mean why wait for tonight. He may not send another message. The last one finished 'I will do no more' which suggests he will not communicate again."

"Still worth checking I think. Can we trust Miss Barnes? It could have been mice scratching or pipes cooling. I don't think she is the most reliable witness."

"But..." Group Captain Turner blew a cloud of smoke into the air, " I thought McBane had heard it as well. They can't both be wrong surely?"

Grainger waved a hand dismissively. "Of course they can. The power of suggestion. Miss Barnes tells McBane she's heard Morse Code, he wants to please a pretty young woman so he agrees with her and that's what he hears too."

"I think you're forgetting that Miss Barnes wrote down some of the message and Miss Frobisher was able to decipher it.

That can't be pipes cooling."

"The Barnes woman may have made it up."

Both Stanley and Turner laughed. "Oh come, come, Grainger. You can't believe that." Turner spread his hands. "What motive could she possibly have for fabricating a message like that. I mean does she have something against Butler?"

"Probably not," said Stanley, "but I think Mr Grainger has something against her."

Grainger's eyes narrowed. "Yes I do. She is a meddler, trying to involve herself in things that are none of her business. I mean all that business this afternoon pretending to have a problem with the undercarriage so she could look for the van. She's getting in the way."

Stanley looked away down the room. "She has good eyes and ears, Grainger, and she is making sure that what she sees is passed on to McBane and then to us. That can't be a bad thing."

An orderly, dressed in a starched white jacket and wearing white gloves, approached the table. He hesitated, coughed quietly. "Excuse me gentlemen,." He addressed himself to Turner. "Sergeant Swallow is in the foyer, Sir. He says it is important he gives you some information."

Turner looked at Stanley who nodded. "Send him in Hawkins."

The orderly disappeared and returned moments later with Sergeant Swallow. The latter looked uncomfortable, out of place, glancing nervously around the room, conscious that he was intruding on an inner sanctum. He stood in silence until the orderly had left.

"What is it Swallow?"

"I've just come from the hangar, Sir. Mr Butler and Mr Healey came demanding to be let in to see the wreckage. Of course, they were denied entry as instructed, Sir, but I think they may cause problems if we don't let them see ...you know..."

"You did right to deny entry, Swallow. Good man."

"Sir. I did have another thought but I'm not sure if I'm speaking out of turn."

Turner waved a hand for him to continue.

"Well, Sir. Sinclair in the hangar, Sir. I was wondering whether perhaps Mr Butler, who became very aggressive tonight, Sir, might have tried to get into the hangar later on last night. Sinclair refused for obvious reasons, there was an argument and Butler hit him on the head."

Turner nodded slowly and looked from Stanley to Grainger. "Quite possible. A good thought Swallow.

"What's McBane doing now? Perhaps he and I should have a conversation with our Mr Butler. We must establish where the leak is, Sergeant, before we can do anything else. We've just been discussing it." Grainger stubbed out the end of his cigar in the ashtray with unnecessary force.

"He and the two women asked me to arrange a car for them. I think they've gone back to the pub, Sir, where I took them last night. But there's no jazz band on tonight."

"Jazz band?" A look of alarm crossed Grainger's face. "They're not wanting to listen to jazz." He stood up abruptly. "I need a car, Swallow. Can you get me one quickly?"

Sergeant Swallow looked to Turner who nodded to him. "If you'd like to follow me, Sir, I'll arrange it. Excuse me Sir, Sir." Having saluted, Swallow made a dignified exit; Grainger was out the door before him.

"There's no time to lose Sergeant. I need to get after them. I'm going to my room for my coat and I'll meet you at the front of the main accommodation building – the one with the big pillars." Grainger hurried away and Swallow followed though not at the same pace.

CHAPTER 22

Lizzie searched for the van as they approached the pub but there was no sign of it. Disappointment filled her. Perhaps they had already left the area, gone goodness knows where. She comforted herself with the thought that they could check some details with the barmaid, Molly...provided she was willing to talk. Robbie McBane opened the door of the pub; Alice and Lizzie followed him. He hovered in the doorway, eyes scanning the bar. It was less crowded than the previous evening but the smell of stale cigarette smoke hung in the air just the same.

"No sign of the roofers. Let's see if we can talk to the barmaid."

Whilst Robbie went to the bar to talk to the landlord, Lizzie and Alice looked around the room. Some locals sat at the bar and others at tables. Just a few RAF personnel were sitting at tables, sipping drinks and talking quietly. The landlord disappeared into the back and a few seconds later Molly came through to the bar.

"Hello. My name's Sergeant McBane. I'm in the RAF Police." Molly's eyes widened. "Don't be alarmed...you're not in trouble. Just wonder if you can help us with some enquiries."

"I'll try but I doubt if I can tell you anything." She giggled nervously.

"Shall we sit down?" Robbie McBane walked over to a table in the blacked out window and pulled out a chair for Molly. Lizzie and Alice hung back to let her go first so that they could prevent any change of mind on her part. But Molly did not seem unduly concerned.

"Molly - you don't mind if I call you Molly do you?"

"No, that's me name. It's fine. What did you say your name was?"

"Sergeant McBane...Robbie and this is Lizzie and Alice who are helping me."

"Nice to meet you all. You were in last night weren't you? For the music?"

Robbie smiled and nodded. "Now Molly, we need to talk to you about last night. It's very important. We know that you played a practical joke on a young man who was on guard last night in a hangar at RAF Cranwell."

Molly wriggled, not knowing at first whether to admit to it or not. "Yeah, we did. We didn't do no harm though...just a bit of fun."

"When you say "we", who was with you?"

"Bob and his mate, Harry I think his name is – bit of a miserable sod to be honest. But Bob's good fun. The chap was a friend of theirs though he didn't seem to recognise their names."

"How did you get onto the base?" Lizzie knew the answer of course but every piece of information extracted would confirm the whole operation and would seal their fate when brought to court.

"They're roofers see, so they had a couple of ladders on the van. It was alright for them but you two'll know that it ain't so easy for us girls. Had to hitch me skirt right up to get me leg over the wire at the top." She laughed. "I told 'em not to look. Mind you it was so dark I doubt they could see anything. No moon last night."

"Did Bob and Harry persuade you to do this, Molly." Robbie felt sure that coercion had been involved.

"Nah, I'm always up for a bit of fun. No what happened was I sneaked out and hid in the back of their van. Bob had said they had to go out and I wanted to know where they was going at that time of night. I mean you can't fix a roof in the dark can you? So they didn't know I was there until they stopped and opened the back door of the van. You should've seen Bob's face."

"And what happened then?"

"Well we crept along inside the fence. We'd got over a long way from the buildings I don't know why. Then Bob said I should sing a song outside the hangar so their friend, Micky Sinclair's his name, would come out and then...I was to...you know..." Molly giggled again but Robbie McBane looked back at her blankly.

"You were to what, Molly?"

"Well you know come onto him."

Lizzie stepped in. "I think Molly is saying that she was to flirt with Sinclair, presumably to distract him was it Molly?"

"Yeah, that's right. I had to keep him busy and then Bob and Harry were going to jump out and surprise him. But I had to...well you know...keep him busy for a bit."

"So where was this happening exactly?"

"Outside the hangar. I had a half bottle of whisky Bob had bought so I took him to the back of the hangar, outside like, where there was no light. I got his trousers off him before Bob gave the signal."

"His trousers? Why?"

"Why d'you think?" Molly arched her eyebrows.

Lizzie stepped in again. "I think the distraction was the temptation of flirtation, Robbie."

He coloured. "Yes of course. I see."

"What were Bob and Harry doing while this was going on?"

"No idea. Just waiting in the shadows I s'pose. The plan was to get him in an embarrassing situation and then surprise him."

"Did they go in the hangar?"

"Could've done. Don't know."

There was a pause which was broken by Molly, keen to finish the story. "Anyway, when I got the signal from Bob...an owl sound...I left Micky there and ran off. He still had the whisky bottle. Bob and I left immediately and Harry came a few seconds later."

"How much whisky had Sinclair drunk, Molly?"

"Oh he only had a couple of swings that's why I left it with him so he could have a nice drink, keep out the cold you know."

"When you say, Molly, that Harry followed a few seconds later, do you mean a few seconds? Could it have been a minute or two?" Lizzie looked at Molly keenly, assessing her truthfulness. She did not seem to have any reason to lie and indeed Lizzie's instinct was that she was not guileful in that way however artful she was where the opposite sex was concerned.

"No definitely not."

"And what was Sinclair doing when you left him? Why didn't he follow you?"

Molly tittered. "He was looking for his trousers. When I took them off him, I chucked them away into the bushes."

"Could Harry have got to Sinclair and hit him?"

"Hit him? Why would he do that? He's a mate of his. Anyway, we could still hear Micky swearing an' that cos he couldn't find his trousers. It were funny. Oh yeah and Bob put on this posh voice asking him where he was and Micky obviously thought it was an officer or something."

"When did he do that?" Lizzie knew that Robbie wanted to verify Sinclair's version of the incident in as much detail as possible.

"That was after he had given me the signal and I'd left Micky. Then he spoke to him in his own voice and told him that I and the whisky were birthday presents from him and Harry. Micky claimed he didn't know anyone called Bob and Harry. Anyway, then we left."

"So Sinclair was still conscious when you left him?"

"Yeah of course. I mean he couldn't have been swearing and going on like that in his sleep. Why are you asking that?"

" Because, Molly, Micky Sinclair was hit on the head last night and he died this morning from a bleed on the brain. So that blow killed him, Molly. He was murdered."

Molly's eyes opened wide. "Murdered?"

◆ ◆ ◆

Sir George Stanley was scowling, holding his empty brandy glass absent-mindedly, his gaze fixed on the coffee table in front of him. Group Captain Turner thought it best not to interrupt his superior's cogitations.

At last Stanley looked up and spoke. "What do you think Turner of what Swallow said? Could Butler be Sinclair's murderer as well as our mole?"

"It's certainly possible, Sir. He had the opportunity and if Miss Barnes and McBane heard correctly, he could be the mole. Perhaps he did go to the hangar and have an altercation with Sinclair. He certainly gets very heated as we have witnessed ourselves."

"Yes we have. I wonder if I should have been more direct with McBane. Trouble is, we can't afford to let anything slip."

The two men fell silent for a while. Turner broke the silence. "Perhaps, Sir, we should have briefed McBane fully."

"Perhaps but that Miss Barnes is very persistent and the two of them seem to have had some kind of dealings before which creates a loyalty between them. If McBane was in the picture, you can be sure Miss Barnes and Miss Frobisher would be and then where would it end? Before we knew it, our mole would have been communicating with Germany and the whole thing would have been a waste of time." Stanley stopped until a sudden thought occurred to him. "Are they courting do you suppose...McBane and Miss Barnes?"

"I don't think so, Sir. I did have a conversation with Commander Trueman, Miss Barnes's boss, on the telephone. I was interested to get some background. She and McBane met at RAF Silverstone last month. The body of a young civilian girl was found and Miss Barnes was apparently instrumental in discovering the killer. She and McBane worked together on the case though, of course, it was McBane's responsibility to investigate with the local police."

"She's certainly a young woman with spirit and intelligence. Won't take no for an answer. Frustrating that at times but, if we're honest, she has qualities we would admire in a man."

"I don't think Grainger would agree with you, Sir."

"Bloody ministry types! I'm not a fan of people who hide in offices and let others do the fighting but, on this occasion, we've had instructions from the very top to go along with this."

"I wonder, Sir, if we should have Swallow question Butler. We could always keep him in custody so he can't communicate. Might be a sensible precaution."

"Best wait for Grainger I think. Hopefully he won't be too long."

◆ ◆ ◆

He had searched everywhere in and around the pub but Hans was nowhere to be found. Bloody man! Why had he gone off like that? He'd just stood up suddenly and walked away from the table without a word. Bob had let him go thinking he'd be back. Just trying to make a point he thought. But he didn't come back. Bob had trudged up the road in the pitch dark from the pub and turned into the street where they had parked the van. With no moonlight, no streetlights and no light escaping from the houses, he could not see if the van was still there or not.

He walked slowly along the road, trying to make out where he was. How far along had they stopped? Just beyond the last row of terraces he thought. He could make out the gate of each house as he passed. Surely it must be along here? But there was no sign of the van. With an initial sinking feeling and then a spurt of anger, Bob realised Hans had done what he said he would do...driven off, probably back to Skegness.

Bob would have to get there somehow.

Unless...unless he handed himself in. How would that play out? A prison sentence certainly but he'd done time before and he could handle it. It would keep him safe and out of trouble for the duration and probably, when the war was over, there would be parole. But Bob knew that his pride would not let him be taken so easily. His wits would come to his aid; they always did. He enjoyed getting out of scrapes. That's what made him so good at what he did. He could bluff his way out of anything and he could certainly talk his way into a lift to Skegness.

He wanted to see the look on the bloody man's face when he turned up at the coast in time for the rendezvous. 'Evening Hans," he would say. "And what have you been doing for the last few hours? Hiding in the long grass while your bollocks froze off? Me, I spent some time with a beautiful young woman. She was soft and warm and very accommodating. And look - here I am, in time for the pick-up. No pressure, completely relaxed.' Bob smiled at the scene he had created in his head.

A few hours at the pub, spend some time with Molly, get talking to some locals and offer a generous amount to someone with a car to take him to Skegness. A brisk walk along the sea defence and he would be in plenty of time. He strolled back to the pub in a better frame of mind.

CHAPTER 23

Hans pulled over to the side of the road to consult the map that Bob had left on the dashboard shelf. The shaded headlights revealed no sign naming the place he was about to drive into. He had no recollection of driving through a village this size two days ago. He switched on the cab light and peered at the map. In the dim yellow light, his finger traced the road he had travelled to Boston and then the road he hoped he had taken out of it. By now, he should have passed three small hamlets and some turnings off the road. "Damn British," he muttered, "removing all the signs."

Going back to Boston, his finger tried another road and he came to a village called Sibsey. That must be the road he was on. It was taking him due North and was well inland. If he followed it, Skegness would be by-passed. Screwing up his eyes, he saw there was a road that went towards the coast from Sibsey and joined the main road he should have been on. He blew out his breath with relief. Driving back through Boston may have been noticed and aroused suspicion.

The van lurched forward. At least he was on the correct side of the road – he kept checking to make sure. All the roads had been featureless, flat, straight for long stretches. With no moonlight revealing the landscape and no road signs, it was impossible to get one's bearings. He knew that the British had removed many to increase the chance of invading troops getting lost.

He found the side road in what he took to be Sibsey without difficulty as it was the only turning on the right hand side. The map showed this should take him to Old Leake, a name he remembered from the briefing they had had just before leaving the submarine. He did have to consult the map again when he came to a T junction. He had to cross this road by turning right onto it and driving a little further South before turning left in the direction of the coast. Once he had reached Old Leake, he started to relax. Just turn left and he was on the road to Skegness.

He was whistling softly as he approached the junction. Nothing was coming either way so he swung the van left onto the main road. He had been driving only a few minutes when he saw shaded headlights appearing from a bend in the road ahead. He leaned forward, peering through the darkness at the two dim pools of light on the road. They seemed to be coming straight for him. Suddenly, the lights bearing down, he realised he was on the wrong side of the road. He braked and yanked the van over to the left. The other vehicle also braked and swerved to the right; they both screeched to a halt only centimetres apart.

Hans sat frozen in the cab. The other driver flung open his door and jumped out, storming round to the driver's door of the van. Hans opened it gingerly.

"What the bloody hell are you playing at? You were on the wrong side of the road."

"I'm very sorry. I was...I'm very tired. I think I lost concentration. I have been working very hard, not much sleep. You know how it is."

Slowly, the other driver subsided, the apology seeming to appease him. "You want to be more careful. You'll kill someone like that. It's dangerous enough with the bloody Germans sending over raiders. We can do without killing ourselves."

Hans noted the accent, very different to Bob's, clipped. This was someone who was used to being in authority. A solicitor or a doctor or..."I am really very sorry. I'm nearly at the end of my journey. I will then sleep."

"You do that. Well luckily no harm done. Go carefully for goodness sake."

"I will. Thank you. Goodnight."

The other driver waved as he walked back to his car. They both reversed and pulled forward onto their own sides of the road. The car sped away and Hans, breathing heavily, let in the clutch. Bob's words were lingering in his brain - how he would give himself away by driving on the wrong side of the road. It was so easily done when one had always driven on the right-hand side. Damn British. Always have to be different. It was just as well that the other driver had not become suspicious. Had he done so, he might have challenged him or alerted the Police. It was possible of course that he may still do so.

◆ ◆ ◆

After uttering that one word, Molly was speechless for a few moments. "But...but, I mean... how could he die?"

"A blow to the head and a delayed reaction from a bleed on the brain. It happens." Alice spoke quietly but with authority. "So Molly, if you know anything, it is your duty to tell us."

"But it was just a bit of fun. I know Bob didn't hurt him 'cos he was with me. Micky was still shouting and swearing when Harry joined us. It can't be anything to do with that. Maybe he drunk the rest of the whisky and fell over. Could've hit his head."

Robbie McBane shook his head. "I'm afraid not, Molly. I've searched the area thoroughly. There's no sign of any blood on a stone or the concrete. Had that happened, there would have been."

"So what's going to happen to me? Me Dad'll go mad."

"You may be arrested for entering a secure area without permission. That will be up to the local Police."

"Police? But it was just a practical joke." Molly's voice ended in a wail of self-pity followed by a silence laden with unpleasant possibilities. The three uniformed people around the table looked at Molly; there was some pity in Alice's eyes but Lizzie was trying to suppress a feeling of contempt. How could anyone be so gullible?

The front door of the pub opened, stopping the conversation. Robbie McBane had his back to the door so did not see at first who had come in. Lizzie stood up and Molly called out, "Bob, Bob, come over here. That bloke, Micky, he's dead."

Before Bob had reached the table, Robbie McBane was on his feet and had slipped behind him cutting off any possible escape through the door. He was significantly taller than Bob, more powerfully built, a physique that had served him well on the rugby field.

"What you talking about? What bloke?"

"You know, last night, on the base."

Bob shook his head very faintly at Molly but he knew it was too late. "He was alive and kicking when we left."

"What were you doing on the base last night?"

"Oh we were just playing a bit of a joke on a mate of ours. It was his birthday."

"It was not Micky Sinclair's birthday yesterday and he did not know anyone by the name of Bob and Harry."

Robbie's voice made Bob turn to face him. "How do you know that? You said he's dead."

"He didn't die until this morning...until after I had interviewed him and found out what happened last night. Someone hit him on the head and he died later this morning from a bleed on the brain."

"Nothing to do with me, Guv'nor. Anyway, what's it to you?"

"He's from the police, Bob."

"RAF Police, Special Investigation Branch to be precise."

"Well nice to meet you...er...Sergeant. But I can tell you now for sure that I did not hit your man on the head."

"But your mate did?" Lizzie stared hard at Bob, determined not to soften her face in response to his charming smile.

"No, he can't of done. We was together the whole time apart from literally a couple of seconds. I'm sure Molly told you all about it. Molly, I'm going to need a ride back to Skegness. Is there a taxi firm or something? Harry's in a sulk. Must've gone off in the van."

"You won't be going anywhere." Robbie McBane drew himself up to his full height. "Robert Edwards, I am arresting you on suspicion of being a German agent and murdering a member of His Majesty's Royal Air Force. You do not have to say anything, but anything you do say may be used in court."

"Hang on, hang on. What're you on about? German agent? I do roofing me. I'm a roofer. Here tell 'em Molly."

"I bloody hope you are, Bob Edwards, 'cos otherwise you've got me in big trouble."

"What's the trouble here?" The large bulk of Molly's father loomed beside them. "German agent? I'm not sure about that Sergeant. Bob and his friend came yesterday morning, checked in, had a meal with us last night, went off this morning to finish the job. Don't see anything suspicious in that."

"Of course you don't, Sir. That's what agents do. They blend in, make themselves look entirely normal. How do you know they are roofers?"

"Well...they've got a van with ladders on the top and it says 'Allen Roofing' on the sides. Seems pretty conclusive to me."

Lizzie was becoming impatient. They needed to get Bob in the Land Rover and back to the base. "The van could have been stolen. It proves nothing. We have other evidence that strongly suggests Mr Edwards is acting on behalf of the German government. We believe they went onto RAF Cranwell last night to sabotage an aircraft."

"Sabotage? But they can't have done. We was just playing a practical joke."

"You may have been, Molly, but were Bob and Harry in your sight the whole time?"

"Well no...but we weren't apart for long. I mean they can't have done anything in that time."

"Did they take anything with them when you went onto the base?"

"They had a metal case but..."

"It could have contained a bomb."

"Bomb? Bob, tell 'em that's not true."

"Course it's not true. This is like something out of a story. I think you've been reading too many spy novels." Bob smiled suddenly. "Anyway, can't stand round here chatting much as I'd like to. Molly can you arrange a lift for me, maybe someone who wants to make a few bob?"

Robbie McBane clamped a hand onto Bob's arm. "You're not going anywhere except with us back to the base. You're under arrest."

Bob tried to shake off the hand but Robbie's grip was too tight.

Lizzie turned to the landlord. "Where's the nearest sizeable Police station?"

"That'd be Boston."

"Can you please telephone them and ask them to intercept a dark coloured van with ladders on the roof bearing the name 'Allen Roofing'. Tell them we believe the van is being driven by a German spy and is probably heading for Skegness."

The landlord's mouth fell open. "Are you serious?"

"Deadly serious."

"Do it please Sir. We can't let him get away." At Robbie McBane's insistence, the landlord shuffled away to make the call. "Right Mr Edwards, come with us."

The sound of vehicle tyres grinding to a halt on the gravel outside made them pause. Seconds later, the pub door was flung open.

It was Grainger. He pushed the door closed behind him, his eyes taking in the scene. "Ah McBane. I see you've apprehended Mr Edwards."

"I have. We're taking him back to Cranwell now for questioning. I've arrested him on suspicion of murder but he may yet be charged with being a German agent."

Grainger smiled. "That won't be necessary, McBane. I'll take charge of Mr Edwards and you can get back to Cranwell and do what you should be doing...finding out who the mole is."

There was hostility and suspicion in Lizzie's voice when she spoke. "Oh and what will you do with Mr Edwards? Let him get away like you've been trying to do all day. It's clear you're working with him. I saw you slip that piece of paper to him last night in here. I don't think we have to look any further for a mole than you."

Grainger did not flinch. "Ah yes, the Miss Marple of the ATA. You are way out of your depth, dear, so I suggest you keep out of this."

"Miss Barnes is right. Everything points to you being in league with Bob and his mate." Robbie McBane had not let go of Bob's arm.

"I am ordering you, Sergeant McBane, to release Mr Edwards into my custody."

Robbie McBane snorted. "You're ordering me! And who are you in the RAF chain of command?"

Without taking his eyes off Robbie McBane, Grainger slowly reached his hand inside his pocket. He withdrew a pistol and pointed it at McBane. "This is my authority. Now hand him over, we're running out of time."

CHAPTER 24

Charles Loveridge eased his Daimler into a space in the car Park of The White Hart Hotel. The Boston streets had been empty as usual. Night life in this part of the World was fairly non-existent at the best of times but now with the war and the blackout, people seemed to prefer to stay indoors. He, however, was determined to attend the monthly Rotary Club dinners. It was a chance to catch up with other key people in the area.

There were already several cars in the car park and he was looking forward to a good meal and convivial conversation. He glanced at his watch. Seven thirty-five. Good timing despite the slight delay en route. The porter took his coat and gestured towards the private bar. The buzz of conversation reached him as soon as he pushed through the swing door.

"Ah, here's Charles. Are you fighting fit? What are you drinking?"

"I'll have a scotch Freddy please. That's very kind. Need something to steady my nerves."

"Why's that old chap? Been doing some dodgy deals?"

"If I had, I wouldn't tell a Police inspector would I?"

"Fair point." Inspector Frederick Sadler pushed the glass of scotch towards him, making the ice cube chink against the side.

"On the way here, I was driving along quite happily, no traffic about at all really, came round a bend in the road and there were headlights coming towards me. It wasn't until I was really very close that I realised they were on my side of the road. I swerved and braked as did the other vehicle and, luckily, we both stopped just a couple of inches from each other's bumpers.

Bloody fool."

"What was he up to?"

"Said he was tired and lost concentration. Lucky he didn't come off the road." Charles lifted the glass and took a sip. The hot fire of whisky slipped down his throat. "That's better. It was a van, ladders on the roof. A workman I suppose doing long hours. Probably shouldn't judge him too harshly. Might have been working on war repairs."

"Well no harm done by the sound of it."

"I suppose not. Nothing that a drop of Scotch won't put right anyway. How's life in His Majesty's Constabulary?"

"It's been very quiet actually. Always worries me that - makes me think that something big is going to kick off. But no, usual boring stuff, a bit of pilfering, a couple of punch-ups."

"I hope you're not looking for excitement. Boring sounds very acceptable to me."

"Man of action I am, Charles. Never really liked the idea of a desk job though sometimes that's what my job feels like."

A bell rang and the gentlemen of Boston Rotary ambled through the double doors to the private dining room. They took their usual places around the long table, standing behind their chairs talking quietly until Mr President called them to order for the Grace. There was a chorus of 'Amen' followed by an outburst of talking again and the shuffling of chairs on the carpet as they seated themselves for a hearty meal...or at least as hearty as rationing allowed.

As he drove away, Hans started to think through what he would need to do. He would drop the van back in Skegness and walk along the sea defence path to the place where they had left the kayak. The problem was the two metal cases and the kit bags. It was too much to carry at once and to make more than one journey would increase the chance of detection and suspicion.

He pulled the van over into the entrance to a field and once more consulted the map. A lane led off the road to the coast itself and came out about a mile South of the point near which they had left the canoe. If he was lucky, the lane would take him to the track that ran along the top of the sea defences and he could drive close to the rendezvous point.. He could drop the cases and bags off by the canoe and then drive the van back to the road and into Skegness as planned. He would just have to risk being seen but the area had looked deserted when they arrived two nights ago so the risk was small.

Switching off the cab light, he pulled away. He drove slowly, his eyes searching the darkness on the right hand side of the road for the lane he needed to take. At last he saw what he thought was the turning and he steered the van into it. As a precaution, he turned off the lights. This made driving even more difficult and he proceeded very slowly, the engine doing little more than ticking over with a soft hum.

A tall shape loomed from the darkness on the right hand side of the track... a tower with large windows facing in all directions at the top. He tensed. It looked like an observation post. No lights showed anywhere so perhaps it was not manned. When he reached it, he dipped the clutch just long enough to read the sign: 'RAF Wainfleet'.

"Scheisse!"

There was one vehicle parked at the base of the tower. He let in the clutch and drove on. If there were observers in the tower, they would have seen him already. He waited for a siren to wail and that vehicle to speed after him but nothing came and the distance between him and the tower grew. Perhaps they were asleep. Then he reasoned that if there were only one vehicle, there may be only one person who could not leave the observation post. Even if the observer had alerted someone else. It would be some time before help arrived.

He drove a little faster but he could not risk coming off the lane or damaging the van by hitting a pot hole too quickly.

At last he reached the end. It stopped well short of the sea at the embankment. Hans turned slowly onto the track at the top of the sea defence and drove along it cautiously. Although no light came from the sky, the sea seemed to give out some, making it a little easier. He saw ahead the bulge of land which he was sure was the point beyond which they had left the kayak. With relief, he at last reached it and stopped the van. When the engine died, he listened.

Nothing. Silence, except the gentle wash of waves on the beach.

Slowly, Hans climbed out of the van and glided to the back. He opened the doors and reached forward to slide the cases and kit bags closer. Perhaps he should leave the kit bags as they were no longer needed but he thought better of it. Leave no trace had been the instruction. He took the two cases first, one in each hand and walked through the long grass until he thought he had reached the place where they had left the kayak. It took him several minutes to find it.

"Das ist gut," he muttered. "If I can't find it, no one else will have done."

His confidence was quickly lost, however, when he saw the grass around it had been trampled. Surely he and Bob had not flattened such a large area? He shrugged. Too late now. The important thing was that the vessel was still there. He re-traced his steps and fetched the two kit bags, placing them beside the cases. Finally, he returned to the van and started the engine. Just a drive to Skegness and another walk along the sea wall, then he would wait to be picked up... with or without Bob.

PC Paul Crowther sighed as he dumped the box of statements onto the desk. Reading through statements might serve to relieve the tedium of a quiet Friday night in the Police

Station. The hands of the large clock ticking monotonously on the wall crawled very slowly around the dial. How many times had he looked at it and it was still only seven forty-five? 'A watched kettle never boils' his Mum always said. Must be true of clocks as well. He lifted the lid of the box and started to read the first statement. He knew by the time he had read all of them that he would be no wiser as to the cause of the fracas that had erupted last Saturday night in The Bell. Everyone would be blaming everyone else, claiming they had no part in it – 'just an innocent by-stander Officer honest'.

His gaze wandered across the room to where Sergeant O'Flynn was examining a document that was probably much more important. The Sergeant always kept the interesting jobs for himself. 'Everyone has to start at the bottom lad. Do the dull things well and the exciting things will come your way.' The words of his Dad. There would only be excitement in this job if he moved to London where all the real criminal action took place.

PC Crowther's thoughts were interrupted by the harsh jangling of the telephone. "Will 'e get that Crowther?"

Crowther stood slowly and ambled across to the telephone. Languidly, he lifted the handset and spoke. "Boston Police Station, PC Crowther here, how may I help?" Suddenly, his slothful demeanour disappeared. He stood upright and reached for a pen and notepad. "How long ago was this.?" A pause while he listened to the voice on the other end of the line. "So on the way to Skegness you think? He would have to come through Boston unless he took country lanes." Another pause. "We'll get onto it right away, Sir. Thank you for the information." Crowther put the handset back on the cradle. His face was flushed.

"Sarge, Sarge. That was the landlord of The Prince of Wales in Leasingham. He's got a sergeant from the RAF Police," he glanced at the note he had made on the pad, "Special Investigation Branch, who asked him to alert us to a possible German agent who is driving a van with ladders on the roof and 'Allen Roofing' on the sides to Skegness he believes. Says can we appre...appr...arrest him."

"German agent? Holy Mother of God. How will we do that on bicycles?" The Sergeant thought for a moment. "Crowther, you need to get on your bike and ride like the fury to The White Hart. Inspector Sadler is there at his Rotary dinner. Tell him about the call. He has a car with him and he can get after that agent. You may have to go with him."

PC Crowther stared at Sergeant O'Flynn. "How will I keep up on me bike, Sarge?"

"God you're an eejit sometimes, Crowther. If he wants ye, he'll take ye in the car."

Sergeant O'Flynn raised his voice. "You're always wanting excitement Crowther. Now you've got some. Get your cape on and leap on your bike." Crowther turned towards the coat pegs. "And take your truncheon with ye."

Fortunately it was not raining. Paul Crowther was glad of that. As his legs whirled on the pedals his mind raced. Yes he did want excitement but, now it had come, he was not so sure about it. His stomach was trembling and he knew it was nerves not excitement. What if the agent had a gun? What if the agent took him as a hostage and forced him to go to Germany? What treatment could a British bobby expect at the hands of the Nazis?

He careered into the car park of The White Hart, swung his leg over the saddle and propped his bike against the wall. A new concern filled his mind. He would have to go in there and interrupt the Inspector's dinner. There would be lots of important people there all staring at him. Maybe reading through those statements was not so bad. He took off his hat and climbed the stone steps. The foyer was warm and comfortable looking. Paul Crowther had never been inside The White Hart but, one day, he thought, he would stride in confidently.

He was shown into the dining room and he shuffled around in the corner until he saw the Inspector. He walked up the side of the room, stopped behind Sadler's chair and coughed quietly. "Um, Sir, Sir."

Sadler put down his glass and turned in his chair. His

rather shaggy eyebrows came together in a frown. "Crowther. What is it?"

Paul Crowther's eyes flicked either side of the Inspector and he leaned forward so he could whisper. "Just had a report that a possible German agent is heading for Skegness, Sir, in a van with ladders on the roof. Sergeant O'Flynn said we should try to arrest him."

Despite Crowther's whisper, Charles Loveridge heard the phrase 'ladders on the roof' and swung round. "Well I'll be damned. That's the chap who nearly crashed into me...you know...on the wrong side of the road."

Inspector Sadler jumped from his chair and called out with impressive authority over the babble of conversation. "Mr President, gentlemen, please excuse me. There is something that needs my urgent attention." He turned to Crowther. "Come with me."

CHAPTER 25

There was silence in the pub. The few locals and the RAF personnel sat open-mouthed at the sight of the gun. Lizzie, Robbie McBane, Alice and even Bob Edwards stared at Grainger. Lizzie broke the silence.

"Well that makes it very clear doesn't it? You're a German agent as well. No need to look any further for our mole."

Grainger flicked his eyes over to her and smiled, a smile of sneering contempt. "My God you think you're clever don't you? When will you learn to stay within your depth. You are well out of it now."

Robbie McBane's face set hard. "You won't use that against me. The penalty for wounding or killing a serving member of His Majesty's armed forces is too high. I suggest you put it away and we can discuss what will happen next. I am taking this man back to RAF Cranwell for questioning. Only when I am satisfied that he is not responsible for the murder of Sinclair and not responsible for the sabotage of an aircraft will I release him. It looks to me as though he is responsible for both."

Bob Edwards chuckled. "I know this ain't a laughing situation, but I did not kill anyone and I did not sabotage an aircraft. It ain't my fault that your lot design and build a plane that blows up."

"How do you know it blew up?" Alice's voice was, as usual, quiet but somehow gained attention.

"Now that would be telling wouldn't it."

"That's enough small talk. Let him go McBane or I will be forced to wound you."

Lizzie was looking around for something close that she

could grab and swing at Grainger's head. Nothing presented itself. Grainger suddenly stepped sideways and behind Alice who was standing closest to him. The gun in his right hand remained on Robbie McBane, as he brought his left arm quickly around Alice's neck. Swiftly, he pointed the gun at her temple.

"I should have realised that you'd want to be a hero McBane. Not such an easy choice now is it? If you don't let Mr Edwards go, I will shoot Miss Frobisher."

Lizzie watched in horror, now even more desperate to stop Grainger. Nothing came to mind. She saw the terror on Alice's face, the anguish on Robbie McBane's. She could see that he knew he was defeated. "Let him go Robbie. You have no choice and Alice is worth far more than Edwards...or Grainger." She turned her angry eyes on the latter. "You will be caught, sooner or later. I will make sure of that."

Grainger smiled maliciously. "Now McBane. Now. Let him go."

Robbie McBane released his hand and Bob Edwards moved his arm about. "You've got a grip like a vice, mate. Must be all that porridge." He walked a couple of steps to be at Grainger's side.

"That's better. Now, I am taking Mr Edwards and Miss Frobisher out to the Land Rover I came in. I am then going to drive off. If anyone tries anything, Miss Frobisher gets a bullet. Provided you do not attempt to detain myself or Mr Edwards, I will release her before leaving. Clear?"

Edwards opened the pub door and Grainger, still holding Alice, backed through it, never taking his eyes from Lizzie and Robbie. He told Edwards to open the driver's door, which was closer to the pub entrance, start the engine and then get into the passenger seat on the other side. He himself backed onto the driver's seat, transferring his grip on Alice to his right arm, and holding the pistol under her chin. Suddenly he pushed her away and she stumbled forward. The door was slammed and with a spurt of gravel from each rear tyre, the Land Rover shot backwards, skidded to a halt and sprang forward, disappearing within seconds down the lane.

Lizzie steadied Alice and put her arm around her. Alice gasped for breath. "We need to get after them, Robbie. Alice, you stay here and we'll pick you up on our way back."

Alice straightened up, sniffed. "I'm coming with you. I want to look in that man's eyes when he's arrested."

"Bob Edwards?"

"No...Grainger."

He was tempted to put his foot down when he turned off the sea defence track onto the lane but he held his nerves in check. He must not do anything that would draw attention to himself if anyone was watching from that tower. He had not switched on the lights of the van so driving in the darkness was not easy. Holding his breath, he slowly approached the tower; he thought he saw a figure in the observation room at the top, a ghostly silhouette, but he could not be sure. It may have been an apparition born from his fear of discovery.

He breathed a sigh of relief when at last he reached the main road and was able to turn North onto it heading for Skegness. Once he was well away from the tower, he turned on the lights which made driving much easier. He would park the van where they found it, if there was space. The owner must have noticed it missing and reported it. He knew the Police must be on the lookout for it. The sooner he could ditch it, the better. As he rounded a very slight bend in the road, he glanced in the wing mirror. There were headlights a good distance from him. They were of no concern. He would be parked up by the time they reached him.

The van crept along the little streets of Skegness. All was quiet and of course no light escaped from the houses. It was eerie, like a ghost town, a town deserted of human life. All the better for him...less chance of being noticed. He found the place easily enough; he had to turn around so he could park the van exactly where they had found it. Killing the engine, he smiled to himself. Just a walk along the sea defence, a few hours wait and he would be going home.

◆ ◆ ◆

The engine in Sadler's Wolseley roared as they sped along the Skegness road. PC Crowther held onto the side of his seat with grim determination, hoping his boss's driving skills matched the speed of the car. Once he had to fling out his hand against the dashboard as Sadler braked to take a tight bend. Thankfully, there were very few of them but Crowther was feeling queasy as the big car swayed alarmingly around lesser bends.

A couple of miles from Skegness, they were able to make out the dim red tail lights of a vehicle ahead of them. Sadler gripped the steering wheel tighter and forced his foot even lower. Slowly the big car accelerated and Crowther prayed there would not be another bend or something else that would cause their early demise.

"That may well be our man," Sadler said. As the buildings of the town loomed out of the darkness, the red lights ahead suddenly disappeared. "He's turned off. Keep your eyes peeled Crowther."

Sadler slowed the car significantly and even more so as they passed the few side streets that came off it. No sign of red lights. They crossed a railway line by the station, the crossing gates fortunately open. There were two roads to head down. Sadler hesitated just a moment and then took the one on the right. This appeared to lead out of the town again. They could see large houses on the right side of the road, facing the sea, no doubt expensive. Just before the houses ran out, Crowther pointed ahead. One could just make out a vehicle parked at the side of the road with ladders on the roof. It was facing the direction from which they'd come.

Sadler stopped the car in front of it and doused the lights of the Wolseley. He took a torch from the glove compartment. "Come on Crowther...and bring your truncheon with you. Be ready. We don't know what we're going to face."

Both alighted from the car, their eyes fixed on the van. There was no sign of any life. "Go round the back, Crowther, and check inside if the doors are open." Sadler himself, felt the warmth of the bonnet and then tugged at the driver's door. It opened without resistance. He checked inside. No sign of anything, no documents, no gun, no bag. The keys, however, were still in the ignition. He shone the torch on the floor of the van so that Crowther could see. There was nothing. They both pushed the doors closed.

"Nothing. That is strange though. You'd expect a roofer's van to have some tools of the trade or some rubbish, perhaps some spare tiles. But nothing. The driver could be anywhere by now." Sadler looked out across the grassland to the sea, his eye travelling southward over the huge expanse of darkness. "Not sure there's any more we can do except perhaps ask at one of these houses."

The two officers walked up the path of the nearest house and rang the doorbell. After some thirty seconds, they could hear footsteps inside. "Who is it?"

"Police, Sir. Just want to ask you a few questions."

The door opened just a few inches and the face of an older man appeared in the gap. Sadler's torch shone downwards so as not to blind him. "Have you got identification?"

Crowther stepped forward holding his warrant card in front of him. Sadler shone the torch on it. A restraining chain was taken off the door and the old man said, "What can I do for you?" The voice was not local, cultured and suggested intelligence. He was old but he was no fool.

"My name is Inspector Sadler from Boston Police Station.

This is Constable Crowther. That van on the road outside your house, Sir, do you own it?"

The old man peered out. "No, I don't. I mean I probably don't look like a roofer do I?"

"Quite so, Sir. Have you seen it before?"

"It appeared a few days ago and then, when was it now?... yesterday morning I noticed it had gone. It must have just arrived. I don't know when exactly but it was not there when I closed the blackout curtains at dusk."

"So you haven't seen or heard anyone creeping about, Sir?"

"Nothing at all, Officer, but my wife and I have been listening to the wireless."

"Well thank you, Sir. Sorry to have disturbed you. If you do notice anything unusual...anything missing for example or out of place...do please ring Boston Police station."

"I will...if I can get to a public telephone box. No one down here has a telephone."

The door was closed and the officers could hear bolts being drawn across it inside. They walked back to the car. Sadler once more scanned the dark landscape. They could hear the gentle sound of the sea beyond the dunes.

"Shall I check around the gardens, Sir? He may be holed up somewhere."

"Needle in a haystack, Crowther. I don't think we're going to find him. Could be anywhere out there."

The two officers stood in silence. It was not cold but Sadler, in his dinner suit, felt a chill from the darkness, the openness, the thought of the warm room he had left and his unfinished dinner. He nodded his head towards the car and began to walk towards the driver's door. Before he reached it, the sound of an engine caused him to look up the road the way they had come. Two headlights were approaching at speed. The vehicle swung around the van and parked behind. It was a Land Rover. Two men climbed out and came close.

"Good evening. Can I help you?" Sadler asked pleasantly.

There was something Inspector Sadler did not like about the confidence of the man in a suit who strode towards him.

"I think I should be asking the questions."

"Do you indeed? I am Inspector Sadler from Boston Police Station. And who might you be?"

"Grainger's the name." He slipped his hand inside his jacket and withdrew a card. "You need to see this but not a word to anyone. I'm just a man from the ministry."

Sadler shone his torch on the proffered document, looked at Grainger keenly to check his face against the photograph on the card. "How can I verify this, Mr Grainger?"

"You can telephone RAF Cranwell and speak to either Group Captain Turner or Air Chief Marshal Sir George Stanley. They know me."

"Telephoning could be tricky out here Mr Grainger. So what's your interest in this van?"

"What's yours?"

"We had a report that a German agent was driving a van with ladders on the roof to Skegness. We've found the van but there's no sign of the occupant. The gentleman who lives here has no idea to whom the van belongs."

"We're after the same man. You're right, he is a German agent. I think I may know where to find him so, Inspector, I suggest you leave this to us. I and my assistant will be able to handle him."

"You need to come with us to Boston so I can make that telephone call."

"Don't be daft man. If we do that, the German agent will be gone, whisked away on a U Boat."

"All the same...."

"What was that?" Bob's voice was an urgent whisper; he swung round and stared across the scrub. "Shush." All four men strained to hear what Bob had heard.

Nothing.

"I swear I heard a cough. Over there," he hissed, pointing South and towards the sea.

"We've got to get after him, Inspector."

Grainger and Bob took off across the scrub, leaping tussocks of grass. They were lost to view within seconds.

"Damn them. They might be legitimate but we need to check. Come on Crowther, we need to get to a telephone as quickly as possible. There goes my dinner!"

Grainger and Bob Edwards, hidden in the scrub, watched as Sadler turned the Wolseley around in a driveway and drove off at speed. They waited until it was out of sight and the sound had died away.

CHAPTER 26

Grainger waited until there was just the sound of the sea before moving South along the defence wall. "We need to find Harry now. It's important that he doesn't see me so we'll have to be careful. I'll walk with you until we're about a hundred yards off where you left the kayak. You then go and see if he's there."

"Blimey. Don't think I'll remember exactly where we left it."

"You'll have to find it, wander around until you do. There's no other option."

"And what'll you do?"

"I'll wait until I'm sure you've found him. If you both stand up, I should be able to see you. Then you must take the cases and kit bags and move them somewhere else unless he's already done that."

"Why's that then? I mean what's the point of lugging that stuff about. It's coming with us in the kayak so…"

"Because you idiot, the Police may be back or McBane, perhaps with several others. It doesn't matter if they find the kayak as everyone already knows about it but it does matter if they find those cases." Grainger was exasperated.

"Alright, alright, keep yer 'air on."

"Keep my hair on? I've a good mind to arrest you and have you put back in prison where you belong. You've nearly messed up the whole mission with your carrying on. You know your trouble don't you? You can't leave women alone."

"I know…I know. It's a great failing. But she was very tasty, that Molly."

Grainger shook his head but said nothing. The two men

stumbled along the track, Grainger as alert as an owl seeking its prey. Bob Edwards wanted to keep his own spirits up. He was disappointed that he had been robbed of another session with Molly. He felt like whistling but knew Grainger would blow his top if he did so. They were some hundred yards off the point as far as he could tell, when Bob realised they must be getting close. He signalled to Grainger who sat down in the long grass at the base of the sea defence. Bob walked on alone.

A minute later, Grainger heard voices and knew Bob had found Hans. Bob seemed to be explaining what had happened as far as Grainger could ascertain and Hans delivered a salvo of German swearing. He was quite right. Bob was an idiot. Had he got the right man for this job? Perhaps not but it was too late now to change it. The mission was nearly complete. A little afterwards, he could just make out two figures carrying things away from where the kayak was presumably lying. The figures disappeared into the darkness.

Grainger let out his breath in relief. He would wait a short while to make sure the Police did not return and then he would leave them to it. All they had to do was wait for the pick-up. Surely Bob couldn't mess that up? He knew that when he returned to Cranwell, there would be quite a scene with McBane but he would simply lay low and let Stanley deal with it. He smiled at the thought of the faces of McBane, Barnes and Frobisher. They would not be expecting him to return.

Robbie McBane hesitated.

"Come on Robbie. We've got to get after them." Lizzie could see the uncertainty in his face. "What's the problem?"

"The problem is a man with a pistol who seems quite happy to use it. You saw how he reacted, grabbing Alice. I can't put you two in danger. If I go, what do I do against a man with a gun. I'm not armed. Should we go back to Cranwell and get some armed men or at least a weapon?"

"By the time we do that, Grainger and Edwards will be gone to ground if not out of the country. His sidekick Harry may already have gone."

They were interrupted by the sudden harsh jangling of the telephone. The landlord moved behind as quickly as his bulk allowed and picked up the handset. "Leasingham 153". He listened intently and then replaced the handset. "That was Sergeant O'Flynn from Boston Police Station. He's sent a PC to The White Hart Hotel to tell the inspector what's going on. He thinks the inspector who has a car will get after the agent."

"But he doesn't know if that's what the inspector will do, does he?"

"I guess not, Miss."

"Robbie. We must go. If we can't find them quickly, we can head back to Cranwell."

"Ok but I'm going to telephone Cranwell first."

Robbie McBane went through the lengthy process of getting put through to Cranwell and then giving a message to the person who answered the call. Robbie had to repeat each part of the message as the person who answered seemed not to understand the urgency. Robbie stressed several times that Turner should be told. "See that he gets that immediately. Understood? We need an armed search party out by Gibraltar Point."

The handset clattered onto the cradle and Robbie rushed from behind the bar. "Let's go."

The Land Rover roared into life and they were soon speeding along the main road to Boston. Robbie was driving as fast as he dared through the darkened countryside. In Boston, there was some hesitation as they did not know which road to take and the Skegness road was not immediately obvious. Once on the correct road, the Land Rover surged forward again.

"We don't know whether they are heading for Skegness but my guess is they will park there and then walk out to the

Point where the kayak was left. They could go down the lane we used when we went to the coast but that passes RAF Wainfleet and they will probably not want to risk that." Lizzie's brain was working furiously trying to think as the fugitives would.

"If they do go to Skegness, they'll be on the South side of the town…the side nearest to the kayak." Alice, squeezed between Robbie and Lizzie on the front bench seat, looked from one to the other for affirmation.

They drove into Skegness and were quickly at the station where they were confronted by the same choice of roads as the police before them. "Go right," Alice said, her navigator's sense of direction giving her confidence. Robbie drove on through the darkened streets until there were large houses only on the right hand side of the road. They saw the two vehicles parked one behind the other. Robbie drove past them slowly and then turned his vehicle so that he was facing the stationary Land Rover.

"Grainger won't be going anywhere with us parked here," he said.

They clambered out and checked the other two vehicles. No one was to be seen and there was nothing in the van. "They must all have gone to the kayak. We need to get after them." Lizzie started to walk in the direction of the unseen grassland.

"We need to be careful Lizzie. There'll be streams and pools of water which may not be visible until we're right on them." Alice did not sound frightened but her natural caution did restrain Lizzie a little. "We must stay parallel to the sea. As long as we stay on the sea defence, we should be ok."

Walking in single file keeping a good yard apart, Lizzie led the way, with Alice next and Robbie at the rear. The only sound was the slow rhythm of the waves washing on the beach and the long sigh of water withdrawing. They could not see very much, barely the track in front of them. The cloud had cleared a little but, with no moon, the stars provided no real light. At last they came to the place where Lizzie and Alice thought they had found the kayak. They moved off the sea defence and down into the long grass, swishing carefully through it until Alice at last found it.

It was exactly as they had left it…except Lizzie thought there was the faintest whiff of tobacco smoke. "I can smell nothing at all," Robbie whispered.

"Women of course have superior senses, Robbie."

"Is that it Lizzie? Well what are your superior senses telling you about the whereabouts of Edwards and Grainger?"

"They're telling me that they are probably fairly close by and may be watching us. Problem is, we'll never find them in this wasteland so I suggest we make quite a noise about giving up and going. We walk away, we drop down into the grass a short distance off and we wait for them to emerge. They will have to do so sooner or later."

"Aye but that could be a long wait. I think I'd rather get back to Cranwell and make sure they're sending a search party. Let's get some manpower out here to help."

"Let's try what I said and we'll wait for what twenty minutes? The search party may arrive in that time."

"I doubt it will. Let's make it fifteen."

"Done. Ok. Here goes." Lizzie raised her voice. "They're not here and we'll never find them in this place. Let's go."

"Ok. D'you agree Alice?"

"Yes. It's cold and miserable out here. The sooner I'm back in the warmth the better."

The three of them walked away until Lizzie signalled. They dropped into the long grass, squatting uncomfortably. By sitting up straight, they could see over the tall stems. Anyone standing would be visible, though they would have to keep their eyes sharp to see them in the gloom.

◆ ◆ ◆

"They're going," hissed Bob. "That's a relief. Didn't fancy

having to lie in the grass all night." Bob started to get to his knees but Hans pulled him down.

"Don't be a fool. It's a trick, the oldest one in the book. They pretend to leave so we show ourselves and then they come for us."

"You've got your gun."

"Of course. But, as you said, better to leave no trace."

"I think they know about us already."

"But they have no proof and they don't know what our mission was. We lay low until I say so."

"So you're giving the orders now are you?" Bob hissed.

"Yes. Look what a mess you've made by carrying on with that girl. Stupid. You nearly ruined the mission." Hans' voice was a low growl.

Both men lay quiet for a long time. After some fifteen minutes, Hans cautiously raised himself to his knees and looked over the long grass. He could just make out three figures stand and walk away, one of them with clear reluctance, looking back. He lay down again and whispered close to Bob's ear. "That's them leaving now. We leave it another fifteen minutes and then we can relax a little."

"We could walk back into Skegness and get a beer. Must be a couple of pubs there, a bit of..."

"No! Absolutely not! Are you mad?" Hans jabbed his finger at Bob. "You are not going anywhere."

"And what about you? Driving off like that and leaving me. I mean, it's damned lucky that I got a lift over here."

"Yes but at what risk? You know they were probably looking for us. Had I not left with the cases, we would not be here now. We may be in a prison waiting to be tried for espionage."

"I keep telling you. I can talk me way out of anything."

"Well you're not talking your way out of this. You are staying here even if I have to use the gun."

"Sod you then." Bob rolled over onto his back. He lay still thinking about his life...and what a life it had been, full of excitement, fun, booze, women... He didn't regret anything which was more than could be said for many. Strange how things turned out though. He had been in prison in this country then on one of the Channel islands yet here he was, very involved in a spy mission of the most importance. He'd probably get a medal when they got back to Germany and, more importantly, a nice big fat dollop of money to keep him in his old age. He'd have some stories to tell the grandkids...if he had grandkids that is...and if he lived that long!

He opened his eyes and looked up. It was just as well it wasn't raining but it would have been nice to be able to see more stars. It was a strange sensation, lying there, knowing the stars were above them somewhere, knowing that the clouds were moving endlessly across the sky even though it was too dark to see them, except when there was a break giving a glimpse of the firmament. How insignificant they were really, like ants crawling across the Earth, alive for just a few moments in eternity, then gone, forgotten, all the worries and cares meaningless. Shakespeare had a line about that – they did it at school. Something about being like flies to the Gods. That's why you had to enjoy yourself, live life to the full, take risks. Tomorrow may never come.

CHAPTER 27

Lizzie was reluctant to leave but Alice said she was feeling the cold. It was the desolate nature of the place of course, the fact that there were German agents somewhere out there, at least one with a gun, and her recent ordeal in the pub where she had been used as a hostage by Grainger that were really troubling Alice. She had shown herself to have courage but everyone has limits and right now, Alice needed warmth, security, comfort. Lizzie put her arm around Alice's shoulders as they walked. Alice's arm crept around her own back showing Lizzie that her gesture was appreciated.

The vehicles were as they had left them. There was no sign of life anywhere. Robbie revved the engine of the Land Rover into life. "Grainger is obviously with Bob and his mate. That confirms it doesn't it? He's an agent too, the mole. We need to get back to Cranwell and find out about the search party. The fugitives can still be intercepted when they try to leave, depending on how they go." He reversed away from Grainger's vehicle, swung around it and the van as they plunged forward. He was driving fast.

They left the town of Skegness behind and Robbie put his foot down harder. The Land Rover lurched rather wildly as he took a bend. "Robbie, I agree we need to get there as quickly as possible, but it may be better if we do so in one piece."

"Not like you to be so cautious, Lizzie."

"Perhaps I'm getting old."

"We're all doing that," Alice offered. "What's the plan when we get to Cranwell?"

"I need to see Stanley or Turner if he's not available and

make sure an arrest party has been sent to Gibraltar Point. I'll go with them if they haven't already left and try to capture them before they escape."

"How do you think they'll be escaping?"

"Dinna know. Boat probably or perhaps submarine as a boat might be detected."

For a while, none of them spoke and then, as they drove into Boston, Lizzie said, "You know I've been thinking about the murder of Sinclair. If Molly is right, neither Bob nor his mate hit him."

"Aye, I've been thinking the same. But Molly can't have remembered events exactly. I mean it takes only seconds to hit someone on the head."

"Agreed, but she was very clear that he was still shouting and swearing looking for his trousers when they left," offered Alice.

"But if they did not kill him, who did?" Lizzie was thinking aloud. "Presumably they did sabotage the aircraft though?"

"Must have done. They're German agents right enough anyway so they still need arresting."

"I agree Robbie. Of course they do."

Robbie stopped abruptly at the main gate into Cranwell and showed his pass. As soon as the gate was open he sped forward and swung into a space in front of the main building. "Right, to Turner's office straightaway."

"If you don't mind, I'm going to go to my room. Feeling a bit tired." Lizzie hugged Alice.

"Do that, Alice. Sure you're alright?"

"I'm fine...just tired."

Once inside the building, Robbie and Lizzie were asked to wait while an airman went to find Sir George Stanley. Lizzie laid a hand on Robbie's arm. "You know I was really worried when Grainger pointed that gun at you."

He turned to look at her and his heart lurched at the concern in her eyes. "Ach, he was never going to pull the trigger.

It was bluff."

"All the same..." Lizzie squeezed his arm.

The airman returned a minute or two later and showed them into a very comfortable lounge. Stanley was sitting with Turner, empty brandy glasses on the coffee table in front of them.

"McBane?" Stanley said simply.

"Sir, there's been a major development. The two of us and Miss Frobisher went to The Prince of Wales pub earlier to question the barmaid there who confirmed that she and the two roofers had come onto the base last night. While we were talking with her, Bob, one of the roofers came in. I was in the process of arresting him when Mr Grainger arrived and produced a pistol which he pointed at me. When he saw I was not going to give up my prisoner, he grabbed Miss Frobisher and held her hostage, pointing the gun at her. He took Bob away with him and we followed a little later. Unfortunately, by the time we found the Land Rover Grainger had used, there was no sign of Grainger, Bob or the other one. We looked around but we could see nothing. I hope you received my telephone message about mustering an armed search party."

"Get your breath McBane. Why don't you sit down?"

"Sir, there's no time for that. If we don't get out there soon and find them, all three will be gone."

"All three?" Turner looked surprised.

"Yes Sir. It's clear that Grainger is working with them and is presumably the German mole." Lizzie placed emphasis on the last word, driving home the message that they had refused to listen before.

"Now hold on, hold on. Where exactly do you think they are?"

"They went to Skegness, Sir, but parked right on the south side on a road that leads out to the sea defence and a vast area of grassland. I daresay they are waiting for a rendezvous with a German sub. We need to hurry, Sir."

"Turner, have you been able to organise an arrest party?"

Stanley turned and looked at Turner; their eyes met.

"Of course, Sir. I'll check whether they've left." Turner stood and left the room.

"Now McBane, Miss Barnes, please sit down. As you can see Group Captain Turner has that in hand so no need for you to do any more on that front."

"But Sir, they won't know where to start searching," Lizzie protested.

"With many men on the ground, Miss Barnes, they'll be able to scour the whole area, watch for signals from the sea, that sort of thing. I think your description of the road is clear enough and presumably they will find the vehicles as you did." Stanley gestured to an empty seat. Reluctantly, Lizzie joined him and Robbie.

Stanley put the fingers of each hand together carefully, forming a cage. "Now, McBane, we really must sort out this mole business."

"But Sir, it's clear that Grainger is the mole…he's working with those two German agents." Lizzie was finding it difficult to restrain her impatience. Stanley was refusing to acknowledge Grainger's role.

"He may not be alone, Miss Barnes. You heard what you thought was a morse code message being sent from Butler's room last night. That must be investigated further. Sergeant Swallow pointed out to us earlier this evening that Butler could also be the murderer of Airman Sinclair. He does get very hot under the collar. Swallow thinks he may have gone over to the hangar to see the aircraft again and was perhaps refused entry. After an altercation, he lost his temper, grabbed a spanner and hit Sinclair."

"What about the whisky?"

"Oh I don't doubt that our roofing friends were on the base and used the girl as bait – just as Sinclair told you. Not sure what they were up to as nothing was taken nor damaged. I'm sure they brought the whisky and perhaps Butler forced some down Sinclair's throat after he had hit him so it looked like he had fallen and hit his head."

"Is there any evidence that it is Butler?"

"Only what you discovered last night. Now, we cannot let this go on any longer. I want you to interview Butler and see what you can get from him. You've got the message he sent and its de-cryption haven't you?

"Yes Sir."

"Get onto it right away please McBane."

Robbie stood. "Sir." He saluted and gestured to Lizzie to follow.

Once outside, Lizzie gave vent to her frustrations. "What is going on Robbie? I know they're not being straight with us. There's something not right here."

"I agree, Lizzie, but let's see if we can get Butler at least to admit he was sending a message to a German counterpart. If we can get him to admit that, he may admit to the murder. We know from what Molly said it probably wasn't Edwards and his sidekick."

◆ ◆ ◆

When Alice entered the main building, Bert Swallow was walking through the foyer. He saw her and approached. "Hello, did you have a good evening?" He glanced at his watch. "You didn't stay out too long."

"No...no...we didn't."

"Where are McBane and Miss Barnes. Still there?"

"No they're reporting to Sir George Stanley."

"Oh."

"I'm sorry Bert, I'm very tired and want to get an early night. We're due to fly back tomorrow."

"Forgive me if I'm being impertinent, but you look ... troubled."

"Yes. I'm not sure how much I should say but if being held

at gunpoint counts as being troubled, then I guess I am."

Bert Swallow's mouth opened and his brow creased. "Oh my God. What on earth happened?"

Tears squeezed from Alice's eyes and Bert laid a hand on her shoulder. "I'm not sure how much I should say."

"Come and sit down somewhere quiet. Can I get you anything? I do have some brandy in my room."

"I'm not one for strong spirits but...perhaps a little..."

Bert swallow's arm went round her shoulders and gently he steered her towards a corridor leading off the foyer on the ground floor. He stopped at a door and ushered Alice inside, switching on the light. Crossing to the bedside table, he switched on a lamp there which gave a softer light when he turned off the main one overhead. He gestured to the bed and Alice sighed deeply as she sat while he opened a cupboard in the desk and withdrew a bottle and two glasses. Alice watched as the brandy splashed into the glasses and she took the glass when it was offered. Her hand trembled a little.

She sipped cautiously and felt the fire burn her throat but it gave a warm glow when it reached her stomach. "Not as bad as I thought." She looked up and smiled weakly at Bert Swallow. "Thanks, it's kind of you."

"What on Earth happened tonight?" Bert said softly. "Only tell me what you think you should."

In short bursts and keeping her voice as calm as possible, Alice told him almost everything, the events in the pub, going out to the coast, the desolation of the place, the way Grainger had betrayed his Country. Apart from taking an occasional sip of his drink, he sat motionless as she talked, his eyes softened by her vulnerability and the gentle light.

"Goodness, that's extraordinary. Did the agents murder Sinclair?"

"According to Molly, the barmaid who was with them on the base, they didn't have time and Sinclair was still shouting and swearing when they left."

"And what happens now?"

"Robbie McBane went to see Stanley as soon as we got back here. He'd phoned from the pub requesting an arrest party to catch them before they escape the country."

"Right. Good idea."

They fell silent. Alice swirled the last of the brandy around her glass and drank it. Bert lifted the bottle and offered it but she shook her head. He poured himself a little more. At last, Alice spoke, her head lowered. "Bert, I'm sorry about last night. I..."

"Nothing to apologise for."

"There is. I was very poor company...it's just that I had an upset before we went out and it put me out of sorts."

He said nothing for a while. "I know how it is. I had an upset too yesterday morning. It does throw you."

Alice looked up. Bert Swallow's face was twisted; he appeared lost in his private agony. Suddenly, he came to and smiled. "Just an issue with my little sister...nothing that won't get sorted."

"Family...mine is my mother."

They sat in silence for some minutes until Bert excused himself. "You'll stay a little longer Alice I hope. I'll only be a few minutes."

"Of course."

When he left, Alice looked around the room. Spartan, functional as one would expect, no softening touches that would grace a woman's room. She stood and walked to the desk. A letter lay open on it and curiosity fought with her sense of privacy for a minute. She leaned over and began to read. Gently she turned the page and saw the plea at the end, the name of the little sister. Poor Bert, she thought, burdened with that and being so distant from her, unable to give comfort. She felt more guilty that she had been so reserved last night. The poor chap just wanted some comfort.

The man mentioned in the letter clearly had no honour, no loyalty to the woman he had bedded. He had taken his pleasure and discarded her. Bert was protective – she had seen that in his concern for herself; that betrayal perhaps accounted for his anger last night. She would treat him more kindly when he returned.

CHAPTER 28

William Butler and Arthur Healey sat together at a table in the bar, not speaking, their pints of beer half drunk and looking decidedly flat. Robbie McBane watched them through the open doorway for some minutes. Healey said something but Butler made it clear that he was not interested in conversation. Perhaps he was sulking about being unable to examine the wreckage of the Meteor. If Healey was disappointed about that too, he seemed better able to manage his frustration.

Robbie McBane approached the table. "Mr Butler. Good evening. I wonder if I could have a word with you...in private."

Butler stood up, lifted his glass. "Lead on McDuff."

Robbie gave a cold smile and led the way out of the mess building and into the main accommodation building. He pushed opened the door of the Library that he and Lizzie had used and looked around. Empty. He flicked on a couple of lights and they sat in two armchairs. This was not the best place for such an interview but perhaps Butler would be off his guard in comfortable surroundings.

"I'll come straight to the point, Butler. Last night, what did you do after the evening meal?"

"I'm not sure why you're asking me that but I don't mind telling you. Healey and I went over to the hangar to check the Meteor once more. It all seemed fine. We came back and went to our separate rooms."

"And did you go out again?"

"No."

Robbie McBane thought for a minute. "Do you know Morse Code?"

"Yes I do. Learnt it in the Boy Scouts like most boys I imagine."

"Do you use it at all in your work...or for any other reason?"

"No. Why are you asking me about Morse Code for goodness sake?"

"Because Mr Butler, last night, I and another witness heard the sounds of a message being sent in Morse Code from your room."

Butler looked dumbfounded. "From my room? How can that be?"

"I imagine you were sending a message to someone. The question is to whom and why did it need to be in Morse Code? The message used a cypher albeit a very simple one that we have been able to unlock."

"I don't know what you're talking about McBane. I would have to have equipment to send a message in Morse. I don't have any such equipment." Butler stood up abruptly, lifting his glass from the table. "I've no idea where this is going McBane or what you're trying to do but you're barking up the wrong tree." With that he walked out.

Robbie had been watching for any tell-tale sign that Butler was lying. There was nothing but, if they could establish he had lied about the Morse Code equipment, that may lead to other revelations. He realised that he should have checked Butler's room for equipment before interviewing him but he wanted to do so surreptitiously and could not be sure that Butler would not return. The problem now was that Butler was on his guard and would certainly conceal any equipment he did have. Robbie McBane's only hope was that Lizzie had found something.

◆ ◆ ◆

Lizzie had agreed with Robbie that while he interviewed Butler, she would go up to the engineer's room and try to get in. She took a towel and wash bag from her own room just in case anyone else was about or she was disturbed; she would simply be on her way to the bathroom. She sauntered along the corridor humming to herself. No one was about. She listened carefully outside Room Six, pressing her ear to the door, and, when she heard nothing, tapped very gently on it. If Butler was inside, it would be loud enough to hear but quiet enough to avoid the sound reaching the ears of anyone in the neighbouring rooms.

Her hand grasped the door handle and, holding her breath, she turned the knob. It turned but the door did not open. Damn. It was clearly locked. That increased the suspicion that Butler had something to hide. What should she do?

Checking the corridor again for any sound of movement, she glided along to Room Five and again listened intently. This room must be Healey's. Nothing. Once more she grasped the door handle and turned; the door opened at the slightest pressure. Again she listened. Should she take the plunge? To be found in the room would be impossible to explain. She could say that she mistook the room for hers but that was evidently ridiculous. Her own room was further along the corridor and the number on the door was plain enough.

She steeled herself and stepped in, closing the door as softly as she could behind her. It was dark as pitch...the blackout curtains prevented any light from outside entering the room. She flicked on the overhead light. Now she would truly be in trouble if found. She must work quickly. She tried the wardrobe, the desk, under the bed but there was no sign of equipment. A briefcase was standing on the floor next to the desk. She picked it up – not overly heavy. Laying it on the desk, she flicked the catches. It was not locked and they flew open. She lifted the lid. There were a couple of letters, unrecognisable drawings but nothing unexpected for an engineer and designer. Opening one folded sheet, she saw what looked like a wiring diagram –

completely meaningless to her and to most people though it had a strange beauty in its symmetry. There was nothing here that suggested a German spy.

She closed the lid and returned the briefcase to its place by the desk. As she straightened, she frowned. There were initials under the handle: WB. How could that be? Had Butler left his briefcase in Healey's room? Then a thought struck her. Perhaps this was Butler's room and Healey was in Room Six. She opened the briefcase again and flicked through the papers. Two letters were addressed to Butler but that was not conclusive. It probably was Butler's briefcase but there could be a simple explanation for it being in Healey's room. She needed something else to indicate that this was Butler's room.

She had just closed and replaced the briefcase when she heard loud footsteps in the corridor approaching. "Oh my goodness," she mouthed. She darted across to the door and flicked off the light switch then back to the bed. Dropping to the floor, she wriggled under it, praying that the footsteps would pass. To her horror, the steps stopped at the door and she heard it open. The light was flicked on again and, with a deep sigh, someone sat heavily on the bed. The springs creaked.

Lizzie lay in dread. There had been no time to check that her feet were not protruding from the end of the bed. Cautiously, slowly, she lifted one foot and felt the toe touch the metal springing on the underside of the bed. She was fairly certain she was hidden. What would she say if she were found? She ran through possibilities but nothing was even remotely plausible. She tried to breathe as quietly as she could and hoped no dust disturbed from the mattress would make her sneeze.

It was agony, trying to keep still, to breath inaudibly. She turned her head to one side so she could see out. All she could see was the bottom of a pair of legs, brown shoes. Did Butler or Healey wear brown shoes or did the feet belong to someone else? Suddenly Lizzie felt tired. She wanted to be out of there and in her own room. The whole day had been exhausting because of the events and the uncertainty. It was like living in a fog, nothing clear, nothing definite, no sense of direction.

She realised that she may not be able to move until the person on the bed went to sleep. That would be a huge risk. How could she be sure he was asleep...unless he snored loudly! She lay still for a long time, she was not sure how long, but it felt like an eternity. What was happening on the bed? The legs had not moved. At last, there was a grunt and the feet moved away. They left her field of vision for a short time and then she could see them moving towards the door. Her hopes lifted. Please, oh please leave the room.

The door was opened and closed again. The light had been left on. She could no longer see the feet so assumed their owner had left the room. She took a deep breath and wriggled out from under the bed, not knowing what she would say or do if she had been mistaken and there was someone else still in the room.

She was on her feet immediately. No one there. Two large steps took her to the door; she listened briefly, opened it and slipped out. She was nearly at her own room when she realised she no longer had the towel with her. She must have left it under the bed. Should she return for it? What if it had slipped off her arm as she wriggled out from under the bed? What if it were draped across the floor, a clear signal that someone had been in the room? It was not her own towel but one that had been put into the room by the housekeeping team. It could not be traced to her though she would have to get a replacement. She decided to leave it there.

Having spent some minutes in her own room, gathering her composure, she knew she needed to report to Robbie McBane. She could not be absolutely sure that Room Five was occupied by Butler but it looked that way. Therefore, the message tapped out in Morse Code the previous night was presumably from Healey.

◆ ◆ ◆

The door opened and Bert Swallow appeared around it. He looked more composed but Alice detected an air of uncertainty about him, something she had not seen on their first encounters.

"Thanks for staying. I didn't think you would."

"I'm not that easy to get rid of."

"As if I would want to get rid of you." He sat on the chair he had vacated.

Alice waited a moment or two. "You referred to your sister as 'little'. Is she much younger than you?"

"No. It's silly really but you know how it is. She's actually only four years younger but when you're kids that's a long time isn't it?"

"Yes, it is. Where does she live?"

"She's up North, never left Newcastle. Trained as a nurse but…"

Alice watched his face which set into a fixed mask. She felt he needed…wanted to talk but she did not know how to unlock the misery he was clearly feeling. At last she said, "Tell me about her."

"Not much to tell, really. What do you want to know?"

"Do you get on well, are you close?"

"We are, yes. Our parents are dead, see. A bomb. There was just the two of us children and we had no uncles or aunts – both our parents were only children. We were close anyway…I always looked out for her being older like…but when our parents passed away, we became even closer. I feel like a parent to her."

"I'm sure you're a wonderful older brother."

"I've tried to be but…but…I'm not so sure now. There is a difficulty…"

Alice did not move, waiting until he felt able to say what he wanted. She noticed his lips quivering as if he was holding back tears. Let them come, she thought, if that's what you need. It does not make you any less of a man.

"How quickly things change. One moment everything's

fine and then something happens and your world changes in a flash."

Alice thought of the news that Bert's letter had brought him, the plea at the end of it. His sister's world had certainly changed and that affected his world because he took his role as her protector seriously. Did he feel, she wondered, as though he had somehow let her down by not being there? Did he feel that she had brought shame on him and their family name? Did he feel as angry about the young man who had deserted his sister as Alice herself had felt when she read the letter?

Alice realised that he did not wish to speak further of it and perhaps needed to be alone. She stood and said she would need to get to bed. She crossed to him, kissed him lightly on the cheek and wished him goodnight though she suspected sleep would not come easily for him.

CHAPTER 29

Eventually, Lizzie found Robbie McBane perched on a stool in the mess bar. He was alone but there were three airmen huddled around a nearby table. She agreed to a glass of sherry but wondered if something stronger might have been a better choice. She looked around. It was like everything else, functional, rather bare, with no attempt to soften the lighting and create a comfortable atmosphere; very masculine.

"I'm sure the housekeeper said it was Butler in Room Six."

"Perhaps she wrote it down wrongly. No trace of any equipment?"

"Nothing. It was definitely his briefcase in Room Five but he might have left it in there for some reason. The fact that Room Six was locked does suggest there's something there that the occupant doesn't want others to see."

"Only one way to find out." Robbie McBane drained his glass. "Come on, drink up. We're going to pay Room Five a visit."

Lizzie swallowed the sherry and followed Robbie from the bar. They walked across the empty concrete to the main building where Robbie went straight to the stairs and mounted them two at a time."

"Slow down, Robbie. I've only got little legs."

They arrived at the door of Room Five and Robbie knocked. A line of light escaped from the bottom of the door. A few seconds later, the door was pulled open and Butler was facing them. "What do you want now? Come with more nonsense about spies and messages have you?"

"Sorry to disturb you, Mr Butler. I just needed to establish which room you're in. This is definitely the room you used last night is it?"

Butler looked at Robbie as if he were mad. "Of course it is. Where else would I use?"

"It's just, Mr Butler," Lizzie explained as gently as she could, "that I was told Mr Healey was in this room."

Butler looked puzzled for a moment then his face lightened. "Yes, I was assigned Room Six but I didn't go up to the room straightaway when I arrived as I went to examine the Meteor. When I did come up here, Mr Healey had mistakenly taken Room Six. As the rooms are pretty well identical, there seemed no need to change. Does that help?"

"Ah I see. Thank you. Sorry to have disturbed you."

"I suppose you think Healey is a spy now do you? Come to think of it, I did think I heard tapping last night but I went to bed early – it was a bright and early start for me yesterday – and I was half asleep when I thought I heard something. It didn't stop me from falling asleep though."

"Well thank you, Mr Butler. Goodnight."

The door was closed firmly and they heard the key being turned in the lock.

Lizzie moved away, followed by Robbie. She paused outside the door of Room Six and listened. The same crack of light appeared at the bottom of the door suggesting there was someone inside but no sound came from the room. Lizzie stood on tip-toe and whispered into Robbie's ear, "Should we knock, search his room?"

He shook his head and pointed down the corridor in the direction of her room. Once inside, he flopped into the single chair and let out a sigh of exasperation. "I guess if we find telegraph equipment in his room, that would be evidence enough."

"It would definitely. Let's do it now, then we can see how Turner's men are getting on out at the coast."

Robbie thought for a moment. "Let's leave it until morning. He's not going anywhere and maybe he'll send another message later. Are you wanting to go to bed now?"

"I'm assuming that's not an improper suggestion." Lizzie's eyes twinkled.

Robbie looked surprised and embarrassed. "No, no, I just meant is it ok to..."

"It's alright, Robbie. I'm just teasing. You can wait here if you want or I can check later and let you know."

"Perhaps best if we do that. I won't go to sleep until you come and tell me...either way. How long will you leave it before you listen?"

"Let's say, I'll go and listen at twenty-three hundred."

He stood and smiled. "That'll be fine. It was about that time last night wasn't it, perhaps a little later. A bientot then."

Robbie left the room, closing the door quietly behind him. Lizzie felt a little pang of regret. She definitely was attracted to him. His unassuming manner, the sadness she knew lingered in his heart, the way she knew he felt about her were all powerful attractions. But she knew she was not ready to commit herself to a relationship with any man. The ghosts of her past needed to be put to rest and that was not going to be easy. Besides, she had an important job to do for the war effort and she was not ready to end that yet.

Soon after Robbie had left, there was a tap on the door. Lizzie was surprised when she opened it to see Alice fully clothed. "I thought you'd gone to bed?"

"I had planned to...an early night was what I needed but... well I bumped into Bert Swallow. He offered a glass of brandy so I decided to take him up on it." Lizzie raised her eyebrows. "Nothing happened, Lizzie, so don't let your imagination run away with you."

Alice sat on the bed and talked about Bert Swallow, what she had discovered about his family, the loss of his parents, no uncles and aunts and only his younger sister. "He's a sad man, Lizzie, lonely. He clearly feels very protective of his sister – the older brother and all that. He seemed very troubled. But when he went out of the room for a short while, I was looking around and I saw a letter, open on the desk. I know it was wrong to read it but I couldn't help it, Lizzie. I was curious about him."

"Ah curious was it?"

"Yes, just that."

Lizzie smiled knowingly. "Curiosity leads to understanding and understanding to love."

Alice blushed. "It's not like that, Lizzie, though I admit I did feel for him."

"What did the letter say? Who was it from?"

"It was from his younger sister...Angela. She was telling him that she has fallen pregnant but she's not married. The thing that was distressing was that the young man, Michael, who is the father said he wanted nothing to do with her...it was her problem."

"Typical men!" The vehemence of Lizzie's response shocked Alice and she stared at her. Neither of them spoke for a few seconds.

"I think you perhaps have suffered at the hands of a man."

"You could say that but I don't want to talk about it."

There was a tone of gentle admonishment in Alice's voice when she said, "Last night, you were telling me that it's good to talk and it was. I found it helpful. Perhaps I can return the favour."

Lizzie looked away while she prepared herself to reveal a little of her past. Alice had trusted her with her own sadness, so it was only fair that she returned the compliment. "In childhood, a family friend, or so everyone believed he was, abused me... seriously. I have only ever told one other person. It didn't help much. There have been other incidents with men more recently, though not as devastating. Men seem to have only one thing on their minds and see us as existing to service their pleasures."

Alice thought for a moment. "All men? I didn't feel that

about Bert Swallow tonight. I was in his room. He could have tried something had he been so inclined. And what about Robbie McBane? He seems a perfect gentleman."

"You're right, Alice. I'm sorry. I just have a very poor view of men...I don't trust them, perhaps don't trust myself not to lash out."

Lizzie was sitting on the bed. Alice stood up from the chair and sat beside her, sliding her arm around her shoulders and pulling her gently closer. Lizzie did not resist though she had to force herself not to pull away. Weakness. She was always afraid of weakness – appearing weak and being weak. She had built her life after the devastation of her childhood on strength, not allowing herself to be dominated, intimidated or overlooked by men. At moments, she wondered how long she could keep that up and Alice's kindness, her gentle concern was threatening to undo her.

"There is so much unhappiness in this World, Lizzie, so many people are suffering. Don't be one of them. You present yourself as very strong but think of the sapling that bends in the wind and survives the storm whereas the mature tree resists and resists until it breaks."

"You want me just to accept the treatment we get?" Lizzie looked into Alice's face, anger welling inside her.

"No Lizzie, I'm simply suggesting that you don't have to fight all the time. There are good men who will love you and cherish you, men who will die for you, men who will over time repair the damage that was done. Don't cut them all out, Lizzie."

Lizzie thought for a minute. "I know I have to come to terms with this, Alice, and that means taking some risks but it's hard, very hard."

Alice leaned closer and kissed Lizzie on the cheek. "I know, I know."

Lizzie sat up straight. "Come with me Alice. We have a little job to do." Lizzie took her by the hand and they walked into the corridor. Still hand in hand, they sidled towards Room Five and, after checking the corridor was empty, stopped by the door listening intently.

Nothing.

Lizzie looked disappointed. The crack of light beneath the door was no longer visible. That meant that Healey was in bed or he was prowling around somewhere. Lizzie led Alice back to her room and explained she needed to report to Robbie. The two young women wished each other good night and parted.

◆ ◆ ◆

Waiting for several hours in the darkness, he felt cold. He was determined though to stick it out, to make sure that they got away without further incident. And that damned man Bob Edwards! There was no telling what he'd get up to next. The two of them should have been well away from Cranwell and its nearby villages long ago. To find they were – or at least Bob – was still at the pub was infuriating. He just could not keep his equipment in his trousers that was his problem.

Ian Grainger once more walked a short way along the track towards Skegness and then back to his former position, swinging his arms around himself in a hopeless attempt to stay warm. He would not have put it past Edwards to have gone into Skegness looking for women. The man had an insatiable appetite for the opposite sex. Not that he himself was impartial to female charm.

He thought of the missions he had undertaken in the past. There had been some very welcome diversions but, he assured himself, he had never allowed anything to distract him from the job in hand. That Valerie though…she had been lovely…blonde hair beautifully styled in the latest fashion…and her perfume…hints of spice and lilac and goodness knows what else lingering behind her wherever she walked. He had drunk it in. And when she kissed him, full on the mouth, her lips moist and yielding, her slim arms around his neck…

Grainger shuddered and shook away the memory that was tempting him to lose concentration. There would be time, he was sure, for future liaisons. Those two young women at Cranwell, the pilot and the navigator, were both attractive but that Barnes woman was so abrupt. There was something wrong there. Where was her charm, her softness, her willingness to flirt with a man? Trying to be a man herself, he thought, doing a job that was a man's job. God it would be good when this war was over and people returned to their normal roles.

He sighed. War changes things, there was no doubt of that. He wondered where Bob and Hans were hiding – probably sitting in the long grass, shivering and praying the pick-up would come soon. Hans would have a hard job keeping Bob there, stopping him from nipping off for a pint or two in a nice warm pub. Had they fallen out? They might have killed each other. So many things could still go wrong with this mission. That damned Scot, McBane, was a problem too. Obviously thinks he's a top detective. Damned nuisance that he had been brought along.

His eyes scanned the cold sea, trying to penetrate the darkness. He could see very little and all he could hear were the waves sighing up the beach and the long hissing withdrawal of their mocking retreat.

CHAPTER 30

When Alice left him, Bert Swallow could have cried out. What a damned thing! He had just been kissed by a lovely young woman who had been so gentle, so concerned, so caring. It was a long time since he had experienced such a moment. But now it was hopeless. How could he pursue her when he had this to sort out? She was due to stay only until the next day. There would be no chance to see her again, enjoy some time in her company, maybe make arrangements to see her in the future though that would be difficult enough.

He himself may not be at Cranwell much longer. But, he reflected, he was so glad of those few minutes in her company, just the two of them talking quietly. He closed his eyes and pictured her sitting on the bed, her pretty, finely-shaped face, her hair so neatly tied, her lovely large eyes exuding warmth.

Why had he let her go? He could have asked her to stay longer but he knew, deep down, that such happiness was denied him. Perhaps Fate decreed that some people should have unhappy lives whilst others enjoyed fulfilment, family, friendship, love. He sat on the chair, staring at the floor for a long time, dwelling on his miserable state and the lovely woman who was lost to him.

After some twenty minutes, his mind turned to more practical things. What should he do? Perhaps when the top brass had left in the morning, he could ask for compassionate leave and go to see Angela. He wished she had a telephone but that was beyond her means. He needed to see her, comfort her with his presence, start to plan the future with her...a new home somewhere she was not known - that was the solution. She could keep the child, say its father had been killed in the war. So many young men had lost their lives no one would question it.

He turned in the chair to see the letter on the desk, still lying open as he had left it the previous morning. The anger that had burned in him all the long day yesterday had dissipated. But he must write a response. Wearily, he re-positioned the chair, took out his writing case and slid his hand over the smooth, brown leather. It was still as good as it had been when new despite its frequent use: he had written regularly, once a fortnight. His mother had treasured his letters. After she had died, he had rescued what he could from the wrecked house. A small suitcase had survived intact as it was under a bed. Inside were photographs, other valued memories and a bundle of letters which he recognised as his.

Sighing, he opened the case and spread it in front of him. Taking the pen, he wrote, stopping frequently, thinking carefully, weighing every word and the impact it would have.

Friday 5th March late

Dear Angela,

I was devastated to receive your letter as you must have been to get that man's…I cannot bring myself to use his name. I am angry but not with you. Perhaps sleeping with him was unwise but you had no reason to think he would leave you and every reason to believe that your relationship would develop into marriage.

You ask me what you should do. It is clear from what you say that you wish to keep the child and, if this is the case, then you must keep it. I know you will be an excellent mother even if you are on your own at the moment. It will not be for ever. You are young, you are attractive and I am certain many men would love you and your child. We live in strange times. There are many women who have lost husbands and are bringing up children on their own. Just think of it like that. You should not worry about what people will think though I

---

know you are very sensitive and may do so. If this troubles you, we can find somewhere else for you to live where you are not known and you can tell people the child's father was killed in action. No one will question that.

We've had a special event at the base today – sorry I can't say what it is – with a very senior officer from the RAF and a couple of other bods visiting for it. They should go tomorrow and I intend to ask Group Captain Turner for compassionate leave to come and visit you. I won't say why, just that you are very ill and have no one else. I could also ask for a transfer to a base nearer home or wherever it is that you go if you decide to move. I think it may do me good to have a change of scene.

It is late now, so I'll finish this letter and get it into the post tomorrow morning. I may even be back before it reaches you but I don't know what Turner will say. You know I have a significant role here and he may want me for other duties. I must confess I feel a great heaviness of spirit, an uncertainty about my future. The sooner I can get away from here, the better I think.

Rest assured, dear sister, I am always on your side and, with luck, I'll be at your side very soon.

Your loving brother

Bert

xx

The wind was still light but it caused him to shiver. He hunched into his coat, hands plunged deep into the pockets, his right one folded around his binoculars. Pulling his left hand out, he checked his watch. It was one fifty in the morning.

There had been no sign of Bob and Hans, thankfully... unless of course one or both had slipped past him or found another way off the grassland. He was sure Hans would not. As a German he would want to get home as soon as possible. Bob was another matter. He was home and might opt to stay here; that would be disastrous to the mission. Bob could have walked South of course, and found the lane that passed RAF Wainfleet on its way to the main road. But that seemed unlikely. It was a long walk to nowhere and Bob at least was a lazy sod. They were probably still huddled down in the long grass somewhere waiting for the signal.

Thankfully, the wind had remained light and there was no sign of rain. It would have been utterly miserable had it been pouring. The things he did for his country! And would anyone appreciate it? Hardly anyone would know about it and those that did probably mis-trusted him. He was after all, as far as they were concerned, just a civil servant, a man from the ministry. He knew Stanley distrusted him. Stanley was a man of action, no real guile to him. That was fine for the role Stanley fulfilled but it was no good for his own.

Grainger pulled the binoculars from his pocket and slowly panned across the sea. It was hopeless as there was nothing distinguishable. He slipped them back in his pocket and resumed his hunched position. He was on the top of the sea defence. That gave him a better view though it did expose him more to the wind. He would, he was sure, be able to see the signal when it came and the response of the agents to it. It couldn't be long now. He waited.

And then his eye caught a flash of light.

Swiftly, he pulled out his binoculars and trained them on the spot from which he thought it had come. He waited, breath held to steady the binoculars. There it was again and this time, he could see a dark shape around it. It must be the sub. A third flash followed. There should now be a pause of some ten seconds. He counted silently. A flash, five seconds, a second flash, five seconds and the third.

The pick-up had arrived absolutely on time. Thank God for German efficiency. Grainger trained his eyes onto the foreshore. There should be answering flashes but he may not be able to see them from where he sat. Another minute followed with no flashes from the sea. Bob and Hans must have answered the signal. Ian Grainger now held the binoculars to his eyes once again, sweeping gently across the foreshore where he assumed the two agents had been hiding. At last he could make out movement, two figures barely discernible, dragging something down the beach to the sea.

A longer burst of light came from the sea, picking out the two figures and the kayak. They would need to keep turning on the light to give the agents a bearing. Without it, they could easily paddle past the sub altogether. There was some delay at the water's edge whilst they climbed into the kayak and then they were paddling out in the direction of the light.

It shone for short bursts several more times, each one illuminating the kayak briefly and the two figures in it, one taller than the other. At last, through his binoculars, Grainger could just make out the kayak bump against the black hull, the two figures being helped out and the metal boxes unloaded. The kayak was swiftly lifted from the water and, within a minute, it had disappeared down the conning tower with everyone and everything else.

Grainger could see nothing after that but he thought he heard a gurgling sound presumably made as the sub sank beneath the surface. He smiled to himself. His job was done. Gratefully, he turned away from the cold sea and walked briskly towards Skegness and the Land Rover that should be waiting to take him back to Cranwell. He had some difficulties to face there but that would, he thought, be in the morning.

The important thing was that the mission had been completed.

Lizzie had lain awake for a long time, tossing and turning. The bed was comfortable enough but her mind was racing. She knew, beneath everything, that she had feelings for Robbie she could not entirely dispel. Her heart trembled at the image of him in the pub facing Grainger's gun. Eventually, she had drifted into a troubled sleep and woke with a start. Grainger's distorted face was leering at her, waving a pistol in the air, threatening at first Robbie McBane, then Alice and finally her.

She sat up until the image had disappeared. By then, she was fully awake and her mind was again churning over all the anomalies she saw in the events she had witnessed since arriving at Cranwell. Bert Swallow's face was lingering in a corner of her mind. She knew it was when they were watching the Meteor accelerating down the runway before the explosion. A flag on a pole at the end of the runway behind it fluttered limply in the morning breeze and she commented on it to Bert. If the Meteor's engines were as powerful as Butler had said, that flag should have been streaming out from the pole. Bert dismissed it but there was something in his eyes which betrayed a knowledge he was not sharing.

The lack of noise she could understand. The jet engines thrust the noise behind the aircraft so one did not hear it until it was at least level. Then the explosions. Why did both engines explode at once? Surely that was an unlikely coincidence? Why did the test pilot who appeared seriously injured when lifted from the plane make such a remarkable recovery? Surely explosions of that magnitude would have caused significant injury?

And then Grainger. Why was he so keen to say it was not sabotage but a fault with the engines? Why was he so keen to make sure Bob and his mate got away? He had been prepared to shoot, she had no doubt, if Robbie had not released Bob. She hoped that the arrest party sent out by Turner had captured them before they escaped. Turner and Stanley had not seemed very concerned; their only worry had been who the mole was and they dismissed the very obvious conclusion that Grainger was working with the Germans, helping the two agents carry out their mission and no doubt communicating with them. Surely they couldn't be working for the Germans too?

But it looked as though it was Healey who was communicating. The Morse Code message she and Robbie had heard the previous night was damning...unless Butler had somehow swapped rooms with him and swapped back again.

At last, she thought of young Micky Sinclair, his marble features lying on the hospital bed, all life extinguished. Was Butler or Healey responsible for that or was it Bob and his mate, despite the testimony of Molly. She was excitable, young, probably a bit scatty and may have confused events, times. And what was the meaning of the words Sinclair thought he had heard from his assailant; 'That's far more sinister.'

Gradually, she began to sort things out in her mind. They still had so many questions to answer. Firstly, the Meteor; sabotage or design failure? Secondly, the mole; was it Grainger or one of the designers? Thirdly, the murder of Sinclair; again there were possibilities. She lay down on the bed, determined that she would sleep but one thought lurked in her mind. Something that Alice had told her after her discussion with Bert Swallow. She could not remember what it was that had struck her.

CHAPTER 31

Robbie McBane walked briskly to the mess. It was early, just seven hundred hours, as again he could not sleep. His mind was full of possibilities, uncertainties, but he had managed to give himself a simple list of actions. He would have breakfast and then interview Healey. He would demand to search his room. No doubt the telegraph equipment would be revealed and a confession would come. When that was sorted, he would see Turner and Stanley and find out what had happened at the coast. He would be furious if Bob, his mate and Grainger had been allowed to get away.

The mess was not crowded and he took his tray and sat at one of the many empty tables. Soon afterwards, Lizzie and Alice joined him.

"What happened at the coast last night?"

Robbie recognised in Lizzie's voice the same determination he felt himself to get to the bottom of things. He had noticed it frequently at Silverstone and several times already at Cranwell. She would not be deterred nor would he wish her to be. "First things first Lizzie. I'm going to interview Healey as soon as possible and see where we get to. Then I'll see Turner and Stanley and ascertain progress."

Lizzie chewed a mouthful of toast slowly. "There's something odd about that Meteor test flight you know."

Alice looked up sharply. "Apart from the fact that it blew up you mean?"

"Indeed. Don't know whether you noticed the flag at the end of the runway. It was hardly fluttering in the light wind and nothing changed when the Meteor set off down the runway. If the engines are as a powerful as Butler said, that flag should have streamed away from the pole with the blast."

"What are you saying, Lizzie?" Robbie McBane looked confused. His thoughts were on Healey and Grainger not the Meteor.

"I don't know but I think...well I wonder if it was a real test."

"You mean, it was not being propelled by the engines?" Alice asked quietly.

"Yes...I suppose that's what I do mean."

"Why would they not use the engines...I mean it was supposed to be a test?"

"Stanley and Turner and perhaps Swallow are up to something, Robbie, that's all I can say. Not sure what and certainly no idea why. Where Grainger fits in, I don't know either but he's in on it."

"But Lizzie," interjected Alice, "why do you think Bert Swallow is involved?"

"Because when the engines exploded, the shock on his face did not look real...it looked staged. And don't forget the pilot was not injured at all although he was carried apparently lifeless from the aircraft. Why was everyone, Butler and Healey included, kept from examining the wreckage for so long? Why was Grainger in particular so insistent that it was not sabotage? How could he know at that stage?"

"So many questions, Lizzie."

"Yes and we need answers. The only people who can give them are those I've mentioned."

"Here's one of them now." Alice half rose, smiled at Bert Swallow when she caught his eye and waved him over to their table. A few minutes later, he joined them with a try of food.

"Bert," Lizzie began.

"Let the poor man at least start his breakfast," Alice said

with quiet firmness.

"Thank you Alice. You're very kind." Bert looked dreadful, his face a dull grey, his shoulders slumped and his whole demeanour depressed, so different to the buoyant personality he had presented on Thursday when they had arrived. He looked at Lizzie. "You wanted something?"

"I've just been saying there was something odd about that Meteor test yesterday. You know I mentioned the way the flag was not affected by the engines and then after the explosion, how could Grainger be so sure it was not sabotage but engine failure?"

Bert took a gulp of tea. "As I said yesterday, the flag is not significant. I can't offer any explanation for Grainger's views, you'll need to ask him yourself."

"If he's still in this country that is."

Bert looked at Lizzie sharply. "What d'you mean?"

Robbie answered the question, anxious to avoid a tirade of suspicions from Lizzie. "Last night, in the pub, I was in the act of arresting the man called Bob – you know one of the pretend roofers – when Grainger strode in and produced a pistol. He even held Alice hostage briefly."

Bert looked carefully at Alice, his face creased with a tender concern. "You missed that bit out last night Alice. Are you okay?"

"I'm fine thanks Bert. I just felt tired. I suppose I didn't really think he was going to use the pistol."

"We don't know what he's capable of doing." Lizzie spat the words like gunshots.

Robbie McBane ignored them. "He took Bob and drove him to the coast. We followed but lost them in that huge area of grassland. It was pitch dark. I was not armed so could not really confront them. We're hoping that Turner's arrest party picked them up before they escaped to Germany."

"Germany!" Bert's single word was not a question and was spoken quietly as if to himself.

They ate in silence for a minute until Lizzie could not stop herself returning to her original question. "Bert, what was going on with that Meteor test yesterday?"

Bert placed his knife and fork on his plate of unfinished food. He pushed the plate away a few inches and rested both forearms on the table. "It was just a test that went wrong. It happens. I can't tell you more than that. You'll need to ask Stanley or Turner."

Robbie signalled to Lizzie to leave it there. She clamped her mouth shut in frustration and asked no more questions. A few minutes passed and then Butler and Healey strolled into the mess, examining the morning's offerings at the counter before taking food to a table some distance from their own. Lizzie looked at Robbie who returned her gaze and smiled.

"Bert, I need to have a conversation with Mr Healey. I could do with a witness. Would you oblige?"

"Healey, why Healey?"

"Something I have to clear up."

"What about Butler? I thought he was under suspicion. The temper on him makes me think he might 'ave done for young Sinclair."

"Aye, Turner said you raised that suspicion but we have no evidence against him on any account whereas Mr Healey has some questions to answer."

"He doesn't seem the angry type. Can't see him taking a swing at Sinclair."

"There's another matter I must explore. Can you help?"

"I can but I must see Group Captain Turner first. Can it wait thirty minutes?"

"I hope so. Looks like he's concentrating on his breakfast at the moment."

◆ ◆ ◆

Bert Swallow waited nervously outside Group Captain

Turner's office. It had just gone eight hundred hours and he knew Turner liked an early start. He wanted to ask about compassionate leave before any other issues arose and made Turner inaccessible or put him in a mood to deny his request. Brisk footsteps clattered on the wooden floor along the corridor and Bert looked in the direction of the sound. He snapped out of his position slumped against the wall. Standing more upright and preparing to salute was instinctive.

"Morning Sergeant. Everything alright?"

"Well actually, Sir, I do have something to ask you."

Turner looked at the ashen face and furrowed brow so different to Swallow's usual appearance. "You'd better come in."

"Thank you, Sir."

Turner waved him to a chair and dropped into his own behind his desk. "What do you want to ask?"

"Well, Sir, it's like this..." Haltingly, with considerable embarrassment, Bert Swallow told him about Angela's letter and their family circumstances, both of them news to Turner who listened carefully. "So I was wondering, Sir, if it's convenient like, if I could take some compassionate leave to go home and see my sister. It would mean a lot to both of us, Sir. I wouldn't normally ask but...but..."

Turner held up his hand. "Can you wait until Sir George Stanley and our other visitors have left today? Assuming they do leave today that is."

"Oh of course, Sir, I didn't mean to go immediately."

"That's settled then. You take what time you need Swallow. I know you won't take more than you need. You're a good man and very important to the running of this base. I had no idea you had suffered such a tragedy as the loss of your parents. You kept that to yourself."

"I like to be professional, Sir. Just get on with the job, that's me."

"Indeed. Thank you Sergeant. Let's just get the final bits of this operation sorted and then you get off."

Bert Swallow rose from his chair but hesitated.

"Was there something else, Sergeant?"

"Not sure if I should mention it, Sir, but Sergeant McBane and Miss Barnes were asking some questions this mornin' at breakfast. I said nothing, like, but I don't know how much longer we can hold them off"

"What questions?"

"That Miss Barnes was asking if there was something odd about the Meteor test. They also think that Mr Grainger is a German agent working with the two that came onto the site."

Turner nodded slowly. "If Sergeant McBane would do his job and find out who the mole is, everything could be revealed."

"He wants me to be in on an interview he has with Mr Healey this morning."

"Healey? I thought it was Butler under suspicion. Well let's hope he can get a confession. We need to plug the leak before revealing anything."

"Understood, Sir. Thank you, Sir." Bert Swallow saluted, turned sharply and left the office, a huge weight lifted from his shoulders. He would be away from Cranwell after lunch probably and he could get a train to Newcastle. He would arrive late but he would be away from... all this.

◆ ◆ ◆

"Are you sure this is wise, Lizzie?"

"No, but I'm going over there anyway. If you don't want to come..."

"I'm coming with you...to keep you under control if I can"

"No chance of that," Lizzie snorted.

It had of course been Lizzie's suggestion that they go over to Hangar Three and see if they could find out anything about the Meteor test. She knew everything was connected in some way but could not fathom it. The wreckage would be guarded but she was confident she could get something out of the guard.

Men's belief in their superiority was their weakness; they could never see when they were being...managed.

Lizzie strode across the apron with Alice having to take the occasional rapid step to keep up. The weather had changed little, the same light wind, the same covering of thin cloud but it looked as though it was breaking. Perhaps as the sun rose, the heat would burn off the cloud leaving a clear day. She would be glad of that as it would make the flight back to Northolt, Brockworth and finally White Waltham more pleasant.

The personnel door at the side of Hangar Three was open and the two young women approached as if to enter. Suddenly a figure loomed in the doorway, rifle held at the hip.

"Stop right there." The command was barked from a face that looked mean.

Instinctively, both Lizzie and Alice raised their hands. "It's ok, we're not coming in."

"What d'you want?" The accent was working class, London, almost a caricature.

I'm Second Officer Barnes and this is Navigator Frobisher...but you can call me Lizzie and my friend Alice."

The airman looked from one to the other, unsmiling. "So what do you want?"

Lizzie treated him to her brightest smile. "We're from the Air Transport Auxiliary. We flew Air Chief Marshal Sir George Stanley up here on Thursday. We'll be taking him back later today...hopefully."

"And?"

"Well we've got a bit of time on our hands before we go so we thought we'd come and look at the wreckage but it looks like it's been repaired." Lizzie pointed behind the guard. Two groundcrew were working on a Meteor which looked pristine, brand new, no sign of any explosion."

The guard looked back and then swiftly forward. "It's a different one."

"Oh, so there's a second aircraft."

"Course. You wouldn't just have one test plane would

you...I mean something might go wrong as it did yesterday."

"Yes that was awful but thankfully the pilot's ok. One does wonder how it was sabotaged."

"Sabotaged? Don't know nothin' about that. Anyway, I'm not allowed to talk about it so you'd best be on your way ladies."

Lizzie started to turn away but Alice took over. "It does look beautiful though doesn't it. So sleek and powerful looking. Maybe we could just get a slightly closer look."

"Maybe...but no."

"What's under the tarpaulin cover at the back of the hangar?"

"That's the Meteor that blew up yesterday."

"It can't do any harm to have a quick peek. I mean it's not as if we know anything about the technical stuff of aeroplanes."

"No point in looking at it then. Bye bye ladies. Enjoy your trip home today." With that he closed the door and they had no option but to leave.

"Wasted journey Lizzie, I think," Alice said but without rancour.

"Perhaps...and perhaps not entirely. Perhaps they had a second Meteor because they knew the first would blow up." Lizzie's eyes were laden with a meaning that Alice could not read.

As they walked back to their quarters, a figure came out of the building which housed the officers' accommodation. A cigarette was lit, the match shielded from the wind and then smoke was blown into the air. It was Grainger.

"What on earth is he doing here?" Lizzie gasped.

CHAPTER 32

Like a horse shying at a fence, Healey had bridled when Robbie McBane said he would need to ask him some questions; rising aggressively from his chair, he demanded what right a Sergeant had to interview him, a civilian.

"You're on an RAF base, Sir, and therefore I have the authority to conduct an interview with you. I can show you the regulations if you like."

Healey had agreed with bad grace but he kept up a constant complaint about being treated like a criminal all the way to the library where Robbie wanted to conduct the first part of the interview. He had agreed with Bert Swallow that he would start on his own and Bert would join them for the room search, the part most likely to give rise to subsequent complaint. Robbie indicated to Healey an upright chair by one of the large wooden tables and seated himself opposite him. He could see that this positioning made Healey uncomfortable. The formality of it, his own coldness, were part of his armoury. He needed to make Healey feel vulnerable, nervous, so he would give something away.

"Do you know Morse Code, Mr Healey?"

"I know of it but I don't use it...couldn't tell you any words except of course SOS."

"You weren't in the Scouts then?"

"No. I was a cub but didn't want to progress to the Scouts when I was old enough. I'd had enough of jolly camping and eating flour and water paste burnt over a fire."

"So you don't use Morse Code in your work at all?"

Healey shifted in his chair and looked away. "No, no...

never had any cause to."

"Could you please tell me your movements on Thursday night, after your evening meal."

"Butler and I went over to Hangar Three to check the Meteor. We were there for maybe fifteen or twenty minutes and then we went to our rooms at about eight o' clock I suppose. It had been a fairly long day and I wanted to rest."

"Did you leave your room at all for any purpose?"

"No."

"No? Not even to use the bathroom?"

"Well that of course but not to go anywhere."

"What did you do in your room? It was quite early when you went there."

"I read a technical paper. Do you want to know what it's called?"

"No thank you."

"It was a paper on helicopters...quite a bit about Sigorsky's VS-300 but focusing on how it works. It's absolutely fascinating, you know, because the rotor blades..."

"I'm sure it is, Mr Healey but another time perhaps."

Healey ignored Robbie McBane's interruption except to change tack. "Yes, my son is very interested in it. I think he may well go into helicopter design when this is all over. Do you have children, Sergeant?"

Robbie McBane noticed how Healey never made eye contact even when asking a question. "No I don't. I'm not married and may never be."

"You should have children. It's wonderfully creative being a parent you know. Difficult to explain how it makes you feel bringing another soul into the World, watching him or her grow, become their own person. It's a very powerful bond...you'd do anything."

Robbie McBane's eyes narrowed very slightly. Healey was being garrulous but, in being so, was he giving something away? The sentence 'You'd do anything for your child' was telling perhaps. "How old is your son, Mr Healey?"

"Nearly twenty-three…birthday is in April. Still seems a child to me but that's a bit ridiculous isn't it? I mean what young men have seen in this war makes them adults well before the official age of majority…twenty-one I mean."

"Is your son serving?"

"Yes but had a hard time you know. Taken prisoner by the Nazis in Northern France back in '40. I pray for his release."

"I'm sure you do but I don't suppose that will happen until…"

Healey looked down at the table. "No…no…but perhaps… you know…miracles happen…"

Robbie let Healey tail off and said nothing. The other man squirmed in his chair, his eyes darting everywhere except at his questioner. At last Healey said, "I think we've got off the point haven't we? What do you want to know Sergeant McBane? I mean you haven't actually told me what you're investigating."

"I'm investigating a leak of information to the Germans."

Arthur Healey at last looked Robbie McBane in the eye directly for a second or two. His mouth was open and terror gripped his face. " A leak?"

"Yes Sir, a leak."

◆ ◆ ◆

Shaking with anger, Lizzie strode into the main accommodation building with Alice fluttering behind her trying to calm her down. No words could do that, however. Bert Swallow was pacing slowly in the foyer, his shoes on the marble floor like the slow ticking of a long case clock. He looked distracted but the anxiety that had lined his face that morning had disappeared. He turned towards them when he heard their footsteps on the tiles and smiled warmly when he realised who it was. His eyes sought Alice's but it was Lizzie who spoke.

"Bert, we've just seen that man Grainger here. What's

he doing? Surely he should have been arrested with the two so-called roofers....I mean Turner sent an arrest party to find them."

"I don't know what the outcome of that was, Lizzie. In fact I don't know anything about Grainger other than he's from the Ministry."

"If Turner has not arrested him, then I'll call the Police. I'm damned sure he's not going to get away with what he did last night. I mean he's got a gun for goodness sake."

"There may be another explanation, Lizzie." Alice held Lizzie's arm as if she could prevent her making the telephone call.

"Perhaps you should discuss it with Sergeant McBane first. I'm waiting here to see Mr Healey with him. He should be out soon. In fact, I'll go and check. Wait here." Bert Swallow plodded along the corridor, tapped on the library door and pushed it open. Lizzie and Alice followed him to the doorway but did not go in. They listened to the voices.

"I hope I'm not interrupting."

"No, your timing is perfect Sergeant Swallow. I've just explained to Mr Healey what I'm investigating. Now Sir, I need to check your room."

"I beg your pardon." Alarm was clear in Healey's voice, the pitch rising even in that short sentence.

"I need to check your room."

"How dare you! What do you think I am...a thief...a criminal of some sort." It was now outrage or rather, Lizzie thought, simulated outrage that infused Healey's tone.

"It's just routine, Mr Healey, so that I can eliminate you from my enquiries."

"Routine, routine? Have you searched everyone else's rooms? Eh? Eh? What about Butler? Have you searched his room."

"Not yet Mr Healey, but I will if necessary. So you can either give me the key or you can accompany me."

Healey suddenly emerged from the room and almost

knocked Lizzie and Alice over in his angry haste. But his face was pale, the eyes betraying fear. Guilty as charged thought Lizzie. Robbie McBane appeared almost immediately afterwards with Bert Swallow behind him. Lizzie caught his sleeve.

"Robbie...Grainger is back on the base," she hissed.

"Not now, Lizzie, I need to be at Healey's room as soon as he enters it. Talk later"

His last words trailed behind him like smoke from a steam train. "Come on Alice, Lizzie said, "let's see what Healey is hiding."

When they reached Healey's room, he was fumbling with the key in the lock, still protesting about the outrageous treatment he was receiving. His protests, however, seemed less convincing, more a case of playing a part than genuine fury. At last he pushed the door open and with a grand gesture, ushered the two sergeants into the room. Lizzie and Alice hovered in the corridor.

"Do go in ladies, please. Why should you be denied a seat at this ridiculous piece of theatre. It may be helpful to me to have witnesses who can vouch for the despicable way in which I, a highly respected aircraft engineer, am being treated."

Lizzie and Alice followed Robbie McBane and Bert Swallow into the room. Robbie started systematically checking the furniture: the wardrobe, the desk drawers. There was nothing in them.

"You do not seem to have any possessions Mr Healey."

"I'm leaving today so I've packed my case."

"And where is your case?"

"Oh it's...downstairs somewhere...you know...ready to go to the aircraft," Healey said airily.

As he was speaking, Lizzie dropped her handkerchief on the floor. She bent to retrieve it and, as she did so, shot a glance under the bed. She saw the suitcase, pushed right back against the wall to make it as inconspicuous as possible.

"I'll need to check it, Sir."

Lizzie coughed quietly and Robbie McBane looked at her.

She nodded her head to the bed and he dropped onto his hands and knees. Reaching one arm right under the bed, he pulled the suitcase into view. "Would this be your suitcase, Sir?"

"Oh I thought...it is but...I thought it had been taken down...you know. But there's nothing in it except clothes and so on."

Robbie McBane lifted the suitcase onto the bed, clearly surprised by its weight. "It's very heavy Mr Healey." He tried to open it but it was locked. "The key please, Sir." He held out his hand. Healey looked at his hand and started to bluster about it being private but Robbie McBane kept his arm outstretched.

At last, Healey reached into his pocket and threw the key into Robbie's hand as if it were insignificant. He turned to the window and began to whistle, his hands thrust into his trouser pockets. Robbie McBane opened the case. He removed a shirt and a pair of trousers, placing them carefully on the bed beside the case. Then he stopped.

"Would you care to explain what this is, Sir?"

Healey turned and looked into the case. "I've no idea. Who put that in there? Did you?" But suddenly he crumpled and flopped onto the chair.

"It looks like telegraph equipment to me...a roll of wire to act as an aerial...and this," Robbie held up a smaller piece of equipment, "looks to me like the device one uses to send Morse Code messages."

Healey stared at the floor.

PC Paul Crowther had forgotten the initial fear of the previous night when Sadler had taken him in pursuit of the German agent. It had been replaced by a new self-confidence, sense of adventure, that he was now doing a job so important to the war effort. During the course of the morning, Sergeant

O'Flynn had become increasingly fed up with his cockiness but Crowther didn't care. He had chased a German agent and had dealings with someone from the secret services – the ministry was all he was allowed to say. He had enjoyed keeping that bit back from O'Flynn, making very veiled references that Mr Grainger was not all he seemed to be.

His daydreams of a career as a member of His Majesty's Secret Services, being sent at a moment's notice to rescue a beautiful, young woman who was crucial to Britain's defence from the hands of the Nazis were interrupted by the harsh clanging of the telephone bell. He swaggered over to it and picked up the handset, hoping that this call might also bring some excitement. He listened for a few seconds and his heart began to race. It was happening.

"Sarge, Sarge. It's RAF Cranwell. They've got a civilian whom they think is a German spy."

"Another one is it? Seems to be a lot about suddenly." Sergeant O'Flynn dropped the report he had been reading on the desk and heaved himself to his feet. He reached out for the handset."

"I can deal with it if you want Sarge. I've got experience now of..."

"Just give me the damn telephone Crowther and get back to work." He put the handset to his ear and spoke with a severe formality. "This is Sergeant O'Flynn of Boston Police. How can I help you?" He listened for a short while. "So let me get this right, Sergeant Swallow. You think you have a German agent at RAF Cranwell. Would this be the same fella as my Inspector went chasing after to Skegness last night?"

The answer was inaudible to PC Crowther who stood as close as he dared straining to hear the other side of the conversation.

"Well you've got to admit, Sergeant Swallow, it seems quite a coincidence to have two German agents in the space of twelve hours. Are they brothers or something?" O'Flynn listened again. "Well, Sir, you'll have to understand that we can't go chasing off after supposed foreign agents without some evidence. I'll tell you what I'll do. I'll contact my Inspector and see what he thinks and then I'll telephone you back. It won't be quick as the inspector is not in the station at the moment. Right...goodbye, Sir."

O'Flynn dropped the handset onto its cradle with a clatter. "Bloody idiots that lot are. Did we find a German agent last night Crowther?"

"No sarge but we did find the van just as they told us and there was no trace of the driver so..."

"So it might have been some poor sod who'd finished work for the week and was glad to get home for some dinner. Damn fools that lot! Right Crowther, as you like all this spy nonsense, you can get on your bike and go tell Inspector Sadler about that phone call."

Crowther's eyes brightened. He already had started to frame his explanation to the Inspector; perhaps a touch of exaggeration might help, a few extra details. Another trip in the Inspector's car at speed would add very welcome excitement to a dull Saturday morning. "Of course, Sarge. Will he be at home?"

"Saturday mornings he plays golf. Be ready for a long walk and be ready for an earful. He had his dinner interrupted last night and will not take kindly to his golf being interrupted this morning." O'Flynn smiled maliciously at Crowther. "Off you go."

CHAPTER 33

Robbie McBane had asked no more. Healey had said nothing. He looked broken. Lizzie almost felt sorry for him but the thought of him communicating with the Germans dispelled that sentiment very rapidly. Bert Swallow had been despatched to telephone the Police. As Healey was a civilian, the Police were the right people to deal with him.

"I'm going to take you to Sir George Stanley. He asked me to identify the mole and to report to him directly. The Police will then take you away to be tried for treason."

Healey said nothing. His lip quivered at the word 'treason' and Lizzie half expected him to start blubbing. Fortunately, he didn't. It was a solemn procession to the building that housed Turner's office, a prisoner being escorted to the scaffold. It may well result in execution. Difficult given Healey's importance as an aircraft designer though and his role in the war effort. Robbie McBane held Healey by his upper arm as much to keep him upright perhaps as to prevent his escape. Lizzie and Alice followed almost marching in step.

None of them spoke.

They preserved the funereal silence outside Turner's office until the Corporal ushered them in. Turner had been in discussion with Stanley and the two men stood as the four grave faces entered. Healey's head was bowed.

"Sir, I have brought Mr Healey to you as I believe he may have been communicating with the Germans. As yet, I have asked him no direct questions on that subject as I wanted to have senior officers present. Given the seriousness of the offence and the possible consequences, it's important that no defence lawyer can defeat any charge that might be brought. We found telegraphic equipment in Mr Healey's suitcase and, given the Morse Code message we heard coming from his room, suspicion must fall on him."

"Quite right, McBane." Sir George Stanley's head lowered just a little, his eyes narrowing beneath a furrowed brow. "Well, Mr Healey, what have you to say for yourself?"

Arthur Healey raised his head, looking with pleading eyes at Stanley whose expression did not soften. "What was I supposed to do?"

Stanley stared at him for a full five seconds, an interval that felt much longer, his lips squeezed tight together as if to suppress an explosion of anger. When he spoke, his voice was quiet, controlled but unmistakably hostile. "What do you mean?"

Healey's hands spread apart in appeal. "My son..." He seemed to choke and could form no words.

"Your son?"

"My son is a...a...prisoner, taken in '40, Northern France. The Nazis have him in a camp you know..." Again Healey stopped.

"And?"

"He was not much more than a boy. I couldn't bear the thought of what might be happening to him. And then...I was approached...as I left my house one morning."

For all his bull-like stance, Sir George Stanley understood when kindness would yield more than threat. "Perhaps, Mr Healey, you would prefer to sit down and tell us about this. It sounds a complicated story."

When chairs had been found and arranged for everyone in a circle, they all sat as if at a polite tea party. Lizzie became aware of a clock on the mantelpiece ticking, its sound becoming more insistent in the silence before Healey resumed.

"This chap, well spoken, quite smartly dressed... in an overcoat... fell into step with me as I walked to the bus stop. We passed the time of day, commented on the weather, that sort of thing and then he started talking about the war and how things were going. I remember, there was a pause and then he said how terrible it was that young British soldiers were in German Prisoner of War Camps and wouldn't it be better if they could be got out so they were available for other war duties. It seemed like a casual remark but of course before long I had told him about William, my boy."

The clock beat like a monotonous drum as they waited for Healey to continue.

"I thought nothing of it. We said our farewells at my bus stop and he walked on. A couple of days later, he was there again. We had a pleasant chat about this and that. He seemed like an ordinary chap on his way to work. It became a regular thing and I enjoyed our conversations when our paths crossed. He said he worked in a Government department but was based in Bristol. I told him what I do, where I work and so on though not of course anything confidential. He sounded interested but didn't press me for anything."

A shaft of sunlight entered the room, growing slowly in intensity, briefly lighting the carpet, the chair legs, before evaporating.

"Then one morning, he said he had learned from his contacts that the Germans were ready to release some prisoners but in exchange for certain…information. I can remember even now the way he paused before saying the last word. I was puzzled but excited. Could this mean that William might be released? He said no more that day about what information might be needed but he did ask me if I would like William to be released. Why would I not? Any parent would want that."

Sir George Stanley clearly wanted to speed the admission. "So what information did they want and what did you supply?"

"At first, he said they just wanted to know what I was working on. I told him that but a few days later, he said they now wanted more. That happened two or three times. I suppose it was a process of reeling me in gradually to make further revelations. Every time, I asked when William would be released. Finally he said that William would be shot unless I supplied plans for the Meteor. I couldn't allow that to happen." Healey lifted his head a little and his eyes flicked first to Stanley and then each person around the circle.

"So you gave away the details of probably the most important development we have at the moment...a plane that could shorten the war considerably...a weapon that could save countless lives."

"I had to save my son's life." Suddenly Healey was belligerent. "Do you have children? Do you? You would do anything to save your child one minute's pain, that's what good parents do."

As he spoke, Lizzie glanced at Alice. She dropped her head suddenly at Healey's last words, her anguish plain. Lizzie reached out her hand and softly gripped her arm. Alice turned her face and smiled weakly.

Sir George Stanley said nothing for several seconds but he stood, the veins in his neck bulging and his eyes blazing. Suddenly, he erupted. "And what about the thousands of other parents who have lost children in the war? What about the sacrifices they have made? What about the thousands who may die because you were not prepared to make that sacrifice? I have children. My son is a bomber pilot who faces possible death every time he takes his aircraft over enemy territory. My daughter exhausts herself as a nurse, treating the wounded." His voice became low, threatening, ominous. "Every day, like thousands of others, I wonder if I will receive news of my son's death. Don't talk to me about the anxieties of parenthood." Stanley turned away in disgust and perhaps to hide the emotion erupting inside.

Turner took over. Contempt filled every syllable. "What about your loyalty to your country?"

"Loyalty...ha...oh I understand loyalty alright. Trouble is it's not simple is it? For whom does one have the greater loyalty, one's country or one's family?"

Stanley turned back to Healey but he did not look at him

directly. He waved his hand in a gesture of dismissal. "Take him away."

Robbie McBane stood up. "I asked Sergeant Swallow to telephone the local police to come and arrest Mr Healey. Hopefully they will be here soon. Perhaps, Group Captain Turner, you could point me in the direction of your cell."

"Cell?" Healey jumped to his feet. For a moment, Lizzie thought he was going to make a run for it but he stood still with a wild look in his eye. Turner explained where the cells were and Robbie McBane once again held Healey's arm. He led him out of the office.

Lizzie took the chance while she had it. "Sir, did you manage to arrest the German agents last night?" Her question was directed at Turner.

Turner looked puzzled at first before a light came on. "No...no...I'm afraid they gave my men the slip. Damned shame but it was like the proverbial needle in a haystack out there by the coast."

"But Grainger didn't leave with them. I've seen him this morning on the base. Why is he not under arrest?"

"Grainger? Grainger? Why ever would he be under arrest?"

"Because, Sir, he helped those enemy agents escape and he held Alice here at gunpoint as a hostage. He is as much an enemy agent as they are."

Stanley, who had been looking out of the window, spun round. His eyes met Turner's and Lizzie noticed the look between them. What was going on? They knew something they were not telling her or Robbie McBane. "You'll need to leave that with us Miss Barnes. Don't worry, we'll sort him out and everything will be made clear later today."

"But Sir, he is...."

"Thank you Miss Barnes, Miss Frobisher." Stanley bowed slightly, the image of courtesy. "Dismissed."

Before Lizzie could protest, Alice pulled her sleeve and more or less turned her to face the door. "Come on," she whispered in her ear. "Leave it."

◆ ◆ ◆

This was not the right image for an aspiring secret agent. PC Crowther pedalled out of the centre of Boston, weaving around the occasional car and nearly colliding with another cyclist. If the powers that be wanted truly effective policing, they should supply him with a car. He knew the car he would choose. He had seen a picture in one of those posh papers in the newsagents. A Jaguar SS 100. The roof folded down so you could 'feel the wind in your hair' on fine days. A big powerful engine would make a satisfying roar as he sped along the highways and byways, chasing German agents. But here he was, pumping the pedals on his old police-issue bike, heading for the golf club which nestled beside the River Witham.

It seemed like a re-run of yesterday night only, this time, the inspector would be extra cross at having another social engagement disrupted. But what could he do? He was just a foot soldier following orders. If Sadler shouted at him, he would let it go over his head. It was not his fault. Even so, it was with some trepidation that he entered the clubhouse. There seemed to be no one about. He coughed loudly a couple of times but no one came so he peered through an open door into a lounge. He walked in, appearing, he hoped, more confident than he felt.

At last, a portly man with greying hair and a white jacket appeared behind the bar. "Good morning, officer. And what can we do for you?" The man's nose seemed to twitch as he spoke, rather like a hamster. Paul Crowther tried not to look directly at him in case he laughed but there was something fascinating about it. Human nature dictates that we cannot avoid tempting laughter to grip us even when we know we should not. The banana skin at the funeral!

Paul Crowther looked out of the window. "I need to speak to Inspector Sadler. Where will I find him?"

The man looked at his watch. "I should think he'll only be on the second hole by now. Left not long ago. If you walk up that way" he pointed to a tree some distance away, "you should find him."

"Thanks, I'll have a look."

As Crowther opened the door onto the expanse of grass, the steward called after him. "Just keep your head down. The way some of these gentlemen play, it's like the Somme out there." He chuckled. Paul Crowther knew his nose would be twitching but, with great self-control, did not look back. He walked in the direction he had been shown and kept his eyes peeled for stray golf balls. Eventually, beyond the indicated tree, he saw the inspector about to take a swing at the ball. Crowther hung back until he saw the arms come down and the ball fly up into the air. He ran forward.

"Sir, Sir."

Sadler twisted round. "Crowther? What the bloody hell do you want? I hope you're not going to ruin my morning."

CHAPTER 34

"I'm not going to leave it Alice and that's that. We cannot let that man get away with it. Stanley and Turner are hiding something and I'm going to find out what."

"But Lizzie…what can we do? You've already tried with Stanley and it was clear that he and Turner won't tell us what's going on."

"Stanley said we'd know later. How much later I wonder?" Lizzie strode on and Alice had to run to catch her up.

"Lizzie, will you please just stop. You don't know where you're going so why are you striding out as if you do?"

"I know, I know Alice, I'm boiling. If I don't walk I'll scream."

"Let's stop and think. What can we do? We could telephone the Police again but I don't suppose they'd take any notice of us."

Lizzie stopped abruptly and turned to face Alice. She seemed suddenly collected, calm, dangerous. "Well done, Alice. That's what we'll do. We'll wait by the gate until the Police arrive and then I can tell them about Grainger."

They now had a purpose and they headed for the main gate. Lizzie went boldly up to one of the sentries and told him the Police were expected very soon. She then made light conversation with him as if there were nothing unusual about the Police entering an RAF base. The sentry looked puzzled by the whole thing but something about Lizzie commanded respect and attention. He did not ask questions but let her talk. After her initial conversation, Lizzie fell silent and she loitered by the gate with Alice who looked uncomfortable and wishing she had not made the suggestion.

Some twenty minutes later, a large black Wolseley turned into the gateway. There was no clanging bell, no skidding to a stop with screeching tyres as Lizzie had expected. It drifted gently to a halt in front of the gate. One of the sentries went to the driver's window and spoke with the occupant who showed him something, presumably a pass. The sentry waved to his mate and the gate was opened. The car eased through.

"Come on Alice. We'll follow it and have a word with them when they park."

The car drove slowly into the base and disappeared behind the Officers Mess. Lizzie and Alice quickened their pace so that they arrived soon after it had stopped. Unfortunately the driver had already walked away into a building, leaving another officer lounging against the car.

"Excuse me, Officer." The young man straightened to his full height and puffed out his chest. Lizzie knew that tell-tale sign of male self-importance – so easy to appeal to. "My name is Lizzie Barnes, Second Officer Barnes from the Air Transport Auxiliary and this is my navigator, Alice Frobisher. May I know your name?"

"Police Constable Crowther from Boston Police Station. That's Boston in Lincolnshire not Boston in the United States." Crowther smiled at his own attempted humour but neither Lizzie nor Alice responded.

"I think you are here to arrest a German spy," Lizzie continued.

"Might be Miss. What's it to you?"

"I'm wondering if you know that there are in fact two German spies on the base. One has been arrested and put in a cell for you to take into custody but the other is still on the base somewhere. Thank goodness you're here though as you can arrest him."

PC Crowther frowned. "Two German spies. Blimey. We seem to be over-run with them. We've come to arrest a Mr Healey. Who's the other one?"

"A man called Grainger. He claims to be from the Ministry but he's very cagey about which ministry. He helped two German agents escape last night."

"Last night?" Lizzie watched the officer making connections...slowly. "Smart looking bloke? Posh accent? Nice suit?"

"Dark hair, not very tall, arrogant expression and manner," added Lizzie. PC Crowther nodded slowly in recognition. "Did you see him somewhere?"

"Last night. We had a call that a German agent was escaping to Skegness so me and the Inspector chased over there. Couldn't find the agent but this chap – Gr...what's his name?"

"Grainger."

"Him. He turned up in a Land Rover with an assistant looking for him. Showed the Inspector his credentials but the two of them shot off after the German before we could check them out."

"Was his assistant quite short, moustache, black hair, bit of a belly?"

"That's him."

"He was another German agent and Grainger was helping him and another man to escape. Probably picked up by a German ship."

"Or submarine," Alice added.

"It's a chance for you, Officer, to demonstrate to your superiors your initiative and courage." Lizzie watched the young man's face brighten and then turn suddenly serious as if trying to cover up his excitement at the prospect Lizzie had painted.

"How do you know this man Grainger is a spy? I mean I can't go arresting him just on your say-so, Miss."

"I quite understand, Officer. Last night in the Prince of Wales public house – do you know it, in the next village – Grainger held my friend Miss Frobisher at gunpoint as a hostage in order to stop the short German agent being arrested. If that is not a clear indication of collusion with the enemy, I don't know what is."

"Gunpoint? It certainly sounds as though he is a spy." Crowther looked across the parade ground to the accommodation block. "I'll certainly have a word with the Inspector when he comes out."

"That may be too late Officer. Surely you want to help the war effort by apprehending a spy?"

Crowther spluttered. "Of course... naturally...but...you know there are protocols, senior officer and all that. I can't just go off half cock you know."

Alice's quiet voice drew his attention. "Well perhaps it would do no harm to question him while your Inspector's dealing with the other issue and then it at least detains him so he cannot escape. I mean, even now, he may have seen your car, realised the game's up and be making his escape."

"That's a fair point Miss. Probably no harm in asking some questions. Where will I find Mr Grainger?"

Lizzie pointed to the building that housed the Officers Mess. "Somewhere in there, Constable. We'll come with you." Lizzie could sense Alice's disagreement but she would not look at her. "This way PC Crowther. I'm sure you won't be a constable for much longer if you can arrest this man."

Bert Swallow lifted the two family photographs from the walls of his room and carefully folded each in an article of clothing before laying them gently into his kit bag. It wasn't much to show for his life in the RAF. The photographs of aircraft he would leave for the next occupant. He knew that he would not return. He would go to Angela and sort her life out. They would probably move elsewhere and he would seek a discharge from the RAF. There would be plenty of work - war repairs that sort of thing.

He sat on the bed. There was time to kill before he could

leave. He would do his usual checks to make sure the aircraft had been properly prepared for any flying there might be. After some lunch, he would see the top brass off and then leave. He would say nothing to anyone, no farewells, no fanfare, no explanations. The word would get round soon from Turner about his compassionate leave. Days would become weeks and they would soon get used to him not being around. Someone else would fill his shoes. He knew he was no more indispensable than anyone else, however much he had tried to convince himself otherwise over the last few years.

He would like to speak to Alice. She was special. He again felt bitterness fill him. Why, oh why did this have to come up just when there was a chance to establish a relationship with a lovely young woman? She was everything he had hoped for... intelligent, attractive, a lovely gentle manner. He almost felt like seeking her out and telling her everything but he knew he could not.

He thought of her carefully managed hair, tied neatly in a bun, her finely-crafted face, the line of her jaw so precise, so perfect and her eyes last night when she had left him, so soft, so full of understanding, compassion. She would make a lovely wife, a superb mother and even the difficulties of her role and his own could be overcome. He could ask for a transfer or she could give up her ATA role and find something close to him.

He allowed himself a few minutes more of dreaming about a possible future before he shook his head to clear her image from his mind. It was not to be. It was just a dream, another fantasy. Wearily, he stood up. His kit bag, now fully packed was on the floor. He left it there and slowly moved to the door. He must present his usual bright face to the World outside, adopt his customary cheery manner, be ready to chivvy his team along with occasional humour. He should have been an actor; his ability to hide his true feelings and play a part were certainly up to that. Perhaps that's what he would do...become an actor.

Robbie McBane noticed how Inspector Sadler looked almost with pity at the sad little man slumped on a chair in front of him. Healey's eyes were on the floor; he was quivering. It was cold in the cell, its blank walls and spartan nature adding to the chill, but Healey was wearing a thick jumper and a coat so it was not cold that made him shake.

"You admit then that you were in contact with a German agent and you passed classified drawings to him?" Healey nodded and a barely audible grunt escaped his lips. Sadler waited a minute before continuing. "The main thing we need now, Mr Healey, is to establish the names of your contact or contacts, both the one who approached you and the person you sent the morse code message to."

Again Healey grunted and Sadler, with an edge to his voice asked that he repeat what he had said. Healey raised his head but not far enough to look either of his interrogators in the eye. "The man who first made contact called himself Mr Green," he mumbled. I've no idea who received the messages. Someone else based in this country as the transmitter was not very powerful. Perhaps the same man."

"Not much to go on is it? I can't believe that you passed secret drawings to someone purporting to be from a ministry in this country without checking him out."

"He showed me a security pass. It looked official."

Sadler turned away in disgust. Robbie McBane asked for a description of Mr Green but Healey was not able to supply anything that would make identification possible. Mr Green was a nondescript ministry-type, well-spoken, of medium height, brown hair greying at the temples, not over-weight

"You can at least give us the wavelength you transmitted on the other night. That might lead somewhere." Robbie McBane turned to Sadler. "We can perhaps set up something to trace the receiver. I'm no technician but something may be possible. Or we can make contact, perhaps ask for a meeting as if we are Healey."

Sadler turned back to Healey. "What I don't understand, Mr Healey, is why you would trust a complete stranger to get your son out of a Nazi POW camp. I mean how did you check out his authenticity?"

Healey raised his head fully for the first time in the conversation and looked directly at Sadler. "I didn't but the possibility of saving my son from death or even prolonged suffering was worth taking." His voice became a whine. "I had to try."

"Does your son know how his release is to be achieved?"

Healey faltered, his lips moving soundlessly for a moment as he understood the implications of the question. "N...no...he doesn't."

"And how do you suppose he will feel when he knows his freedom was bought by his father's betrayal? He will think of the hundreds of fellow British soldiers suffering still in Nazi camps while he walks freely along the street." Sadler's voice was rising. "He'll wonder how many people will die because this War will be prolonged by your selfishness. And what about your fellow engineers and designers? What will they make of your betrayal?"

Healey said nothing and then mumbled, "I did what any parent would do."

CHAPTER 35

PC Crowther strode towards the building to which Lizzie had pointed; she and Alice followed. As he reached the entrance, his pace slackened. Lizzie could see him swallow hard, his steps faltering, clearly nervous. Poor man, she thought, he is out of his depth but needs must.

"Straight through here, Officer." Lizzie walked past him and pushed open one of the two oak doors. Both were glazed, small neat panes of glass with bevelled edges that distorted the view of the interior. She held open the door for him and Alice and then nodded towards the reception desk at which a corporal sat. He stood as they approached.

Crowther stood tall and cleared his throat. "Ah, good morning. I am Police Constable Crowther from Boston Police Station. I'd like to speak to a Mr Grainger. Where would he be?"

"He was down here earlier, Officer, but I'm not sure where he will be now. Let me check the Officers Lounge. Please wait here." The corporal smiled more to himself than to them and strolled away. The three of them stood awkwardly in the foyer, PC Crowther looking about him at the elegance of the place. A few minutes later, the corporal returned leading Grainger. When the latter saw the two young women with the police officer, his face broke into the arrogant smile so familiar to Lizzie and Alice.

"And what can I do for you Officer?" Before Crowther could reply, Grainger continued. "Didn't I meet you last night at the coast with your inspector...what was his name...S..."

"Sadler, Sir. I have been given information that you held this lady here as a hostage at gunpoint yesterday evening to enable a German agent to escape."

Grainger laughed, a short bark, and then his expression changed to one of fury. "I have a job to do, Officer, and I can do without interfering women. I am accountable to someone considerably more senior than you and therefore I do not have to explain myself. I spoke with your Inspector Sadler last night and showed him my credentials with which he was satisfied. That is enough for you."

"Credentials can be forged." Alice's sudden interjection drew the eyes of everyone in the foyer. The corporal hovered behind his desk and looked nervously at the scene in front of him.

"Yes but mine aren't. And what's it got to do with you? You're not in the Police nor the secret services. How dare you question my integrity." Grainger breathed in slowly and deeply. When he resumed, his voice was quiet, controlled but laden with menace. "So, Constable, if there's nothing else, I'll return to my paper."

"Nothing else?" Alice's voice was as quiet but filled with anger. You held me hostage with a gun to my temple. That might be acceptable in Nazi Germany but it is not acceptable here. That man...Bob...that you took away. He is a German agent. He was on the base the night before last. He may have killed Airman Sinclair. What is that if not betrayal of this country?"

Grainger's amused smile returned. He stepped closer to Alice. Lizzie tensed waiting to spring at him if he tried anything. "I am sorry I had to hold a gun to your head but I had to make McBane release Mr Edwards. There was no danger to you – the safety catch was on – but I knew McBane would do anything I asked if he thought a young woman was in danger. You see, he wants to be a hero does young McBane. He would have taken a bullet rather than let Edwards go, but he would never let harm come to you. I suppose it's quite admirable really but I did what I had to do."

"So you're admitting that you enabled Edwards, a German agent, to escape?"

"That's right, Miss Barnes. That's exactly what I did."

PC Crowther looked confused and alarmed at the same time. "So, Sir, you admit you helped a German agent escape?"

"That's right, Constable."

"In that case, Sir, I am arresting you on suspicion of treason." Crowther took a step forward, grabbed Grainger's arm and swung him around. In a deft movement of his other hand he whipped out handcuffs from his tunic and clamped them on Grainger's arms behind his back. They closed with a satisfying clunk.

◆ ◆ ◆

Bert Swallow pushed the door of the Sick Bay open tentatively. He stepped inside and let the door swing shut with a soft swish behind him. The corridor that faced him was stark, sterile...bare walls, a hard floor and that unmistakable smell of hospital. Was it the cleaning fluid they used or the drugs? The smell was of antiseptic, seeming to stress this was a place of hygiene, order, no nonsense tolerated. That was good but it felt alien to him, as if he were an impostor. He knew of course why he felt that way.

He took a few steps along the corridor. He had been in here before – the previous morning and some months before that but he wondered whether he should have come. Why had he come? There was nothing to be done here but he had not been able to resist the pull. He had to find out why, what happened. Sinclair had been alive yesterday morning. It was not right that he had died.

A nurse stepped out of a side room and spoke. "Sergeant Swallow. Back again? What can we do for you?"

"I came...I came to ask about...Sinclair."

The nurse's face did not soften. A wisp of dark hair escaped her hat, the only thing out of order in her impeccable appearance. But there was no warmth, none of the kindness one would expect from a woman of her profession.

"Yes, Sinclair. Very sad that."

"How did he die? I mean he was alive when I visited yesterday morning...when Sergeant McBane talked with him too." As the nurse explained how a blow on the head had led to a bleed on the brain, resulting in a delayed death, Bert Swallow watched her face. It was plain, rounded cheeks disguising the bone structure beneath, taking away definition of her features. The eyes were slightly sunk, a nondescript greyish colour. There was something self-satisfied about her whole demeanour, a woman who was confident in her own expertise. That was good, of course, but where was the doubt, where was the remorse that one of her patients had died in her care?

"Thank you Nurse Jarvis for explaining that." He hesitated.

"Was there something else, Sergeant?"

"I wonder....could I see the body? I know that sounds rather morbid but he was in my unit and I'd like to say my farewells."

"I'm afraid the body has been taken to the mortuary in Boston, Sergeant. I'm sure they would let you see him there. I'm told he lived up North somewhere so I guess he'll be taken there to be buried."

"I see. I have to go away later today – a problem I have to sort out. I would have written to his parents...family...not sure if he was married actually...but I won't have time..."

"There's no need to worry about that, Sergeant. Group Captain Turner's office will handle all that."

Bert Swallow half turned away but again hesitated. He wanted to shout, he wanted to demand why they had let Sinclair die? It was crazy that a man who had been alive the previous morning had died a few hours later, whatever she had said about a bleed on the brain. Surely he can't have been hit that hard if he was able to talk the following morning? "Of course," he said, "yes, of course. Well thank you Nurse for your help."

"That's quite alright Sergeant but now...if there's nothing

else, I must get on."

"Yes, yes." Bert Swallow nodded to her and backed away as if from a royal person, before turning and fleeing from the building.

◆ ◆ ◆

"What the blazes are you doing? You cannot arrest me. Your superiors will know about this and by God you'll know about it then. Get these things off me."

Grainger was shouting, his voice reverberating from the walls of the foyer. The corporal disappeared from behind his desk. Crowther, still holding onto Grainger's hands, looked at Lizzie in alarm.

"Don't take any notice, Constable. This man is a bully as well as being a German agent. He's just trying to bluff his way out of it. I suggest you take him away with you and lock him up in your cell. He's a civilian not a member of His Majesty's Armed Forces and is therefore your concern." Lizzie looked at Grainger.

He snarled and then bellowed, "You really are stupid. I'll see to it that you are booted out of the ATA. Trueman must be mad ever to have let you enter."

The front door swung open. Inspector Sadler and Robbie McBane hurried into the foyer, staring in disbelief at the scene that confronted them. "What's going on, Crowther?"

PC Crowther did not relinquish his grip on Grainger's arm but he faced his superior. I have been given information by these ladies here that this man is in fact a German agent. He held Miss...Miss..."

"Frobisher," Alice supplied.

"...at gunpoint yesterday evening in order to get a German agent away from Sergeant McBane. That man who was with him last night...you know, Sir, by the coast, was not his assistant but a German agent. Mr Grainger here has admitted it."

Sadler looked from Crowther to Grainger then at Robbie McBane. He was clearly totally baffled. "Mr Grainger, you showed me your identity last night and said you are a member of the Secret Services...the British Secret Services that is."

"I am and I don't take kindly to your turnip-picker here slapping handcuffs on me. Get them off." He pushed his arms out as far as he could behind him. "Why can't you lot let me get on with my job?" The shout was full of anger, not an appeal.

"Did you hold this young woman at gunpoint yesterday evening, Sir?"

"Yes I did. I had no choice because of that wretched interfering Scotsman." Robbie McBane squared his shoulders. Lizzie could see he wanted to hit Grainger...as she did herself. The arrogance of the man was astounding.

"I think you need to offer an explanation, Sir." Sadler spoke quietly, firmly but his eyes betrayed contempt. Lizzie realised he shared the dim view that she, Stanley and plenty of others had of secret agents. How could anyone trust a man who dealt in subterfuge, deceit, and downright lies? The antipathy she had felt towards Grainger almost from their first meeting twisted her own view and she looked forward to him being put down, arrested, tried and sentenced at least to a long prison term. The Country could do without his type.

"I don't have to explain myself to you nor to anyone else. I take my orders from the highest authority in the Land and as soon as I can get through to that person, you will be regretting that you let your carrot-cruncher here loose with a pair of handcuffs. He's been put up to it of course by her." Grainger's eyes drilled into Lizzie. She was determined not to flinch and met his gaze but inside she had to confess the naked hatred there almost made her wilt.

They stood in a hostile circle and no one spoke. At last, Robbie McBane said, "I think Inspector Sadler you should take Mr Grainger in for questioning to your Police Station. Perhaps a night or two in a cell will reduce his arrogance and encourage him to co-operate with our enquiries."

"That's exactly what I'm going to do."

If Grainger had shouted before, it was nothing to the indecipherable bellow of rage that greeted this suggestion.

"You'd be better to come quietly, Sir. You don't want to make a fool of yourself."

Hurried footsteps approached along the corridor from Turner's office. Group Captain Turner was followed by Sir George Stanley and the corporal scurried along behind them. The two senior officers took in the scene. Stanley's face softened into the merest hint of a smile, his blue eyes twinkling. He quickly removed it when Grainger shouted again.

"Sir George, will you please get these imbeciles out of my hair? I've had enough."

Sir George looked around the cluster of people in the foyer. "I think it's time for an explanation. Inspector Sadler, please ask your constable to release Mr Grainger. I think it's best if you all come to Group Captain Turner's office. This has gone on too long." He turned on his heel and began to stomp away, turning to fling a final command over his shoulder. "Oh and Turner, arrange for someone to get Butler here. Don't want to have to go through it twice."

CHAPTER 36

Bert Swallow knew he should not have come but he could not stop himself. Before he left for the North, he needed to know about Sinclair's death. Apparently, the barmaid, Molly, had been adamant that Bob Edwards and his sidekick could not have murdered Sinclair. She said she was either with Sinclair or with Bob Edwards all the time. The only possibility was that Bob's mate, Harry, had done it. He must have done. What other explanation could there be? Bert knew he just needed to convince Molly that her recollection of the time between her leaving with Bob and the moment Harry joined them was longer than the two seconds she had claimed. Mind you, two seconds was long enough to hit someone over the head.

Slowly, he climbed down from the Land Rover and approached the door of the pub. It was lunchtime so perhaps would not be too busy, though, being a Saturday, it may be. He pushed open the door and ducked inside. Just a few locals sitting around, mostly at tables. Molly was behind the bar. She looked up and gave a broad smile when she saw him.

"Now then, Sir, what can I get you?"

"Just a small beer, please." She bustled about taking a glass from a shelf at the back and poured his beer.

"You don't normally come in at this time of day do you?" Her smile broadened, her eyebrows lifting, as she placed the glass in front of him.

"No...no, I don't." Bert tried not to respond to her flirting but the temptation was strong.

"I expect you get fed up with that lot up there don't you? I mean all those rules and regulations and stuff. I couldn't be doing with it meself."

"Molly, I need to ask you some questions about the other night."

She seemed unconcerned. "Which night you talking about?"

"Thursday."

"Thursday?" She seemed not to recognise there had been anything different about Thursday. "Thursday...oh yeah, I remember. What d'you need to know? I mean I've already told that Scottish bloke about it and answered his questions. I don't know nothin' else."

"I just need to go over it again. You went onto the RAF base that night with a man called Bob Edwards and his friend Harry."

"That's right. It was a laugh." She leaned forward conspiratorially over the bar, her ample bosom visible in the opening of her blouse. "They wanted to surprise their mate. I'd say we achieved that alright. But sorry to hear the poor sod died."

"I think you told Sergeant McBane that there was not time for Harry to do anything before he joined you and Bob after the ...surprise."

"That's right. A couple of seconds at the most."

"How can you be so sure about that, Molly? I mean, when things are happening quickly, it's hard to be precise about time. You said two seconds but it could easily have been five or ten, couldn't it?"

"Well I suppose so... but I'm sure it was only a couple of seconds."

Bert Swallow took a sip of his beer and Molly went to the sink to wash a couple of glasses. He waited until she had turned towards him again. "You do realise Molly, that it is an offence to enter an RAF base without express permission?"

She laughed. "Yeah but we weren't doing no harm, just having a bit of fun. Don't think anyone would be interested in that."

Bert's voice became harder. "Do you know what happened

on Thursday night?"

"How d'you mean. I've told that Scottish one what we did."

"There was a young airman guarding a plane. He was hit on the head and died as a result of his injuries. The only people who could have done that are Bob, Harry or...you."

Suddenly Molly became angry. She flung down the tea towel she had picked up. "You're not pinning that on me. I never done nothin' and neither did Bob. I'm certain Harry couldn't have done that because young Micky was still hollering looking for his trousers when Harry joined us."

"Perhaps they went back afterwards to finish the job?"

"Well Bob certainly didn't 'cos he was with me...in his van." Molly's chin jutted forward and her eyes were bright with indignation. "I like a bit of fun and I know we shouldn't have been on the base but doing somethin' you're not supposed to is half the fun ain't it? It's the most excitement I've had 'ere in years."

Bert Swallow took another long pull from his beer. He contemplated the towelling beer mat on the bar in front of him. "I don't know whether you realise this, Molly, but Bob and his mate are German agents. They've been helped to escape to Germany. You could be charged with aiding and abetting foreign spies. I think you may need to adjust your account of that night. There is no other explanation."

"Well there was some peculiar carrying on last night. That Scottish fella arrested Bob but another guy came in with a gun and took Bob away. It was a right do I can tell you. But," she leaned forward over the counter again to make her point, "I know people, I'm a good judge of them and there is no way that Bob would hurt a fly. He's a lovely bloke – bit of a lad, yes, but he just wants to have fun. And I can't believe he's a German agent." She straightened and her eyes narrowed. "Harry, now he's a different kettle of fish. Something dangerous about him but he can't of hit that young bloke on the head. Like I said, Micky was still shouting and hollering about his trousers when Harry joined us. That's what I know and I'm sticking to that, however much you want to pin it on Bob and Harry."

Bert Swallow shrugged. "As you wish, Molly." He threw down his last card. "You should be ready when the Police come to arrest you. Bob and Harry have escaped but you have not." He lifted his glass and drained the remaining contents. "Look after yourself, Molly, because no one else will."

Molly's mouth was open wide. "Arrest me?" but Bert Swallow left the pub letting the door bang behind him.

◆ ◆ ◆

They sat in silence. There had been some sorting out to find enough chairs. Lizzie's eyes flitted around the ragged circle: Stanley standing at the front with Turner, Grainger, lolling back in his chair which he had pushed back to distance himself from the others, William Butler, his face like stone, Robbie McBane, legs crossed, looking troubled, on the verge of anger, Alice, as calm and apparently composed as always, Inspector Sadler sitting erect, expectant and Crowther shifting uneasily in his chair, looking uncomfortable, out of place.

Stanley cleared his throat. "What I'm about to tell you will make some of you angry. That is understandable but I want you to contain your feelings until you have heard the full explanation. You will, I know, feel that you should have...indeed could have been told this before but there is a very good reason why that was not possible."

He looked around the circle of faces, his squat frame set firmly on his feet which were planted slightly apart. "I will start at the very beginning. We have of course been developing the Meteor for some time. You know from the briefing the other night, how important this aircraft is to the war effort. As far as we know, it is the only jet aircraft under development in any Allied country. It is crucial that the Germans are not able to steal our technology and improve their plane to compete with it."

The urge to shout that Grainger had done exactly that was almost too strong for Lizzie to suppress. She glared at Grainger but he was looking out of the window, unconcerned by the proceedings.

"About a month ago, we discovered from one of our agents in Germany that some details about the Meteor had been obtained by the Germans but he did not know how. It was of course top secret so it meant it had to be someone working on the design of the aircraft or the new engine. We needed some way of persuading the Germans that the Meteor and its engines were not ready for service and we needed to find out where the leak was."

He paused, for several seconds while he examined the carpet. When he looked up, his face was set hard. "I'm not a fan of subterfuge. I'm a direct man and I like to operate directly. If you have an enemy, destroy him, that's my view. But there are powers higher than me and it was decided, at the highest level of Government, that a trick was needed, something that would convince Jerry that he need have no concerns about the Meteor. I'll ask Mr Grainger to tell the next part of the story. You need to know that Mr Grainger is from The Directorate of Military Intelligence, Section Six."

"Thank you Sir George." Grainger slowly rose to his feet. His voice had resumed its characteristic arrogant drawl. "I am described as being from the Ministry, because my role is essentially secret. I am charged with finding ways of persuading the enemy that things which are false, are true and vice versa. That means at times enabling things to happen that some of you may find abhorrent. It means, at times, working with people even I find abhorrent. But such abhorrence is fine for those who live in a secure World where right is right and wrong is wrong. In my World, things are often turned on their head. I do things that you would regard as wrong because the result is a good far greater than any crime committed in achieving the goal."

"That sounds like just clever words to me." Lizzie had not

been able to help herself.

"Ah Miss Barnes. A spade is a spade and so on...Spare me your righteous anger at least until you've heard me out." Grainger had turned to look with disdain at Lizzie and now turned back. His eyes were bright; he was enjoying himself.

"As Sir George said, it was decided at the highest level that we needed some way of convincing Jerry that the Meteor did not work. Enter Mr Bob Edwards. Before the war, Bob Edwards was a criminal, part of a notorious gang called the Jelly Gang because they used gelignite to blow open safes. Things started getting hot and Bob left the mainland to continue his career in Jersey. He was arrested, imprisoned and then the Germans invaded. Whilst in prison, he persuaded the Germans that if they released him, he would return to these shores and act as a spy for them."

Silence amongst the group. PC Crowther sat forward in his chair like a child riveted by a ghost story.

"We knew about it, of course, and were ready to arrest him as soon as he landed but, to his credit...I think...as soon as he was dropped by parachute into Norfolk, he made his way to a Police station and handed himself in. After some considerable investigation and assessment of his character, we decided to accept his offer of acting as a double agent. You see, Bob Edwards is a chancer, a man with the gift of the gab, someone who never seems to be concerned by anything and who will grab any situation and turn it to his advantage. His biggest fault is that he's a womaniser and that can be a big liability. He nearly ruined this operation because of it...that girl from the pub, Molly is it?" Grainger shook his head.

"So let me get this straight." Robbie McBane uncrossed his legs. The Germans sent Bob Edwards to sabotage the Meteor but he was really working for us?"

"Not quite, Sergeant, but working for both sides is part of it. Let me please explain how we had used Bob before and very successfully I might add. In February, you may have read about the sabotage of the Mosquito factory in Hertfordshire. The Germans believe that one of their agents blew it up, a belief that we encouraged by releasing photographs of apparently massive damage. In fact, Bob Edwards, with our encouragement, slipped over the fence one night and blew up some minor buildings away from the main factory. He returned to Germany and was treated as a hero, his credibility as an agent absolutely secure."

"Blowing up one Meteor is hardly going to impress the Germans though is it?"

Grainger smiled. "Quite right, Inspector. So he did not blow it up." There were protests around the circle and Grainger held up his hands. "Bear with me, please. I will reveal all."

CHAPTER 37

Molly stared open-mouthed at the door. She was not given to worry but she could feel a tightening in her chest, something between a fluttering and a pain. Bob and Harry murderers? That couldn't be true. She was certain Harry had joined her and Bob while Sinclair was still shouting about his trousers. Harry couldn't have hit him. And why would he want to hit a mate anyway? It made no sense. It was all a bit of fun. Why did that Sergeant bloke come to the pub trying to make out Bob and Harry killed Micky? And German agents? What absolute nonsense! Bob certainly didn't have the guile to be a secret agent.

What should she do? She felt a twinge of panic. If the Police did come calling, she needed to get her Dad on her side. What had Swallow said? She could be arrested for entering an RAF base unauth… something. She needed to warn her Dad and then she needed to find Bob and Harry to prove they were not to blame.

She heard her father's heavy tread on the wooden stairs from the cellar. Seconds later he appeared in the bar, blowing noisily.

"I swear those stairs get steeper every day."

Molly put on her sweetest smile. She knew he could not resist the little girl act. "Daaad?"

"Yes?"

"I've just had a very strange visit from a Sergeant at RAF Cranwell…not the one who was in last night…but he has been in here several times before. I recognise him."

"So what? Hope he bought a drink."

"Yes…just a half…but…the thing is, um, you know those

266

two roofers?"

"Bob and what's 'is name? Yeah."

"This Sergeant fellow said they were German agents."

"I know. I was there last night remember."

"But...they can't be surely? I mean they were nice blokes, well Bob was anyway."

Molly's father looked up from sorting bottles behind the bar. "I thought you'd taken a shine to 'im."

"Maybe. But Dad they're roofers from Skegness. I bet if we went over there, we'd be able to find them."

"Why?"

"Because I want to check that they're not agents...that they didn't tell me a pack of lies."

"I wouldn't know how to start finding them. But I tell you now, I'm not gadding over to Skegness on some wild goose chase. Let the Police deal with them. Nothing to do with us."

Molly was silent for a while. Absent-mindedly, she moved chairs closer to tables. "There's something you should know, Dad." She didn't wait for a response but he did look up. "The other night, I went with Bob and Harry in their van to play a trick on one of their mates who works on the Base. We climbed over the fence and had a bit of fun with him. That sergeant who came today said I could be arrested for going onto the Base without permission. But I mean, it was a bit of fun, that's all. I can't be arrested for that can I?"

"You silly girl. Course you can. What did you do that for? Ain't you got any sense?"

"But we didn't do anything...you know like we didn't pinch anything or damage anything."

"Makes no difference. Well if the Police come, you'll need to deal with it. Don't look at me to stop 'em." He flung the last bottle he was stacking into the rack and stomped into the kitchen.

She had to do something. She couldn't just leave it. There was no way she could get to Skegness on her own. By the time she got a bus there and did some asking around, she might miss the last bus back. Her dad would have a fit anyway when he found out where she had gone. Perhaps she should go to the Base, speak to someone senior, tell them what actually happened, tell them that Bob and Harry can't have murdered Micky Sinclair.

Five minutes later, Molly, in overcoat, gloves and headscarf, was cycling towards RAF Cranwell. The wind was not strong but it had gone round more to the East since yesterday bringing with it a definite chill. Cycling kept her warm though and she pressed on, thinking about what she would say when she got there. She needed to use her charm on the sentry, she knew that much. She allowed herself a brief smile. Men...they were all the same. They couldn't resist a bit of female charm and maybe some flirting.

At last, she approached the gate. She undid the bottom buttons of her coat so that it fell either side of her. She then slid her skirt higher up her thighs so that, as she pedalled slowly towards the gate, more of her legs would be visible. The eyes of the sentry hungrily settled on them. She hopped off her bike and stopped in front of the gate. The young sentry looked embarrassed.

"Morning, Officer." A bit of flattery helped too. "I have some important information which I would like to give to your commanding officer." She blew out hard and smiled, lowering her eyes a little.

"Right Miss. Well if you tell me what it is, I can pass it on."

"It's far too important I'm afraid...secret...about the airman who was murdered the other night."

The sentry, Ben Wallace, of course knew about Micky Sinclair. Word travels quickly in a closed community such as an air base. "Well I dunno, Miss. It's not usual to let civilians in unless it's been arranged beforehand. You know what I mean."

"Of course but...what's your name Sergeant?"

"No, Miss, I'm not a sergeant just an airman. Airman Wallace."

"That's a bit of a mouthful. You must have a Christian

name." She edged closer to him and smiled, looking into his eyes and pouting her lips. She could see him falter, his feet shuffle on the ground.

He looked away. "It's Ben, Miss."

"What a lovely name. I'm Molly...from the pub at Leasingham...you know, The Prince of Wales. I can get you a drink on the house when you're next over...Ben."

"That's nice, Molly, but I don't think I can let you in."

"Why not just phone through and explain I have important information about Sinclair's death. I bet they'll want to hear it."

Ben Wallace shrugged and went into the small gatehouse. Molly watched him lift the telephone receiver and, leaning as far forward as she could, hear him ask to be put through to the corporal on duty at Group Captain Turner's office. She knew how to get her way. She always did.

From an office near the gate, Bert Swallow watched the young woman being escorted to the building that housed Turner's office. His hand shook slightly as he placed his mug of tea on a table.

Grainger's glance skated over the assembled group. "We had word from Bob Edwards a couple of weeks ago that he had been tasked with returning to this country to get more information about the Meteor. They wanted pictures of the engine and the aircraft. We knew we had this test flight coming up and we...I ..suggested he came here. It meant that he could take still photographs of the engines and aircraft but I also suggested he took a film of the test flight. I said he should make sure he brought another agent with him."

"Why so?" Inspector Sadler again.

"Because, we needed a second agent to be able to verify to

the Germans that the pictures had been obtained by stealth and that they were genuine. This preserved Bob's status as a trusted agent. Then the subterfuge proper began." Grainger turned to Group Captain Turner. "Your story from here, Sir."

Grainger slumped back in his chair and Turner stood, looking slightly awkward. "Like Air Chief Marshall Stanley, I am uncomfortable with these...ruses. I'm a fighting man and believe in a fair fight." Lizzie noticed Grainger look away as if he thought Turner was naïve.

"Two Meteor aircraft were delivered to this base some days ago...at least I should say one complete aircraft and one dummy – real on the outside but without engines. We had a very small team, led by Sergeant Swallow under the strictest secrecy, prepare the second aircraft. Mock engines were created and fitted, engines that were nothing like the real ones and hence which would give no one any clue as to how the real ones worked. That aircraft was fitted with large batteries and two electric motors linked to the wheels."

Turner glanced nervously at Butler. "You, Mr Butler, examined an aircraft when you arrived. That of course was the real one. The dummy was under a tarpaulin at the back of the hangar. After your second inspection with Mr Healey, the two aircraft were switched. Now Bob Edwards was not tasked to sabotage the aircraft but to photograph it and film the test flight. The dummy aircraft is what they filmed. Bob knew that would be the case but his German fellow agent did not. Explosives were fitted in the morning inside each of the mock engines." Turner looked around nervously. Butler was staring at him.

"Yesterday morning, the dummy aircraft was rolled out for the test flight. It appeared to accelerate down the runway and then blew up. That was being filmed by Bob Edwards and his fellow agent from a secluded part of the airfield. There was never any danger to the pilot, we made sure of that but he acted badly injured for the sake of the film the Germans would see."

"I thought it wasn't real," Lizzie blurted. "Bert Swallow's shock when it blew up seemed unconvincing and he glossed over the flags when I pointed them out."

"The flags, Miss Barnes?" Sir George Stanley swivelled his thick neck and gazed at Lizzie.

"As the Meteor started down the runway, the flags at the end – in its wake – hardly changed. If the engines were as powerful as Mr Butler said, those flags should have been streaming out from the poles."

Sir George Stanley smiled to himself and nodded. "Well observed."

"So you sabotaged the plane yourselves?" Robbie McBane spoke with slow and menacing deliberation.

"That's correct, Sergeant. And now I'll hand back to Mr Grainger."

Grainger stood again. "It was crucial that the film taken of the test flight showing the Meteor engines blowing up was taken back to Germany and that the two agents could testify as to how it had been obtained. The Germans will now believe, we hope, that our new aircraft does not work. They will relax, have a laugh about the hopeless English, while we get the Meteor into service and use it to smash their aircraft over France. So, I'm afraid I had to ensure that they and their cargo made it away from these shores...whatever the cost."

Robbie McBane and Lizzie shot to their feet at the same time. "You held a gun to the head of Alice Frobisher to prevent Edwards being arrested. Are you telling me, you would have used that pistol?"

Grainger looked McBane in the eye. "Yes, Sergeant, if you had forced me to."

"How on earth can you justify that?" Lizzie almost screamed.

Grainger paused before replying. All eyes were upon him. "If this mission had failed and the Germans had found other ways of getting the truth about the Meteor, if they managed to sort the issues with their own jet fighter – which of course they probably will do at some point – how many of our forces, our civilians would have died?" His quiet voice began to rise in volume and pitch. "Ten, a hundred, a thousand, ten thousand? What is one life when compared with so many?" He stepped close to Lizzie. "I'd put a bullet through my own brain if I thought it would save so many." He turned away and stared out of the window. His voice was barely more than a whisper. "I'm sorry, indeed I am sorry Miss Frobisher. It would have grieved me to cause you any harm but, as I said, I'm engaged in a part of the War where desperate measures are sometimes required, where the normal rules don't apply."

"I understand, Mr Grainger. Your apology is accepted."

"Thank you...thank you." He subsided onto his chair.

Robbie and Lizzie also sat down. Silence fell on the room for what seemed an age but was only a few seconds. Then William Butler broke it. "Why on earth was all this kept from us? Had we been told, there would have been none of this... this... anger... this misunderstanding."

"Yes that's the hard part...not one which Turner and I found easy," Stanley said. "But you'll remember I said we knew we had a mole. All the aircraft design team fell under suspicion as it was the plans for the aircraft itself that had been leaked. We now know it was Healey but we did not know that until this morning. Had we told others about the dummy Meteor, we would have given away our own subterfuge. That could have been passed to the Germans and they would know the whole thing was a hoax."

"So you didn't trust us?" Butler made no attempt to disguise the disgust in his voice.

"I'm afraid that's how it is. We had no idea whom we could trust."

No one spoke for a long time.

CHAPTER 38

Trust, such a small word but such a major issue. Who could one trust in these dark days? Not the news it seems, managed as it was by Government agents. Lizzie had seen the coverage of the sabotage at the Mosquito factory. It had been utterly convincing but it was a fabrication.

Lizzie looked at the faces in the circle, some like Butler's screwed up with anger and hostility, others like Stanley's embarrassed. The only one who seemed unconcerned was Grainger, the architect of the whole fiasco. Was such deception permissible? Does war allow normal values to be set aside in favour of lies and subterfuge?

Lizzie wanted to scream "no" in answer to her question but a nagging thought prevented her. Perhaps against an enemy like Hitler, anything was permissible. Winning was essential for the good of humanity; such a monster could not be allowed to succeed. Her understanding had changed in an instant, as if an earthquake had opened a huge crack in the ground. The anger that had filled her moments before had left her. She felt the silence needed to be broken, the conversation needed to move on.

"Can I just clarify something? How is it that Bob and Harry had access to a roofers' van that nobody seemed to miss?"

"The van they 'discovered' was arranged by myself. It was parked in Skegness ready for them with ladders already on the roof. And, yes, before you mention it, I did slip Bob a piece of paper with information such as the name of the guard."

Lizzie said nothing for a moment. "What happens to Mr Healey now?" she asked quietly, making sure no resentment tainted her voice.

"I will question him over the next few days and see if we can establish whom he was contacting. If we can discover that and send another message, we can provide the Germans with confirmation that the Meteor failed. We can perhaps gain some advantage from Healey's betrayal." He paused and looked more directly at Lizzie. "And, by the way, well done for picking up that message he sent. It was observant of you and crucial in discovering our mole."

"Goodness Mr Grainger. That sounds like a compliment."

He smiled briefly at her. "Well yes. I suppose it's useful sometimes to have a nosey female around."

"I see it hurts you to admit that women can be useful. Still at least you won't have to suffer my flying on the return journey. It was obviously very difficult for you to have a female crew."

He shrugged. "Needs must..."

Lizzie wanted to continue the conversation, challenging Grainger about his attitudes to women, but there was a sharp rap on the door followed by the entry of the corporal who stepped close to Turner and spoke quietly in his ear. Turner frowned and replied. The corporal left the office and a minute later returned with a young woman - Molly. When she saw the assembled group, she blushed and looked anxiously around the room.

Turner brought a chair from the side of the room and set it down in the circle. "Do please sit down my dear. The corporal tells me you have information about the death of Airman Sinclair."

"Yeah, that's right. Um...well...I may as well be straight. Me and Bob and Harry, that's the two roofers from Skegness, climbed over the fence the other night to play a joke on Micky Sinclair. Well least they was going to play the trick but I sort of went along for the ride – didn't know what they was up to until we got here. I didn't know Micky but the idea was to flirt a bit and give him a drink for 'is birthday. So we climbed over the fence and I...you know...had a bit of a cuddle and then after that, we left."

Her words flooded from her mouth and Stanley looked bemused. In an attempt to slow the deluge, Turner asked her how they had climbed over the fence.

"They used the ladders, the ones they had on top of the van. I mean being roofers they would have ladders wouldn't they?" The torrent resumed. "The thing is, I was with Micky or Bob the whole time, so it can't have been him that killed Micky and anyway they were mates and Harry can't have hit 'im 'cos Micky was still shouting, looking for his trousers, when Harry joined us. If he'd have hit him, Micky wouldn't have been shouting would he?"

Robbie McBane gently interrupted. "Molly, you told us this before. So what's different?"

"That Sergeant - you know the one who was with you the other night when we had the band in the pub – came to see me a short while ago and he was saying that Bob and Harry are German agents and that I needed to change my story 'cos I couldn't be remembering right. But I know what happened. I was there and I'm sure Harry never done for Micky. And why would a pair of roofers be German agents?"

She stopped suddenly.

"D'you mean Sergeant Swallow?" Robbie McBane was frowning. "Why would he be visiting you?"

"Dunno but it was very unpleasant, threatened me with prison and things."

Grainger sat forward. "Molly, I have to tell you that Bob and Harry are in truth German agents. They are not roofers."

"You was the one with the gun in the pub yesterday evening wasn't you?"

"That's correct."

"So you're a German agent as well are you?"

"No Molly, I work for the British Government. It's a long story which need not concern you but it was essential to the war effort that Bob and Harry left this country."

"I don't know about all this agent stuff but I know what happened the other night and neither Bob nor Harry hit Micky.

And if I have to be arrested for breaking into the base, then you'd better do so now but it was just a bit of fun."

"That's up to you, Group Captain Turner. Unauthorised entry to a base is of course an offence and we could charge the young lady but I don't see why she should face charges when the other two have got away scot free." Sadler looked daggers at Grainger.

Grainger sighed in a rather histrionic fashion. "As I've explained, Inspector, there are times when national security over-rides everyday norms. It was essential that the two agents returned to Germany with the..." he glanced at Molly, "... evidence."

"I agree with you Inspector. We have no wish to press charges against you, my dear, but please ensure it does not happen again." Turner paused before continuing. "So if neither Harry nor Bob killed young Michael Sinclair, who did?"

Lizzie looked at Alice and their eyes met. "Michael? Michael... of course. Micky would be a Michael. What was the name of the young man mentioned in that letter you saw Alice?"

"Michael."

"Sinclair was from the North-east wasn't he?"

"Aye, he was. Newcastle I think," said Robbie.

"Where does Sergeant Swallow live, Sir?"

Turner shrugged but Alice responded. "His sister lives in Newcastle."

Lizzie was now sitting bolt upright. "Robbie, what was it again that Sinclair thought he heard his attacker say?"

"That's far more sinister."

"That's far more...or perhaps it was...'That's for me sister'...said with a North east accent, it could easily have been that."

Robbie McBane nodded, recognition lighting his eyes. "I think you've cracked it Lizzie."

Lizzie stood up. "Robbie, you need to talk with Bert Swallow."

"He asked for compassionate leave this morning...a

family issue...but I asked him not to go until all our visitors had left. Swallow can't be involved surely? He's an absolute brick, utterly reliable and loyal," Turner protested.

"That may be the problem, Sir." Alice stood up. "Loyalty... it gives rise to conflicts within each of us."

Turner lifted his phone and asked for Sergeant Swallow to be brought to his office. Inspector Sadler and PC Crowther took their leave with Grainger as they needed to take Healey to Boston Police station where he could be questioned. Molly was thanked by Sir George Stanley and Lizzie noticed how she was shown out of Turner's office with surprising courtesy. Even the very important are perhaps susceptible to female charm. For a moment, Lizzie wondered if she should use that more often but she dismissed the thought; from childhood, she had refused to play that game. That was about women making men feel important, powerful; she would not allow herself to be diminished by doing so, though she had to admit, at times, she had made use of the tactic.

Stanley glanced at his watch suddenly brisk. "When we've seen Swallow, Turner, perhaps we can have some lunch and then we must have the Meteor test. I want to be away as soon as possible."

"Quite so, Sir."

They sat in silence, Stanley, Turner, Robbie, Alice and Lizzie. It was as if there were too much to digest. Alice was deep in thought. Lizzie guessed her mind was on Bert Swallow. Could it be that Micky Sinclair was the man who had let down Bert's sister so badly? Could Bert, gentle as he seemed to be, have taken out his anger on Sinclair. And Bert had been angry on Thursday evening. She knew Alice would be hoping for another explanation.

At last there was a knock on the door. The corporal entered and, approaching close to Turner, whispered in his ear. He left and Turner addressed the group. "It seems that Swallow can't be found at the moment."

Robbie McBane jumped to his feet. "We need to find him

before he leaves. Come on."

Without waiting for an answer, he strode towards the door. Lizzie and Alice followed at speed but Turner and Stanley sat motionless, stunned by the sudden activity.

◆ ◆ ◆

It was the shame he could not face. Eyes upon him, the high regard in which he knew he had been held, being stripped from him like clothes torn off. How could he face that? Better to go with his reputation intact.

Bert Swallow watched the training flight assembling on the apron in front of the hangars. Tiger moths for initial training, a batch of new trainee pilots, probably with a few hours solo flying under their belts. It would be messy but easy and certain, provided one held one's nerve. There was the rub. Could he do it, knowing what the outcome would be for him... but also for whichever novice pilot he encountered? What was the alternative? It needed to look like an accident but...he had a contingency; he patted the pistol in his pocket.

He hovered in the shadow of a hangar. No one would find it strange to see him there but if he was going to do it, he needed to be closer to the runway. Perhaps he could make it look like he was inspecting it, making sure it was ok after the Meteor explosion. That was it. He began to walk across the airfield, heading for the point where the aircraft would be approaching their maximum speed but had not left the ground. He felt remarkably calm, almost happy that he was going to take some action, action that would end this turmoil in his mind.

Robbie McBane, Lizzie and Alice erupted from the main buildings. "Check the gate Lizzie. Make sure he hasn't left already."

While Lizzie ran across to the gate and established that only the Police and Molly had left in the last hour, Robbie headed for the accommodation building with Alice in tow. She was trying to talk to Robbie between gulps of air.

"We mustn't....assume any...thing, Robbie. I can't... believe Bert...would do anything...like that."

Robbie McBane took the steps up to the huge palladian columns two at a time. But, just as he reached the top, there was a shout from Lizzie. He wheeled around and saw her pointing across the airfield. From his vantage point he could see the figure walking across to the runway. It certainly looked like Bert Swallow.

"Let's go," he called to Alice as his feet clattered down the steps.

Alice turned and followed him. He was running and she could not keep up with him. Lizzie joined her and though a little faster, the space between them and Robbie increased.

"What's he doing out there?" gasped Alice.

Lizzie saw the Tiger Moths on the apron, engines running, a training flight ready to go. Instantly, she realised what Bert Swallow intended. She stopped running and shouted to Robbie. "He's going to jump in front of a Moth."

As soon as the words had left her mouth, Bert Swallow turned, looked back and at the same moment engines roared. The first Moth rolled forward onto the runway, the others lining up behind. Bert Swallow was not yet at the runway. He began to run.

The first Moth gathered speed, its propeller invisible but for the dark circle in front of the aircraft. Robbie McBane shot forward as if fired from a cannon, his legs powering him over the ground, his arms pumping. Lizzie saw then the rugby player he had been, totally focused on the line, an imaginary ball under one arm. He was closing the gap between himself and Bert as was the Moth.

Alice had stopped too and was staring in horror. "All three will meet at the same point. Both Bert and Robbie will be killed."

But just before Bert reached the runway, Robbie flung himself forward in a flying tackle. Bert went down, the Moth roared past and left the runway followed by the others. Bert and Robbie lay on the ground. Suddenly Bert wriggled free, was on his feet, a pistol in his hand pointing at his own temple. Everyone froze.

CHAPTER 39

Slowly, Robbie McBane rose to his feet. He took a step forward.

"Stop right there. I'll do it."

Alice and Lizzie walked forward as cautious as deer leaving woodland for open pasture. They stood either side of Robbie.

"Bert, don't be a fool. Put the gun down. We can sort this out."

There was a short bark, an attempt at a hollow laugh. "Sort it out? This can't be sorted out. It's over...I'm finished."

"No, Bert, you're far from finished." Lizzie's voice was imploring, full of sympathy."

Bert said nothing but closed his eyes and raised his elbow slightly so that it was at right angles to his head. He screwed his eyes tight shut, and they watched in horror as his hand tensed, preparing to squeeze the trigger.

"Bert, Bert." Alice, gentle, calm. "Before you die, please tell us what happened, the other night, what happened to Micky Sinclair?"

Bert's arm relaxed a little and his eyes opened. He looked close to tears. "I didn't mean to, I didn't. It just happened." Despite the uniform, the pistol in his hand, he looked and sounded like a young boy, caught doing something wrong, damaging the picture that was a wedding present to his parents perhaps.

"You were angry that night, Bert. Was that my fault?"

"No...no... well perhaps in part. It's a lonely life, stuck on this base miles from anywhere. I so long for companionship, a wife...a family. It's rare that I meet a young woman, a lovely young woman such as you. I was disappointed, I admit, but that was not the main reason."

"Angela, then?"

He looked directly at Alice, his brow furrowing in surprise. "How...?"

"I'm sorry, Bert. It was unforgivable of me but when I was in your room and you left briefly to go...you know...I couldn't help noticing the letter on your table and I read it."

"The letter?"

"From Angela. I can understand how angry it made you."

"She's my little sister. I promised her and myself that I would always look after her. It made me furious that he just dumped her like that...had his fun and then left her to face the consequences alone. I'd thought, see, that if she married and was settled, I could then find a wife and settle myself. But now I have to put my happiness on one side to look after her."

As gently as he could, Robbie McBane spoke but the gruffness of his voice jarred after Alice's softness. "So what happened Bert?"

"The man who dumped her was Micky Sinclair. After bringing you back on Thursday from the pub, I thought I'd have words with him. I knew he was on guard at the hangar. So I went over there. He wasn't in the hangar, he was outside it, taking a swig from a bottle. I couldn't stand it. He'd betrayed Angela and now he was betraying his uniform. What kind of man can be so cavalier?"

"Did he see you there?"

"No. He was facing the other way, looking for something, perhaps something that had dropped from his pocket when his trousers came off...I dunno. Anyway, I saw red. It was like a volcano erupting inside me. All the misery of my life, losing my parents, no chance of happiness, Angela distressed because of him. I know he wasn't to blame for my parents but it felt at that moment that he was the enemy."

"So you went into the hangar and picked up a spanner."

"It was on the bench close by the door. I didn't stop to think. I picked it up, went outside and hit him on the head from behind. He went down without a word. I wish, how I wish I had challenged him first. Then maybe I wouldn't have felt any need to use the spanner. Perhaps I would have hit him with my fist and he would still be alive. I didn't even get the satisfaction of telling him what a bastard he was."

"As you know, I found the spanner but assumed it was one of the German agents."

"I know. Handy that for me. But how did you find out? It was that girl was it? Molly...from the pub."

"She was so sure that neither Bob nor Harry could have done it. When you visited her, tried to get her to change her story, she was determined to make sure we knew it can't have been them. But it was Alice and Lizzie who made the connection...Michael in Angela's letter and Micky."

"You'd make good spies you two." It was not resentment in Bert Swallow's voice, but a grudging admiration.

"I'm sorry Bert...but..." Alice looked down, unable to meet Bert's eye.

"Ah well. It's done now isn't it. No remedy except this." His elbow lifted again and he closed his eyes.

"No Bert. You cannot do this. What about Angela? How will she cope without you?"

"I'll be no good to Angela locked in a prison for the rest of me life or swinging from a hangman's rope."

"Bert, listen to me. You're a good man. You were under pressure. A court will understand that. You could say it was accidental...you thought it was an impostor come to damage the Meteor...that's it an impostor. There were German agents on the base that night. You took action to protect our secret weapon. No jury is going to convict you with a defence like that."

Bert's arm relaxed again. He smiled wryly. "Nice try Alice, but it won't work. You know the truth, Robbie and Alice know the truth and, most importantly of all, I know the truth. I cannot live a lie for the rest of my life and I cannot expect you to do so.

I cannot face the disgrace of a court martial, being found guilty, death or imprisonment. I had hoped to make my death look like an accident, take the secret of Sinclair's death to the grave but you prevented that Robbie...you and your rugby tackle."

There was silence for several moments before Alice spoke again. "I want you to know, Bert, that I like you a great deal. Whether that in time would turn into love, I don't know but I ask you not to take this way. I understand about the shame but do you want everyone and especially Angela to be ashamed of your memory. What will everyone think? A man who had great loyalty to his sister, loyalty to his country and his armed service infuriated by Sinclair's betrayal of his duty, but a man who did not have the courage to face up to what he had done. That's not you Bert. It's not the man I have begun to admire."

Slowly, with the grace Lizzie had observed in her, Alice moved forward, her eyes on Bert's, holding him with their warmth. She stepped right up to him, stood on tip-toes and kissed him gently on the cheek. As she did so, her left hand moved up to his right hand and, grasping it, twisted it upwards. There was no resistance.

Bert Swallow sank to his knees and let out a howl. "What have I done?" Alice dropped beside him and cradled him in her arms.

Lizzie and Alice had eaten very little for lunch and their subdued mood remained as they waited in the viewing area with personnel from the base to see the Meteor fly. Robbie McBane had taken Bert Swallow into custody and was occupied taking a statement from him. Bert was a broken man, that much was clear.

At last Lizzie took the risk of asking Alice about him. "Did you...sorry do you like him...Bert I mean, Alice?"

"Yes. I felt for him and I suppose pity is one route to liking, perhaps love."

"I suppose even a good man can do bad things."

"True. Murder is clearly wrong but the motive for it was good. Loyalty is far preferable to betrayal. Sinclair was a philanderer. He deserted Angela and he deserted his post to enjoy Molly's charms. That would enrage anyone."

"What of Healey? Was he a good man?"

"In some ways, yes. His loyalty to his son was unequivocal and it clashed with his loyalty to his country. He chose his son. That's understandable and to some extent I admire it."

Lizzie wondered whether to ask another question or whether it would be too intrusive. As usual, she decided to take the risk. "Do either Bert or Healey's actions make you think of your mother?"

Alice did not respond immediately. "Of course. My mother would not lift a finger to help me or defend me. I am sure of that. She is entirely driven by self-interest."

The statement was simple but delivered with such certainty that Lizzie did not feel she should contest it. How miserable for Alice to have such a vacuum in her life! She said nothing but slid her arm around Alice's shoulders. There was the slightest sob from Alice and no more. The two young women stood close together, unmoving until disturbed by Robbie McBane approaching them. He looked troubled.

"I wish Bert had taken your suggestion, Alice, but he was determined to tell the truth. He will be able to plead extreme provocation and that he had no intention to murder, so may escape the death penalty but his career in the RAF is over and he will certainly face a long prison sentence."

"Such a waste," murmured Alice, "but it proves he was an honourable man. He'd rather tell the truth than lie."

"It does," agreed Lizzie. "Strange isn't it what war does? I can even see Grainger's point of view. Sometimes in war, one has to do things that in normal circumstances would be considered unacceptable. Let's hope it's all worth it."

They stood in reflective silence as the hangar doors slowly rumbled apart. The tow truck appeared with the Meteor behind looking as sleek and impressive as the previous day. With the change in wind direction, the aircraft would start it's run from the buildings end of the runway. The truck stopped close to the point where the apron joined finished. The tow bar was removed and a group of airman carried out final checks. A ladder was put against the side of the plane and the test pilot, ungainly in flying suit and helmet, climbed into the cockpit.

The area was cleared of personnel. They heard the engines start, a roar that had been absent the day before. Slowly, the Meteor edged forward, centred on the runway. It stopped for a few minutes and then, suddenly, the spectators were shocked by an even bigger sound, like thunder but continuous. Lizzie felt it as much as heard it, her insides gripped with excitement and fear.

The aircraft leapt forward as if fired from a catapult. It gained speed with incredible rapidity until it was streaking along the runway, away from them, thrusting the engine noise back in their faces. Seconds later, its nose lifted and it shot into the air at an unbelievable angle, climbing away from them and disappearing for a while into the cloud. But they could hear it somewhere above them, the sound at times fading and then returning with renewed force.

All the spectators stood with open mouths but unable to speak. At last Lizzie found her tongue. "Did you see it? It's amazing. I can't believe how rapidly it climbed. Just like a rocket as Butler said."

"Extraordinary," whispered Alice to herself.

"Was it worth all the trouble?" Robbie McBane looked doubtful.

"I suppose time will tell"

The sound of the aircraft faded to nothing as it flew somewhere in the vast dome of the sky, far away from them soaring like a hawk before stooping to its prey. And then Alice pointed to a dot in the distance way beyond the airfield. It grew bigger quickly, taking the shape of an aircraft but it was soundless. Even as it passed over the edge of the airfield, there was no noise, just a shape streaking low and fast, so fast one could barely track it. And then it was past them and the noise returned as loud as before, growing in intensity when it suddenly climbed. The sound was with them for several seconds after it had disappeared into the clouds.

"Breathtaking," said Lizzie. "I'd love to fly one."

"Aye well maybe one day. You need to work on Stanley. I think he likes you."

Lizzie was surprised and did not reply so Alice did on her behalf. "Is that a touch of jealousy I detect, Sergeant McBane?"

"Perhaps..." he smiled, "but Lizzie and I have an understanding."

"When I've flown a Meteor and Germany has been defeated, maybe there will be time for...you know..." Lizzie stopped, feeling her cheeks redden.

"We should not wait. We can't know what's around the corner. Think of poor Bert. That's something I've learned this trip...take your chances while you have them."

Lizzie smiled shyly up at Robbie and gave him her arm. He pressed it close to his body and squeezed her hand. He then took Alice in his other arm. They walked in step back towards the buildings.

HISTORICAL NOTE

The Meteor did indeed have its first test flight on 5th March 1943 at RAF Cranwell near Boston, Lincolnshire, piloted by Michael Daunt. The engines had of course been tested and the plane had been through taxiing trials before this date. It was built by the Gloster Aircraft Company and its Chief Designer was George Carter. Originally, it was supposed to have turbojet engines designed by Frank Whittle but, because of production problems, it was fitted with two de Havilland Halford H1 engines designed by Frank Halford.

The Meteor was the only Allied jet powered aircraft to see service in World War II and thus was an important asset to the British and Allies. Its top speed at 30,000 feet was between 450 and 470 mph which compares very favourably with the Spitfire's 330 mph though of course that aircraft was of massive importance in the Battle of Britain.

The Germans had developed the Messerschmitt ME 262, originally as a piston engine aircraft but then using jet engines. It had its maiden flight in July 1942 but, as Sir George says in Chapter 7, there were problems with its development. It came into service in mid-1944 almost at exactly the same time as the Meteor which commenced operations on 27th July 1944. The prototype Meteor that had its first test flight in March 1943 did have a problem with yawing in flight and so the rudder was increased in size. Otherwise it was a highly effective aircraft that, with modifications, flew in operational service until the mid-1950s.

This novel is of course fiction. As far as I know, no one involved in the development of the Meteor was a traitor and there was no subterfuge to convince the Germans that the Meteor was a disaster. However, one part of the story is based on fact but is so extraordinary that I'm sure many readers will think it is the least probable part.

The character of Bob Edwards is based on a man called Eddie Chapman who started his career as a criminal with the London based Jelly Gang. The gang's speciality was blowing open safes using gelignite. At the start of the War, to evade British justice, Chapman went to Jersey but he was imprisoned for burglary. He was still in prison when the Germans invaded; he did a deal with them and said he would be their agent. They dropped him by aircraft into Cambridgeshire, a fact known to British intelligence but they did not have to arrest him because, as soon as he landed in England, he handed himself in.

He agreed to become a double agent and to convince the Germans that he was their man, the British agreed he should put into operation the assignment the Germans had given him to blow up the de Havilland Mosquito factory in Hertfordshire. Extensive 'debris' was created using wooden models so it looked as though a bomb had exploded in the main power plant. It even fooled many of the factory's own workforce! The British secret services planted a story in the Daily Express, ensuring that the Germans would see it as an authentic piece of sabotage. Chapman was even awarded the Iron Cross, Germany's highest medal, for it!

Eddie liked the high life and was especially partial to women. He wrote three books about his exploits and two further books have been written about him. A film, The Real Eddie Chapman Story, was made about him in 1966 but Chapman was disappointed by it. He died in 1997.

ALSO BY KEVIN O'REGAN

The Lizzie's War Series

New Swan Stone February 1943 and Lizzie discovers the body of a young civilian girl at RAF Silverstone. Can Lizzie help find the killer despite the ghosts of her past?

"A brilliant read...a real page turner."

Eager for the Air, the third book in the Lizzie's war series is due for publication in October 2024.

The Dresden Tango

It's 1889 and nearly 1800 poor Irish migrants arrive in Buenos Aires to start a new life. The trials they endure are focused on nineteen year old Rose and Patrick, a young priest. Can they save each other from despair?

"This book is absolutely compelling; I could not put it down."

Order the e-book or paperback now from Amazon.

ACKNOWLEDGEMENTS

I first came across the important role that the Air Transport Auixiliary (ATA) and especially its female pilots played in World War II when reading 'Spitfire Women of World War II' by Giles Whittell. It is an account of the real women who flew aircraft from factories to operational bases and other non-combat missions such as ferrying important people around the country. I am very grateful to the Air Transport Auxiliary Museum for providing such a wealth of information on their web-site (atamuseum.org) and at the Museum itself which, though small, is well worth visiting. It is at the Maidenhead Heritage Centre.

Once again I would like to thank Fred Lockwood, Patrick Sanders, Mark Kenny and Jane Wilkinson for their very valuable feedback on an earlier draft. Finally, thanks are due to my wife, Carrie, for her patience and encouragement.

Printed in Great Britain
by Amazon

37941514R00165